I0670045

Particles
a novel

SHAWN MIHALIK

Asymmetrical Press
Missoula, Montana

Published by Asymmetrical Press, Missoula, Montana.

The author would like to thank, for their help with this book, Joshua Millburn, Colin Wright, Ryan Nicodemus, Josh Wagner, Jessica Williams, Kelli Carney, Robert Brown, and Cynthia Cook.

Library of Congress Cataloging-In-Publication Data
Particles / Shawn Mihalik — 1st ed.
ISBN: 978-1-938793-85-1
eISBN: 978-1-938793-86-8
1. Broadway. 2. Technology. 3. Pornography. 4. Loneliness. 5. Particle Physics.

Cover design by Colin Wright
Cover photo by Joshua Weaver
Formatted in beautiful Montana
Printed in the U.S.A.

Publisher info:
Website: www.asymmetrical.co
Email: howdy@asymmetrical.co
Twitter: @asympress

ASYM METR ICAL

To Paige Ferro

The conception of the objective reality of the elementary particles has thus evaporated not into the cloud of some obscure new reality concept, but in the transparent clarity of a mathematics that represents no longer the behavior of the particle but rather our knowledge of this behavior.

—Werner Heisenberg, "The Representation of Nature in Contemporary Physics"

We're all messed up in the head.
Every human being starts incurring psychological damage as soon as they exit the womb.

—Stoya, *The Morning After Podcast,* Episode #72

Particles

A BRIEF HISTORY

NOTHING IS NEW. EVERYTHING THAT is happening has happened before, in some time or place. In other universes some things happened that haven't happened here in yours—but still they happened. I know this now. I am acutely aware of everything. It hurts, to see it all and feel it all. I see your universe and I see every inch of mine and all the corners of the other ones, all the histories and the futures. And yet when it comes to who I am, or who I ever was, I am not clued in. My existence extends so far beyond that now.

The change had been coming for a very long time, but the impetus of the world's greatest change came probably, in retrospect, when this one massive technology company released two products, both of which were at the time called revolutionary by the world community and early adopters (late adopters didn't use the term revolutionary themselves because, by definition, by the time the late adopters had adopted the technologies, the technologies were all but ubiquitous, and the revolution was long over). These two products consisted first of what was at its release called a smartphone and second of a tablet computing device. Worth noting is that neither the smartphone nor the tablet were the first smartphone or tablet to be released onto what was then referred to as the consumer market and what is now just called The Market, with capitals, in some place or time; both smartphones and tablets had been attempted by other massive technology companies several times, but for some reason no device had been able to capture the hearts of the humans that made up the consumer market in quite the same complete and enduring way as the ones created by the massive technology company that ultimately built the ones that did. It's hard to quantify exactly what it was about this company's products that made them so well loved and widely adopted, but to say they made an impact would be an understatement. Phones, by the way, as in the concept of a handset that allows a person to dial a number and be near-instantly connected with another human being, had been around for over a hundred years before the release of these two products, although for most of their existence up until that point the handsets had been anchored to gargantuan receiver boxes which themselves had to be anchored to a wall in two separate places.

In the years after the release of these two products, other massive technology companies suddenly "got it" and started releasing their own smartphones and tablets that were far better than their previous efforts. There was a sort of philosophical debate that proliferated among the technological, historical, and scientific communities as to what exactly would happen now that these technologies had achieved significant cultural penetration. Some argued that the state of technology and the ways humans lived their lives would continue to evolve at an ever-increasing (exponential, some said) rate, while others posited that these new technologies were only a fad, that the novelty would wear quickly off and the net impact of them on the world would, once future generations looked back, be effectively nil.

It turns out that the groups on both sides of the argument were pretty much wrong, and what happened was that in most respects the state of technology stagnated. Some massive technology companies tried to make further innovations, notably in the field of what was dubbed "wearable tech"—things like glasses with always-on heads-up displays and watches that relayed notifications and even self-tying shoes that the wearer could use to send electronic mail by typing with her toes (the self-tying feature stuck around for longer than the toe-typing, almost a hundred years, but then one luxury shoe company switched back to conventional laces and well that was that)—but in the end the products of each of those attempts were realized to be too intrusive into the lives of human kind, although things like the glasses were still purchasable and used by certain niche communities (e.g. rock climbers, winter sports enthusiasts, construction workers) when engaging in certain tasks. If they looked back on it, philosophers and historians might have realized that smartphones and personal media tablets were technological steps along the same vein as the wheel. Think about it: the wheel is still in constant use and its design has remained essentially unchanged since its invention. Smartphones and tablets were the same—they were the perfect incarnation of their respective technologies and improving upon them had no point. Although, it's worth noting, "smart" was eventually dropped from the term smartphones and they came to be called just phones (and a specific individual's was typically referred to as one's "personal phone") because after a few decades there were no so-called dumbphones left for differentiation.

Speaking of wheels, cars—indeed, the whole of the transportation situation on, and off, planet Earth—also remained relatively unchanged and uninnovated since that time. Planes became faster and roomier. Cars gained self-driving options and had them for hundreds of years, but most people elected not to use them except in special situations because, driving, it turns out, is an enjoyable and relaxing activity for all but the road-rage inclined, who, it's worth noting, have other, deeper problems, and scientific studies have backed this up. In fact, when, maybe seven hundred years after the introduction of the self-driving car, one U.S. state (of which there were at the time 51, before the destruction of Puerto Rico by Unified Korea) tried to make the exclusive use of a vehicle's self-driving feature legally the only way a person could drive, the violent backlash nipped that motion in the proverbial bud. Also, trains simply ceased existing (and I realize I probably shouldn't have brought up trains at all since, because they haven't existed for some long time, you probably don't even know what they are, but I suppose now I have to explain: trains were this incredibly limited form of transportation, limited in that they required the use of special powered rails to operate and were therefore confined to said rails' fixed courses, that stuck around as a major mode of transportation for an amount of time that is, when you think about it, mind-boggling).

Natural disasters, as they are so inappropriately named (because here's the problem with the moniker: if they're so natural—and rest assured they are—then what exactly makes them a disaster? Most deaths are not labeled "disasters," and the only difference here is that the deaths are often en masse, but they're still natural, i.e. a part of life) continued as they always have since the Earth's formation. Volcanoes continued to erupt, tectonic plates continued to rub against one another, tornadoes and hurricanes still formed in seemingly random places. So, yes, the Earth's geography changed in innumerable ways, but the collective result of the change was small.

Another interesting thing that happened was that man continued to go into space for a time, although he never made it out of his own star system, and some still wonder if he ever will. He established colonies on the moon and on Mars, but the impracticality of continuously resupplying these colonies led to the eventual abandonment for a long time of any further plans for manned and even most unmanned interstellar travel. Although the good news is that in the last few decades certain parties have begun to once again stress the importance of space exploration for mankind's future, prompting nations like the United States and Russia to fund their respective governments' space programs, and certain massive technology companies are actually beginning to get into the space game as well, with manned commercial space flights planned and on the imminent horizon, which is good, because it will probably take some time to regain the knowledge that was lost when man stopped his interstellar efforts billions of years ago, time he probably can't afford to waste, so it's good that he's got cracking on the issue.

Also, most terrestrial diseases were found cures or treatments for, creating a sort of golden age of medicine that lasted for a long time until the pace of medical and other scientific advancements slowed to a stand-still (because there were no longer any diseases that needed curing), which then gave the various microscopic life forms time to regroup, to fortify their efforts, to become once again stronger than humans and to once again attack with impunity, meaning that people started dying from things like cancer and HIV and even severe cases of the flu, again. Which of course caused the medical community to step up its game, but because the entirety of historical medical records were lost some time before 13.8 billion years ago, there is, like with space travel, some catching up that must be done. Penicillin was only rediscovered about a hundred years ago.

An important question is: Why was the entirety of historical medical records lost? Well now that's interesting.

One of the biggest changes that occurred with the introduction of smartphones and personal media tablets was the way humanity read books. Physical books, as in bound paper entities, were usurped in popularity by electronic books (shortened to ebooks) until eventually nearly every paper book in existence was destroyed by either natural means (natural means being the ordinary decay that comes with use and existence) or deliberate incineration and virtually all books (and medical records, scientific research, etc.) were read in electronic form on phones and media tablets. This was fine, in theory, but then at some point a solar flare, which tend to happen as your sun gets older and grows even if by an immeasurably small amount, caused a drastically large amount of recorded data to be wiped from existence. Hence the loss of the knowledge of various cures that at this point hadn't been used for a long time (also the knowledge of nuclear weapons, all of which had been dismantled in a landmark moment of peace long before). Of course what were still being used were various forms of technology like phones and tablets and cars, and nobody was killed or physically harmed by the solar flare, so the people who made these things and thus had knowledge of how to make these things were perfectly fine, and the flare didn't permanently disrupt the planet's electrical systems or anything like that, so besides the data loss, the world went on mostly as normal for a little while. But of course with time almost all of the informational knowledge that wasn't lost, i.e. the historical knowledge that was inside people's heads but that wasn't in most's heads very vividly because let's face it who really ever pays attention when being taught history, became warped or altered and in most cases forgotten completely, and humanity, after existing for a long time in a condition of what one may call utopia, grew confused and angry and distressed, and this led to this weird phenomena where the state of humanity regressed and certain historical incidences (e.g. wars, philosophical, artistic, and religious movements) repeated themselves. But none of it mattered, because in time that sun went nova, and then, after billions of years, all the suns. And new stars came together in the aftermath, until eventually the whole thing just went kaput like a flame that's lost its fuel, except there was still some gas there, lingering, and a spark, because it all happened again. And again. And again.

Everything is real. Everything is new. The whole of it is fractured. Of this I am acutely aware.

ROUTES

PENNSYLVANIA ROUTE 28, SIGNED INTO existence in 1927 when America was a bigger place, was not initially conceived as a major metropolitan highway, and that is its most significant problem. Every morning and every evening the stretch of road from Kittaning all the way to 279 transforms into a busy mess of cars and pickups and semis as workers commute to and from their jobs both in the city proper and in the many factories and mills that flourish in the surrounding townships. During today's particular rush hour, through the snail-paced traffic a so-blue-it's-almost-black Volvo speeds. The car, which was built at least a decade ago and which, as evidenced by the chipping paint and alarming amount of rust around the door frames and undercarriage, is not holding up well, entered the highway somewhere near Harrison Township at close to four o'clock this evening.

The sky has all day been dull and grey and overcast, but once the Volvo merged with the traffic on 28, what was at first just a spirit-dampening display of less-than-perfect weather evolved into a slightly less perfect drizzle. Within a few minutes it escalated into a downpour. Now, as the Volvo passes the Cheswick exit, the downpour is something more like a deluge of Noahic proportions. Visibility is nil. The rush hour traffic, which was already slow, is further impeded by the weather and, for all practical purposes, has ceased moving in either direction. But still the aging Volvo speeds, taking every gap and opening, using the highway's shoulder for purposes for which highway shoulders are not intended. The Volvo speeds, and at twenty miles per hour, compared to every other car on Pennsylvania Route 28 on this Thursday afternoon in 1991, it is a jet, the sonic kind, on wheels.

Inside the vehicle, which sort of sputters and coughs as it moves along, Bernard Gilpatrick grasps the steering wheel with the fingers of both hands, his knuckles white and the calluses on the upper part of his palms in danger of being torn off by the friction of the tightness of his grip; the friction of hard work created the calluses, and the friction of anxiousness and frustration and excitement will be their undoing. He relaxes his grip a little, like a person who has his hands around the neck of a man he does not intend to kill, only scare, but Bernard cannot scare the Volvo into speeding up the flow of the traffic it is already being made to subvert. He taps the fingers of his left hand on the outside of the steering wheel's circumference. *Drum, drum, drum. Badum, badum, badum.* But he is not tapping, though, is he? He has not loosened his grip at all. The *badumming* is the drumming of his heart, and not in some figurative way, like in a way that's meant to signify romanticism or to cause people to swoon and think *Oh Bernard's heart is drumming because he's in love or something how sweet*, but literally, like as in it beats, because that is what hearts do, and it is beating faster than normal, both because Bernard is nervous and because he is having a small heart attack—so small that he will never know about it, not even when the sequel comes years later and his cardiologist puts him on statins—that he's been having for the last several minutes.

In normal traffic, the drive to the University of Pittsburgh Medical Center would take him maybe twenty minutes, but as the situation stands now, even with his, from his perspective, manic display of vehicular control, he has been on the road for thirty. He is worried he will arrive too late, but he isn't sure. He doesn't know how long it takes to have a baby. How long does labor last? Did they tell him that? Is that one of the things he's supposed to know as father-to-be? As the husband? He should have been on the road sooner. There was a ten-minute gap between the moment he received the phone call (his supervisor, Mr. Clark, called to him from the doorway of the loading dock, phone in hand, while Bernard was arranging product in the bed of a delivery truck: "Hey, Bernie! Your wife's in labor. You want I should let you off early so you can get to the hospital or whatever?") and the time he arrived at his car. This gap can be accounted for by his fainting (the beginning of the tiny heart attack that he will never realize has happened), his recovery a few minutes after hitting the ground (Mr. Clark will later lament that he didn't call an ambulance after the fainting, and that if he did Bernard would almost certainly have gotten to the hospital faster, that is, on time), and his subsequent tripping over his booted feet as he ran from the warehouse to his car.

Bernard Gilpatrick is a large, solid man. He is only a hair shorter than most doorways, and sixteen years of manual labor has counteracted a steady diet of bologna and mustard sandwiches, lending his frame a powerful musculature. His dark brown hair is flecked with strands of grey, his round face a showcase of three-day-old stubble and pronounced pores and unruly eyebrows. Maria always says they, the eyebrows, are *endearingly* unruly. He once mentioned trimming them a bit, tidying the longer hairs that curl up a little too high, but she won't let him, knows he doesn't really want to, and she's right— he's content with the length of his eyebrows. It isn't like he has a unibrow, which, if he had one, he would most definitely shave or wax or do whatever that thing is people do to their unibrow. In grade school he knew this Asian kid who thought everyone had a unibrow but their parents shaved them for them, like his did for him, and after meeting that kid, Bernard, who wouldn't go through puberty for another year and so didn't know what follicular surprises his head had in store for him, vowed to never, never, be seen with a unibrow, which again, fortunately, he doesn't have. In every trait of his bearish masculinity he is secure.

From somewhere behind him a horn. A sign in front of him says NARROW SHOULDER AHEAD, and indeed about a hundred feet down the road he can see, just barely through the monsoon, that the space between the guardrail and the right lane grows narrower by a significant amount. It would be impossible to fit a car through that space, even the Volvo, which is so small that a man as large as Bernard driving it is comical, visually. The Fates are forcing him to rejoin the flow.

Which—*flow*—is a misnomer. If rivers flow then the cars on PA Route 28 are drops in an unmoving pond. Red drops and silver drops and black drops and blue (like the Volvo) drops and a copper-colored drop and even white drops and pale yellow drops. Bernard slows and lists to the left, cautious but hopeful. He idles, waiting, and when traffic crawls forward a dozen feet he turns the wheel, inching the front of the car toward the newly created gap, but the car behind the gap closes in, its driver flashing its brights and making a rude gesture to which Bernard does not respond—he's never been one for rude gestures. He drums the wheel for real while waiting for traffic to crawl again, for another gap to open. The mini heart attack he doesn't even know about ends. It lasted long for a heart attack so small. Some of his anxiousness subsides and his breathing comes easier and he feels a general sense of lightness wash over him. Is this portentous? Is it a sign? An extra-sensory acknowledgment that his wife, at the hospital, has given birth and all is well? It is. Yes, yes it is. Maybe. Three-and-a-half more minutes he sits at the edge of the shoulder, in front of the narrow-shoulder sign, the Volvo's front end turned toward traffic, blinker signaling desire to merge, the rain crashing on his windshield and his wipers batting it away. Twice in that time another gap opens; he is allowed into the second gap by a driver who probably realizes it doesn't matter if there is one more car in front of him.

Maria isn't even supposed to be having the baby at UPMC, and she isn't supposed to be having it now, either.

They planned the whole thing out with Doctor Eckstein, as if these things always happen in the most ideal way: Maria would go into labor a month from now, on or very close to her due date, in the middle of the night. Bernard would be lying there in the bed next to her, asleep, and he would be waked by her whisper and a feeling of wetness creeping across the sheets toward his side of the bed. "Bernie," she would whisper, "my water broke. It's time." They always say "It's time" when they go into labor, women do, the antecedent obvious and needing no clarification. Bernard's heart would flutter, because this—"It's time"—would mean his daughter is on her way. He would panic for a moment, internally, saying nothing, and Maria would repeat again, "Bernie." And he would snap to it, just like that. He would say, "Got it! Yes, let's go. Are you ready? I'm ready. Do we have the go-bag? Oh where's the go-bag?" And the go-bag, packed with two changes of clothes for Maria and two for the coming baby and a robe and a small blanket and a fuzzy little knit cap and diapers and a few other things, would be by the door, because that's where Bernard had put it, and so he would say, "Wait, it's by the door. Okay, let's go. Wait, I'm not dressed. Forget it—I'll just put on slippers. Let's go." And Maria would say, "Bernard, calm down. Get dressed. The baby isn't coming right this second. You get dressed and I'll call Doctor Eckstein and then we can go." And Bernard would get dressed. Maria would get dressed, too, and even manage to put on makeup, in the time it took Bernard to get ready. He would grab the keys and they'd head out the door, he reaching back through the doorway, grabbing the go-bag because he'd almost forget it before locking the door. He'd drive them to Allegheny Valley Hospital, which is located only miles from their home in Natrona Heights, twenty-four miles northeast of Pittsburgh. Doctor Eckstein would be waiting; he would say something like, "She's only dilated *this much.*" Bernard probably should know how much she was supposed to be dilated, but he keeps forgetting these details, so in his mental projection of how things are supposed to happen some of the specifics are fuzzy. Then Doctor Eckstein would tell them it would be a few hours, after which he would deliver a healthy baby girl.

But of course, instead, Maria is having the baby now while Bernard sits in the middle of a monsoon, her water having broken while working at the PNC headquarters downtown. She usually works at the local branch in Natrona Heights but was today attending a corporate meeting. Her maternity leave was supposed to start in three weeks.

Bernard inches the Volvo forward. In reality, it moves fifty feet, but from a big picture perspective inches is the appropriate word today. Lightning flashes across the sky. Two cars in front of Bernard is the car that before refused to let him back into the flow, that made the rude gesture. It is a white LeBaron. Bernard sees a bolt of lightning strike the LeBaron, blowing the thing to bits—another what would have happened. The lightning never leaves the sky and the LeBaron still sits there, stuck in a sea of vehicles, same as him.

When he will think about this day in the months that follow, Bernard will not be able to with any amount of certainty say exactly how long he was on this stretch of 28, how long he waited; he will know only that it was too long, that he should have done more, done something, to either get out of there or move that traffic forward, to change the flow of time. But of course those will be ridiculous thoughts, the troubled rumination of a broken-hearted man, and anyway, his memories of this day on 28 will, eventually, fade to mere impressions, and he will come to view today as a tragic sort of blessing, something poetic and beautiful, and he will realize what a lucky man he's turned out to be. And then, of course, decades later, when he thinks about the day in the rain on 28 . . . I just don't know what to make of it anymore. How does it go like this?

But that's later. Now, after the sitting and the inching and the eternity, the rain stops. While it started slow, escalating over the course of hours, when it ends it just ends. Done. Pebbles pounding on the glass and the metal and then nothing. No need for wipers or even, as the clouds break apart and the sun peeks through, headlights (although Bernard, like of the drivers around him, keep his headlights on, because in Pennsylvania the law requires headlights be turned on in construction zones, no matter the time of day or the weather, and PA Route 28 is, it seems, a perpetual construction zone, which, by the way, is the cause of the dense and mollasical traffic, the construction is, not the weather). And things start to move, as in forward, as in at a reasonable pace (because, in an act of nonsensical serendipity, when the rain stops the construction stops, too, the workers tossing their tools to the side of the work area and pulling their big machines out of the two lanes they were congesting, and going home).

But so then the Volvo coughs, and chokes, and dies.

For the first time in his life Bernard wishes he had one of those cellular phone things that the businessmen always carry around. He managed to move the car nearly a mile before it stopped working, so he is once again on a part of the highway with a shoulder of normal width. He lets momentum take him to the side of the road, where he flicks on the emergency lights. The dash lights up when he turns the key. The starter makes a sound like turning over. The temperature gauge reads at acceptable levels. From the hood, smoke does not rise. Bernard's knowledge of cars is, like most men his age, acceptable, but not complete. He can change his own oil and often does, installed new bulbs himself when the left taillight went out last year, can jump the battery by putting the vehicle in neutral and pushing it (preferably at a slight downhill angle) a few feet and jumping in and turning the ignition. But he is not, when he pops the hood and stands over it and stares for several minutes, able to tell why it sputtered and died and won't start again now.

And while Bernard stares in desperation at the insides of his broken Volvo, his wife is in the hospital in the city having a baby, a baby who at this moment is nameless, and not exactly conscious in the traditional sense and has just escaped into the world, and the first thing the baby hears is this question:

"Why isn't she crying?"

It's a common question asked immediately after a birth (although the baby doesn't know that), and so is often lampshaded in fictional productions, notably film, and because of this, most people then assume that, because it's a question that is asked in works of fiction, it probably isn't one that is asked often in real life, which is to say most people assume that when a baby is born, it begins to cry immediately (or even has been crying since the womb), but this is almost never true, because in the womb babies are swimming in a viscous amniotic soup and so do not breathe in the traditional way, and when they exit the womb they need a moment to assimilate to inspiration and expiration. A doctor or a nurse usually assists with this by clearing the nasal canal of obstruction.

A thin, hard rubber tube is inserted into the newborn's nose. Suction. She begins to cry, a small, hollow, but alive, cry.

"Here's your daughter, Maria. Here she is."

Warmth. A heart beating against her new skin through a welcoming chest. Serene breath on her tiny face. A nose inhaling her new-baby smell (which is not the smell of baby powder, not at all).

"Oh, she's beautiful." Words more exhaled than spoken.

"She is, though, isn't she?"

"Doctor Eckstein, do you see that? There's . . . blood . . . on the infant."

"Yes, I see. Okay. Maria . . . ? Maria, I'm going to need you to hand your daughter back to the nurse now, okay. Just for a moment, okay. We'll get her right back to you."

"Why . . . what's wrong?"

"We'll get her right back to you. We just need to check something. Barbara?"

"There's no sign of an external bleed. The baby's okay."

"My baby's okay? She's alright, right, Doctor?"

"She's just fine, Maria. She's beautiful. Barbara, get the child cleaned up; take her to the nursery. June, page Doctor Pennybrook 911 and get him an OR prepped for an emergency laparotomy. Maria, I need you to answer a few questions for me, okay? Are you in any pain . . ."

When you're born, you have no expectations. But if you were capable of having expectations, it would be reasonable of you to assume that you would be held by your mother for more than eleven seconds; that after your cord was cut, you'd be wrapped in a blanket and then placed in the arms of your father; that you would see the woman who gave birth to you again sometime after you left that room; that you would suckle her breast; that she would hang your schoolwork on the refrigerator; that she would watch you graduate; that she would cry when you left for college, and again at your wedding; that she would be there for you. You would not expect, and you do not expect, to be carried away by a strange old woman with bad breath down a long hallway with washed-out lights above you—light, light, light, light, light—perfectly healthy and strong, and for your mother to die of an obstetrical hemorrhage—in this case specifically a tear in the uterine lining that must have happened not long before the delivery process, the doctors decide, or else they would have caught it—in an operating room one floor below.

WHY THE GIRL WENT TO THE BUS STATION

THE GIRL STANDS IN FRONT of the doors to Greyhound's Pittsburgh station on Eleventh, hands in her pockets, a cheap backpack slung over one shoulder and a red gym duffle on the ground beside her. The black cotton hoodie pulled up over her head serves two purposes: One, it protects her face from the mid-spring weather, which this year has been colder than normal, more like early spring or late fall; and, two, it cuts her off from the rest of the world—it is her cocoon. Brown hair pokes from beneath the hoodie's hood, the wind catching it and tossing it about. The girl hugs herself.

She supposes her being here is a product of her own actions. Inside, her guilt wars with rebellion and determination. Determination to prove to her stepmother that everything she (her stepmother) has ever said or believed is wrong and ugly and evil. Rebellion against all she's ever known. Her head still aches from the night before, and just when she thought she might finally be getting over it, the yelling brought it back. She picks up the duffle and pushes through the glass doors.

They keep it dark in the Greyhound station at night, probably in order to avoid interrupting the delicate circadian cycles of weary bus-bound travelers. There are lights on, but they are the dim and warm halogens spaced sparsely around the terminal's open layout—the emergency lights, the girl thinks, although she's never actually seen an emergency light turned on because she's never since and excepting her birth been in an emergency (although tonight might qualify as an emergency if nothing else)—not the bright, fluorescent lights that are probably kept on during the . . . but no, no there are no florescent lights in the terminal at all, the girl realizes. The dim halogen bulbs are the lights, the only ones, and the bus station's ceiling is made of glass so during the day travelers will have natural light. Real light. The girl longs for something real. She approaches the ticket counter, the line to which is nonexistent. There is no one behind the counter, and then there is a man, an overweight man with a goatee wearing a greasy polo. The girl flinches as he says, "Help you?"

It is not cold in the bus station like it was outside, but the girl shivers as she speaks. "I need a ticket to New York," she says.

"City?" The way he says it, she isn't sure if he is asking What city? or if he's confirming she wants to go to New York City, as in NYC, as in the Big Apple.

"New York City, yes," she tells him.

The man yawns. "Bus schedule's behind me on that board there," he says. "See it on that board there? Next bus New York City leaves 'marra morning. Six-oh."

It's like he's speaking a different language, this man, one without certain English syntax, and not just Pittsburghese, as the dialect of southwestern Pennsylvania is affectionately called, but something more. "Oh," the girl says. "I can't . . . well, that's okay. I, yeah, one ticket for New York City still. Please."

The man sighs. He pecks at what looks like a cross between a modern desktop computer and an ancient textile machine. "New York's a shitstorm. You got any luggage 'n'at?"

"I've got a bag here. And this backpack."

"Backpack's fine. Place the bag up here on'is scale here, would ya?"

The girl doesn't know what scale he's referring to.

He gestures. "On'at there. That metal platform there."

She sees the counter. She heaves her bag onto the metal surface. She packed the bag in such a haphazard and hurried manner as she made her unplanned (oh but really she'd been planning it, way deep down she'd been planning it all along) escape that she finds it difficult to picture what unmatched clothes and random effects she's stuffed in there. The man plucks some keys, like actually plucks, the girl could swear, like flicks them toward himself rather than types.

"Twenty-two-point-eight pounds," the man mutters. "That's fifty greens."

"Fifty dollars? Why?"

"Gas n'at. Every bag added to the bus has a hefty effect on gas mileage."

"Right."

"So then that's the bag plus the ticket is one-thirty-fifty-seven."

The girl digs into the deep single pocket of her hoodie, producing seven twenty-dollar bills, fresh from the ATM. She hands the cash to the man, who plucks and pecks some more at the computer. The computer beeps repeatedly and then seems to scream like a handheld drill, and from some unseen printer a ticket is produced. The man slides the ticket across the ticket counter. "The bus'll be here at 6:05. Boards at 6:20. Departs at 6:30. It'll leave without you if you ain't on board. No refund on the ticket. Have a nice night."

"Right." The girl takes the ticket wearily. She picks her bag from the scale and turns away, scanning the terminal for the bench that looks the most comfortable. But then she turns back. "Is there any coffee around here?"

"'Ere's an instant coffee machine by the bathrooms. The Starbucks next door opens at seven."

Seven, of course, is too late. And the watery bitterness of instant coffee she isn't sure her still-poison-flushing body can stomach. She resumes her bench searching.

"Hey, kid," the man at the ticket counter says, and against her instincts, or perhaps because of them, she turns to him again.

"Yes? What?"

"Why you going to New York? I mean you're what? How old?"

"I'm eighteen."

"Bullshit."

A pause. "I'll be eighteen in three weeks." Why she tells the fat, greasy guy this she'll never know, except that her preconceived notions about certain things, like men, and women, have been recently demolished.

"See now *that* I believe. You don't look young, though, I don't mean to say. Like you could be eighteen, if you wanted to be, looks-wise 'n'all. But I could tell. Got a knack for these things. So, why then?"

"Why then what?"

"Why New York?"

"I'm . . . visiting family. My . . . aunt."

"See, now that's more bullshit. But anyway, be careful, kid, is all. New York's a shitstorm."

The girl backs away. "Right," she says, one last time. She picks a bench by a potted tree in the center of the terminal. Using the backpack as a pillow, she lays across the bench, placing the duffle on top of her like a heavy blanket. From the hoodie's deep pocket she pulls her BlackBerry. It still has service, has not yet been shut off, but of course there are no messages, no texts or missed calls—how could there be when they don't even know she has a phone. If they did know, she wonders, would they call? She sets the alarm for 5:45. She falls asleep with one arm in her pocket, cradling the BlackBerry, and the other looped around the duffle's strap so no one can try to take it without waking her. She's going to New York because New York sounds like a city she could be happy in.

SUGARCANE

IN ONE UNIVERSE, AS HE stands there off to the side of that stage in that theater, where the lights have just gone down and where 1700 seats are filled by almost 1700 humans in their nicest clothes and where detail after detail has been rehearsed and tweaked and made to be as close to perfect as possible for the better part of the last year, Jonathan Bread is suddenly aware that his life is about to completely and irreversibly change. There's a sound, deep and short, that echoes throughout the building as one of the stagehands makes the first turn on the crank that will bring the curtain up. A man, or maybe a woman, in the audience coughs twice. It's difficult to tell a person's gender by the sound of just two coughs. Bread thinks it's a man, but he's not sure. It really could just as easily be a woman. Bread wonders if she's attractive, thinks about what kind of body she has, what her ass is like sitting in the semi-comfortable chair of one of Broadway's smaller theaters. But is she even in one of those chairs? Maybe she's got box seats, and so she's sitting in a chair that's far more comfortable than he'd originally assumed. Oh, god, Bread thinks, this woman is incredibly wealthy, so wealthy that she's got box seats to a Broadway show, and here she is, bored as hell before the play has even started, coughing, so as to say without saying, get on with it. Oh, god.

The curtain is still coming up, but there are no more loud noises, just a steady creaking of metal gears, the sound of which is quiet enough that it reaches only the ears of the stagehand turning the crank and of Jonathan standing there off to the side. The first scene's actors are in place behind the opening curtain. On cue, music starts: various stringed instruments played with bows accompanied by chilling electric guitar and clashing cymbals and a triangle. The play was written to be edgy and anachronistic, so even though the whole thing takes place in the mid-eighteenth century, the music is modern and loud.

Called *Sugarcane: The Man* from its very inception fifteen years ago when Bread was in college, the play has gone through some fifteen drafts. In this, its final incarnation, the show's plot revolves around a 25-year-old Indian slave named Raj who is working on a sugar plantation in Great Britain. Raj falls in love with the 17-year-old daughter of a fellow slave, this fellow slave being twice Raj's age and also Asian, and so Raj and the girl, with the girl's father's blessing, decide to make a break for it and sneak aboard a boat bound for America. The girl's father, who is ill by this point, gives them all the money he has, which he's kept stored secretly for many years in the lining of the only jacket he owns. Attempting more than once to escape the plantation, Raj and the girl fail each time, and during their third and final attempt, the plantation owner decides they simply aren't worth the trouble and orders them both killed. The girl's father, in a heartbreaking display of love that isn't actually all that heartbreaking, when you stop to think about the fact that he is by this point very very ill and will die soon anyway, disrupts the execution and is himself violently killed, and Raj and the girl escape to America and live happily ever after. *Sugarcane: The Man* was originally intended to be a musical, but after Jonathan Bread convinced Andrew Lloyd Webber to sit down for lunch a couple years ago, hoping to get him to write the music, and Webber told him the script was good but he had better things to do than work on something written by a man nobody had yet heard of, Bread decided it shouldn't be a musical anyway, and so he rewrote the lyrics as regular dialogue.

Sugarcane will be considered Jonathan Bread's masterpiece, his greatest work, for thousands of years to come, despite its short first run.

The curtain is open and the music has reached its loudest point thus far—it's a breathtaking fanfare. If the woman in the audience is still coughing, Bread can't hear her. He releases the breath he's been holding since the curtain started rising as Hugh Jackman, in what has the potential to, but will not, become a Tony-winning performance, speaks Raj's first words: "Oh, woe is the life I lead, and the toil I toil. And the work I am forced to do is laborious and hard, but the face of a woman's heart's love keeps me living."

Certain portions of the play's dialogue will not be without their critics in the coming millennia.

After the play is over, the cast and crew gather for an extravagant party with the goal of celebrating the hard work they've been putting into this thing for the past many months, the extraordinary and exhausting effort they've each invested in making *Sugarcane* a success, and that very success, which they've assured themselves will come, so good is the show and their performance of it.

And indeed, at the party, the initial reaction to the play is overwhelmingly positive. Jonathan Bread wanders about the room, which isn't small and is lit brightly but decorated with soft colors that diffuse the light, a glass of fine pink champagne in his left hand, congratulating the cast members as he walks by. He thanks Mr. Jackman graciously, shaking his hand and patting him on the shoulder, and Jackman says he's happy to be in such a grand production and can they do lunch someday soon. Bread tells the girl who played the girl in the play that she did wonderful, kisses her hand and reminds her how lovely she is and tells her she's got such promise, which is the same thing she's been hearing over and over again at this party from everyone who approaches her. *You were wonderful. Beautiful. Surely this is the start of an incredible career.* She smiles each time. She's twenty years old and until only recently she was waiting tables at a restaurant in Times Square. Bread speaks briefly with reporters, reviewers for the *Times* and *SF Mag* and others. He speaks to business men who appreciate a good Broadway show, various celebrities.

Finally, Jonathan sneaks off into a corner and downs the glass of champagne, which he's been carrying without drinking a single sip of, in one loud gulp. If he were to take a moment to be truthful with these people, he'd speak to them of the complete and total overwhelmingness of the evening's response. He'd never dreamed that all this. . . . Except he had dreamed—all humans dream of things like these, but never in the most ambitious of those dreams does one expect that it all will actually happen, that one will achieve such success and praise, that one will create so great a work. And even now he wonders how great it could really be. Certainly all here tonight are deluding themselves, or they're pulling Bread's leg, ribbing him, joshing him, whatever—certainly the play was awful and they hated it. Certainly Jonathan Bread hasn't actually arrived.

Merrel Whippo, the man named on the playbill and all the posters as *Sugarcane*'s producer, comes up to him, two glasses of champagne in his hands. He's a genuinely kind man. He's balding, but gracefully, and he's shaved his greying hairline down to within an eighth of an inch of his tanned and moisturized scalp. He wears these black-rimmed glasses on his face and a bit of extra weight around his mid-section. His tuxedo is black and traditional, but his tie is purple and *this close* to being overly large. He holds one of the champagne flutes out to Jonathan. "I saw your glass was empty," he says, "and well, I figured you'd need a full one, if you're going to make a toast."

Jonathan Bread is thirty-six years old when *Sugarcane* premiers on Broadway. Bread was born in Akron, Ohio, shortly after the start of its rebuilding. His parents are Glenn and Nora Bread, two kindly people who, at least in this reality, are alive and well and still live in Akron but have come to New York for this very special night, tickets paid for by their son. He looks around for them but doesn't see them, which isn't surprising because, while he made sure they were on the list for this after-party, Jonathan knows his father has in recent years developed a tendency to grow particularly nervous around large groups of people, and occasionally he becomes downright scared and forgets things—his doctors are fairly certain he's in the early stages of Alzheimer's, which is a shame because he's only sixty-two—and so Jonathan had a feeling his parents might not end up coming to the party, but that's okay because he saw them both before the show, and they have plans for brunch tomorrow before they catch their afternoon flight back home out of JFK. Jonathan Bread's face is still youthful—some call it a baby-face, which he dislikes; his hair is full and dark and curly, and he slicks it back with a water-based pomade, the brand of which has changed every few months since he was a teenager because he still doesn't think he's found one he quite likes; there are, despite his boyishness, gentle signs of aging around his eyes and mouth and on his forehead, subtle lines that are the products of laughter and crying and furrowing his brow in concentration while hammering out a frustrating scene late at night under the influence of too much Scotch. He's relatively fit. He doesn't work out but he has sex a lot with beautiful young women, and the aerobic intensity of his particular style of fucking keeps his muscles tight and toned, even if the tone is diminished slightly by a thirteen percent body-fat level. He's worked for ten years in theater and television, first as a stage-hand and then as an assistant set designer and then as a script editor for a popular serialized crime procedural. All the while, he rewrote and rewrote and rewrote again his script. The script was rejected by an entire industry before Merrel Whippo, the producer of such stage classics as *At the Bread Shop*, *Ira on the Island*, and *Frogs!*, decided to give it a chance. Even Merrel was at first reluctant to back Jonathan's project because it was no longer a musical, and Bread insisted that he could make it a musical, that it had been a musical before and he still had that earlier draft of the script; but Merrel just looked the pages over silently while Jonathan sipped nervously at his coffee in that Tribeca cafe. And then finally, mercifully, Merrel looked up and smiled and said that, on second thought, the fact that *Sugarcane* wasn't a musical was refreshing, and he'd be happy to back the production with his own money.

Bread reluctantly takes the flute of bubbly pink liquid and smiles. "If you insist," he says. "But you know I hate public speaking."

"It can be short," Merrel says. "You know they want to hear something from you. All of them do."

Merrel picks up a spoon from a nearby table of little cups of *flan de leche* and taps it against his own glass. "Everybody!" he calls out, and the conversations in the room cease one by one until there are just a few and then none at all and everybody is silent and staring. "I want to thank you all for the hard work you've put into this project. I took a risk last year when Jonathan came to me with his script about a poor Indian slave and a beautiful young Korean girl and their love, but I've also had the utmost confidence from the beginning, and you've all shown me that confidence was well placed."

There's applause and a few cheers, and a couple actors shout out good-natured jibes at Merrel's expense. Merrel laughs. "Thanks, Hugh," he says, "We'll talk about that later." And everyone laughs at that. "But now," Merrel says, "I think Jonathan would like to say a few words, and I'm sure we'd all like to hear them."

Bread smiles uneasily. When he told Merrel he hates public speaking, he wasn't lying, wasn't being modest. If he could talk about things with, like, his voice, he often says, he wouldn't need to write about them. He starts to speak, but the sound that comes out of the back of his suddenly dry throat doesn't exactly sound like any English word. He pretends to cough into the top of his balled-up fist and tries again. "I—"

They're all looking at him. The actors. The actors' understudies. Crew. Journalists and critics. Celebrities. The air is cool in this room, still and quiet. Jonathan hadn't noticed how big the eyes are of the girl who plays the girl in the play. They're big, but they're also very blue, not hard like ice but understated like calm water. Her hair is dark, the color of almonds. She's so small. She seems to be staring at him more expectantly than anyone, and why not: she carried the show—its success rested on her shoulders more than anyone's. The next morning, in its review of *Sugarcane*—"fantastic, but with a few small flaws this reviewer is confident will be worked out for later runs of the show"—the *Times* will call her the next Zhang Ziyi.

"I worked on this for a long time," Bread says, "a very long time. It's been my dream for over ten years, and I know this dream wouldn't have been realized without each and every one of you." He raises his champagne flute high and tips it toward Merrel, who's still standing beside him, and then tips it back toward everyone else. "To *you*."

Those in attendance raise their own glasses and drink and break out into loud and genuine applause.

The party goes on for a couple more hours, but not too late, because, after all, they've got to put on another show tomorrow. The show's first week will be performed entirely by the principle cast before switching next week to a schedule of three shows a week with the principle cast and two with certain key rolls filled by the understudies, and this schedule will go on for at least the next two months, after which point the fate of the show's first run, i.e. whether it will continue or go on hiatus or be cancelled altogether, will be decided by Merrel and his financial compatriots. After the toast, the talk at the party becomes less about the show and more about friends and colleagues catching up with one another. Jonathan finds it refreshing. He wonders how he'll feel in the morning. His work on *Sugarcane* is essentially done—from this point on, the actors and stage managers will keep things going. His creation is in their hands now and the hands of those who choose to watch the show. With this night, his life has changed, yes, but will he feel it? Does change, he wonders, actually mean different? More questions not unlike these he asks himself as the night goes on.

The next morning, Jonathan Bread wakes up just after nine o'clock and rolls his naked body over, turning his face into the sunlight. He's not really hungover—he had only the two glasses of champagne and then a whiskey sour—but his mouth is dry and his head hurts mildly just above the right eyebrow. Sometimes, when turning into the light like this, he winces or blinks uncontrollably, but today he smiles and inhales deeply, taking the light in through his smile.

The noise he makes when turning over is maybe too loud, because there's a rustling sound from behind him, and he feels the soft hand on his upper thigh, right near his ass, and hears the woman in his bed breathe the same as he did, as if she too is trying to inhale the glorious morning sun's warming rays. He turns to her. His mouth is like sandpaper, but it becomes more like wet sandpaper as he moves his tongue around inside it and the salivary glands start doing what they're supposed to do. "Morning," he says.

Her name is Melissa. She's about twenty years old. She's an understudy for the girl who plays the girl in the play, but she got the job weeks before she and Jonathan started sleeping together, so when they sleep together, which is for the most part all their relationship consists of, there's no guilt for either party. She didn't sleep with him to get the job. There is little emotional connection here except for that which comes from good sex.

They simply enjoy the human contact that each other's presence provides.

"Morning," she replies.

They make love or have sex or fuck wildly, whatever you want to call it, for the next twenty minutes. The majority of that time is spent on foreplay and kissing each other's bodies in various places and in various ways, but the last five minutes or so are filled with intense thrusting, with Jonathan on his knees on top of the mattress and Melissa on all fours in front of him and then threes because she puts the palm of her left hand up against the headboard in front of her to steady herself while Jonathan moves against her and inside her. They both like this particular position because of the pleasure it facilitates, but what it doesn't allow for is some sort of eye-contact, some depth of soulful contact in addition to depth of penetration. Melissa's long, straight dark hair sticks against her shoulders and back and Jonathan wonders if it might be a good idea to manually turn down the automated thermostat after they're finished. They climax in sequence, first Melissa and then Jonathan, and then they both fall over onto their backs on top of the mattress and bed sheets, breathing heavily but invigorated more than exhausted.

Jonathan stumbles out of the bedroom, which, he thinks now, is a bit small. He walks into the kitchen and starts the coffee, pouring a scoop of beans into the grinder and grinding them and pouring the ground beans into his six-cup coffee pot. He has a French press that he uses more than the coffee pot, but the clock says 9:27 and he has to meet his parents for brunch at a quarter past ten, so he doesn't quite feel like he has time to use the French press, and besides he'll get to have some decent coffee there, at brunch, maybe an espresso. As the smell of hot coffee begins to fill the apartment almost immediately, the pot bubbling audibly, he fills a saucepan with water and puts it on the stove, turning the burner all the way up. Jonathan's apartment is open: the kitchen and living room occupy different parts of the same space with no wall separating them; there's a round glass table that seats four on which sits a laptop and Melissa's purse and Jonathan's phone and keys and wallet. The living room space has a couch and chair and a glass coffee table that matches the round dining room table. On the coffee table is a magazine Jonathan has never read and a seven-inch white plastic tablet computer that acts as his reading library and also controls the television that hangs on the wall. There's art on the other walls. The only window in the place is in the bedroom, but it's a large window. Jonathan's been here for almost two and a half years. His lease ended five months ago and he's been renting month-to-month since then, and he's thinking he should probably look for a new and at least a little bit larger place within the next few days.

Jonathan walks towards the bathroom by way of the bedroom and passes Melissa, who looks up from her phone and smiles at him. "I'm going to shower," he says, "but I'll be quick. There's water on for you."

In the bathroom he turns on the shower and lets the steam begin to build while he uses the toilet. He looks into the mirror and wonders if he should brush his teeth, if brushing his teeth *now* will ruin the taste of his coffee and if the coffee will ruin the minty effects of brushing his teeth, or if he should wait until after he's had a cup, but he knows if he waits he may forget, and he'll leave the house with morning breath only slightly overpowered by coffee breath. He doesn't actively make a decision about this. He pulls the shower door open and steps into the humid cubicle and under the hot spray.

His mouth is pretty much back to proper moisture levels and the sex got his blood pumping so that the last of the dull morning above-the-eye headache recedes, vaporizes, into nonexistence when the hot water, which he likes almost scalding, hits his skin. He's thinking about nonexistence as he lathers, about obsolescence and irrelevance. The one thing he's been working on the entirety of his adult life is, as far as anyone is concerned, finished. It will live on and everything, and it will take work to keep the thing alive for months and hopefully years to come, but of that work he's already done his part. He looks at the bottle of the body wash he's using; it's dark blue with one of those caps that just won't stay properly shut after you've opened it for the first time. The point is what exactly should he do now? What should he work on? In what ways can he continue to move his life forward? He knows, can feel, that at this point things will start to accelerate, to exponentially increase, to—what's the term? —snowball.

In the decade-and-a-half since he began pursuing his dream of writing a big, famous Broadway play, he's eschewed certain personal desires, like travel and close personal relationships. He went to Paris once, but for only four days because he couldn't afford to take more time than that from the set-design job he held at the time, and he thought he'd find inspiration there but mostly he just found food and the Eiffel Tower. His physical relationships have been many and often, but he's given little real time to the idea of settling down with someone or even spending any sort of meaningful time coming to feel anything for them. Now might be the time to start; after all, he could ease off on the hard work a bit and things will still snowball. It's the day after the premier and he's not sure if he feels any different and yet he feels so very different. He likes Melissa and her company and decides she should come to brunch with him this morning.

He shuts off the water, turning the chrome knob to the left all the way until it doesn't turn any more, and grabs the big white fluffy towel on the shelf outside the shower stall and towels off his hair and his face and his feet before stepping out onto the fuzzy blue bathmat in front of the sink. He wraps the towel around his waist and shakes a dollop of moisturizer from a bottle into his hand and rubs his palms together and rubs it over the significant stubble on his face. His beard takes a long time to grow and he hasn't shaved in weeks just so he could have that amount of stubble hip and trendy celebrities often have in time for the premier.

"Hey," he says as he opens the bathroom door and walks into the bedroom. "I don't know what sort of plans you have for this morning, but I'm having brunch with my parents at this great place on Franklin and I'd love for you to come. They have great French toast and—"

She's not in the bedroom, but she made the bed for him. He checks the apartment's other room and she's not there either. Her purse is gone and the half-empty cup of tea she was sipping at is on the counter by the sink. She has left already, which isn't surprising or anything—they rarely stay for breakfast when they stay over, no matter how much he'd often like to make breakfast for them.

Jonathan sighs. He shrugs his shoulders nakedly and then puts on clothes from his small apartment's single small closet: A black t-shirt and dark-blue jeans and a brown zip-up sweater he likes because the protagonist of this one action film series tends to wear something similar in two of the films of the series.

Brown leather wing-tipped boots. It's technically spring but the weather is still more like winter in the city and so the temperature is still cold. He has to be at the restaurant in about twenty-five minutes, but it's only three blocks from his small apartment, so he has time.

He pours out the half-empty cup of tea and rinses the glass and fills it again with coffee and carries it to the sofa, where he sits and puts one leg folded across the other's knee relaxedly and picks up his media tablet with his empty hand and opens up the *New York Times* application and feels like his father—reading the news in the morning with his cup of bitter coffee and one leg crossed over the other. He resists the urge to turn to the culture section and instead skims the front-page stories, reading the one about that recent earthquake on the other side of the world more completely than the rest. He checks the one social network to which he belongs but which also he isn't very active on. His follower count has overnight gone up by three thousand five hundred and nine, and he thinks *holy fuck*. He gives in and switches back to the *New York Times* and taps on the table of contents and on the culture section and sips his hot coffee.

The reviews of *Sugarcane* are stellar apart from a few anomalies, but there are always going to be anomalous opinions when you're dealing with this sort of thing. Tastes in all things are completely and utterly subjective. Taste in music is subjective. Taste in film is subjective. Taste in comedy is subjective. Taste in things like literature and trashy novels and game shows and certain technological things like mobile operating systems and hardware are subjective. And tastes in clothes and personal style and sexual positions and how much foreplay is not enough foreplay before moving on to the main event and things like which city is the best city to live in for aspiring young creative professionals (whatever the hell that means these days—Jonathan, being no longer aspiring or young, wouldn't know) and sculpture and paintings and collage and television are all subjective tastes. Taste in Broadway shows is subjective. But just because taste in these things requires a definitive amount of subjectivity doesn't mean there aren't certain aspects of some specific examples of each of these things that are so widely enjoyed by a large enough percentage of the general human audience to be blanketly called good. *Sugarcane* is good is the popular consensus among the critics who saw its premier.

"Did you read the *Times*?" Merrel asks eagerly from the other side of the phone signal. Bread walks down the street as a light flurry of mid-spring snow falls onto his navy wool peacoat and onto the lenses of his glasses. Each flake is more like a collection of flakes, puffy and large, pausing on a surface for a moment, frozen there, and then melting and disappearing as if it never was.

"I did. I read the *Times*." Jonathan says into the phone.

"What about the *Post*? Did you read the *Post*?"

"I didn't read the *Post*."

"Did you read the *Journal*? Or the *Globe*? Or the *Voice*? Or the—"

"Woah now, Merrell. Calm down. I read only the *Times*. I almost didn't even read that, barely had time, but."

"They love you, Jon!"

"They don't love me," Jonathan says, sidestepping two men who are carrying a couch from a moving van to a building across the sidewalk. "They love the play. They don't even know who *I* am."

"Don't know—? Aw, fuck, Jon, did you even read it? They love you. They mention you like a dozen times."

Jonathan laughs. Merrel calls him Jon only when he's excited because that's when he forgets Jonathan hates being called Jon.

"Listen to this," Merrel says. "And I quote: 'Bread has, with his debut play, proven that the American theater arts are entering the dawn of a new era, an age where whimsy and storytelling and genuine tugging at the heartstrings matter more than catchy scores or clichéd lyrics, where dialogue and character are king.' What do you think of that, Jon?"

"I think first that calling anything cliché is just cliché in itself anymore, but I'm excited—"

"That was from the *Guardian*, Jon! Even the British loved it, love *you*."

Jonathan smiles to himself. He's trying his best to remain modest and humble, etc. Truth be told, he's speechless.

"You're going big places, Bread," Merrel says. "You're doing brilliant work. They love you."

Things that are not subjective, as far as Jonathan Bread is concerned: that money doesn't grow on trees; that satisfaction is not something you seek out or purchase but something you choose; that love is an addiction initially caused by the release of the chemicals dopamine, phenethylamine, and norepinephrine and then carried on by a variety of side effects of that initial chemical release, including a lowering of serotonin levels; that certain wines are better than certain other wines (Malbecs, for example, are far classier and therefore tastier than Merlots, and this is indisputable) and that cheap wine doesn't necessarily mean bad wine; but that cheap coffee on the other hand is generally terrible; the origins of the universe; the moralistic wrongness of certain acts—acts like rape and child abuse and murder; the fact that other certain acts are moral grey areas; that baseball caps should be worn only by those who play baseball; that sports are sometimes entertaining and that the skill of a few rare athletes is admirable and even impressive, but that generally the hullabaloo caused by and attention given to such things is misplaced and a waste of time on a humanly detrimental level; the laws of physics; the fact that some serious, major things have been happening climatologically in recent decades; the deliciousness of the contents in those little silver-pouched juice drinks.

Jonathan Bread arrives at the restaurant and speaks to the *maitre'd*, who points out to him his parents—they have already arrived and are sitting at a square table with four chairs by the wall, sipping coffee, and Jonathan joins them at the table and now he's waiting for the waiter to return with coffee of his own and recommending the French toast to his parents.

"It's delicious," he says, pointing to the French toast's spot on the menu, a graceful single sheet of laminated paper.

Jonathan's mother, Nora, says it sounds good, reading the description: two croissants, halved for a total of four pieces, dipped in an egg and cinnamon and vanilla mixture and then grilled with butter and finished with dollops of homemade vanilla whipped cream, sugar powdered in-house, and berries (the berries vary depending on season and availability). "But your father can't have any sort of bread. The doctor says he needs to stay away from gluten because studies have shown that gluten can exacer . . . exacer . . . contribute to his . . . you know."

"Alzheimer's," Glenn Bread says. Nora winces, but Glenn waves his hand. "Please. I know what I have, and I'm not uncomfortable talking about it."

"Sorry, Glenn," Nora says, rubbing her husband's big shoulders. "It's just I'm still . . ."

Jonathan smiles. This is the third time since his parents have been in the city that they've had a conversation like this one. He reaches across the table, placing his hands on both their hands. "I'm glad I got to see you two," he says. "But now then, what sounds good, Dad?"

Glenn grunts. He picks up his own menu. He mutters. "My damned name is Bread and I can't eat bread. Ridiculous."

Glenn and Nora Bread make an attractive couple. They've both aged gracefully and both faces have this effervescent glow. They each have far more grey hair than black, but Nora is as thin and fit as she ever was, and Glenn still has the broad muscular shoulders of his youth.

The waiter comes back around, dropping off strong, aromatic coffee for Jonathan in a large pink mug, and asks if they're ready to make their selection. Jonathan and Nora both order the French toast, and Glenn orders eggs and bacon and, after being chided by Nora for several seconds to "get something healthy, Glenn," adds a bowl of fruit. They all ask for orange juice with their meals. The juice has been fresh-squeezed that morning back in the kitchen, the menu says.

They wait for the food, sipping their coffee. They don't speak, but Jonathan looks around the dining room. It is bright and open and airy. The tablecloths are white. The walls are a soft pink with little floral accents printed faintly on the wallpaper every few feet, except it's not that antique sort of floral print Jonathan always thinks of when he remembers his grandmother's house—it's floral but modern, in a quaint and pleasant sort of way. The waiters wear black or white shirts with white or black buttons; the buttons on the black shirts are white, but the buttons on the white shirts are black. It's the same with the bow ties in that the waiters with white shirts have black ties, etc. The contrast is visually interesting—each button is a vortex against the fabric, black holes and white black holes—and the fact that there are both black and white options makes Jonathan wonder if the individual waiters have a choice as to which color they're going to wear or if the colors are assigned. The split between white shirts and black shirts (and therefore buttons and ties) seems to be an even one. They're probably assigned. Such things are always assigned. The glassware is clean, crystal. The coffee mugs are the same pink as the wallpaper, sans floral prints, and are also aesthetically pleasing in a modern way. Jonathan sees some of the customers currently eating brunch have ordered tea, and there are medium-sized kettles on the white tablecloths of those customers. Brunch is very popular in the city on the weekend. *Sugarcane* premiered on Friday night, and so today is Saturday. Brunch is especially popular on Saturday. Jonathan wonders if the silence between himself and his parents, and the silence between his mother and his father, as they wait, are the kind of silence that comes from awkwardness, from having nothing to say to another person, from being alone, or the kind that comes from being so comfortable, so familiar with another human being, that nothing need be said. He doesn't know.

Jonathan's phone, which he has left on the tablecloth next to his coffee, buzzes. The screen lights up and he fights the urge to check the thin device, but he fails, and he sees Merrel has texted him: *The London News! I told you the British love you.* Jonathan shakes his head and grins.

"Who's that, dear?" his mother says.

"It's just my producer," he says. "He keeps bothering me about the play's reviews."

His father looks at him. "And—?"

"And they're good."

"Ha!" Glenn says. He turns to his wife. "I told you, Nora! I told you our son's an artist. They love him."

"And well of course they do, dear," Nora says. She puts her hand on Jonathan's. "The play was wonderful. We haven't said it yet this morning, but we both thought it was wonderful."

"Thank you," Jonathan says, and then the phone buzzes again. His mother takes her hand off his.

"You tell your producer you're out with your parents and to leave you alone," she says. "Or better yet, you turn that nasty thing off now why don't you. I never did like phones."

"Don't like phones?" Glenn says. "Nora, that's like saying you don't like wheels. Or . . . or fire. They've been around as long."

"They haven't been around as long, Glenn. The wheel is what, like billions of years old?"

"Thousands."

"Okay, fine, thousands. And you're telling me the phone is pretty much the same?"

"I was being hyperbolic."

"And just how do you remember things like the age of fire or how to correctly use words like hyperbolic but forget where your keys or shoes are so often that your doctor says you have an actual bona fide medical condition? How is that? Explain that to me."

The sound of his parents' amicable row is lost on Jonathan as he goes to silence his phone. But the message isn't from Merrel. It's Melissa. *Sorry*, it says plainly.

Jonathan turns the phone sideways and texts back as his parents fade with the rest of the restaurant to the edge of his perception. *What happened?* he types. *I thought maybe we could have breakfast. My parents are in town.*

She replies quickly. *Im sorry*, she says again. *I had things to do before preparing for this evenings performance.*

Jonathan's thumbs dance on the screen. *It's okay. I understand. We're all busy.*

Tonight? her next message asks. *After the performance?*

Of course. Always, he types, and then: *Your place tonight?*

After he hits send, the phone's screen just sits there staring at him. His parents have stopped talking. Finally the animated speech bubble pops up: *Can we do your place again, actually. Mine is just a mess and I havent had time to clean things up with the play and everything.*

Jonathan's parents have stopped talking about phones and fire. He can feel their eyes on him. *Sure,* he types, and he hits send, and the phone's screen goes black as he locks it.

"Did you tell your producer to leave you alone?" his mother asks.

Their waiter refills their coffee mugs, pouring from a silver carafe that is the same modern metal as the tea kettles on the tables with tea kettles. He brings their food a few minutes later on a black plastic tray. He places the tray on a wooden tray holder while he moves the plates from the tray and in front of their respective orderers on the table. Will there be anything else at the moment? No thank you; we're fine. It all looks delicious.

And so they eat.

The french toast is not as good as Jonathan remembers it, but Nora seems to be enamored with hers. To Jonathan the croissant seems stale, the eggs it's been dipped in underscrambled and undercooked, the powdered sugar too finely powdered and the berries (raspberry) out of season, the whole experience underwhelming, not as he'd imagined it would be. His mother cuts each bite with what can be described only as giddy anticipation and savors each one slowly. When questioned about his level of satisfaction with his bacon and eggs, Glenn grunts good-naturedly. "They're bacon and eggs," he says. The orange juice comes from fresh blood oranges and, all agree, is delicious.

"I forgot to ask," Jonathan says as they take the cab south to JFK. "How was the hotel?"

His parents wanted to stay with him during their visit, and in fact they'd never seen his place before, but the apartment was just too small, he told them, so, since they were going to be in town for only two nights, he put them up in one of the more expensive hotels he could afford.

"It was nice," his mother replies.

Jonathan can't tell if she means it. His father is asleep on her shoulder on the right side of the cab. Jonathan is on the left. His mother in the middle.

Growing up just outside of Akron, which when Jonathan was born was in the early stages of its federal-funded rebuilding after Quake Irvine's devastation nearly thirty years before (it was the first time the National Geological Association had ever seen fit to name an earthquake, but the damage had been so catastrophic, the quake itself so powerful, that certain interest groups had lobbied the NGA to do just that, arguing that a failure to name such a massive Act of God would be nothing but spitting in the face of the divine), provided little opportunity for moments of opulence in a young person's life. Indeed, the rebuilding and refortification effort took nearly twenty years, and so even though now the city is considered one of the most prosperous and culturally significant in the country—sixth in line in fact next to New York, Chicago, Las Vegas, Colonial

Williamsburg, and Missoula (which also faced a significant natural disaster, a freak tornado that eyewitnesses swear looked nothing like a tornado at all but that still sucked into its maw a quarter of the city twenty years ago)—as he was growing up it was nothing but a fenced-in cluster of slowly rising metal towers, and those who lived outside that fence had little in the way of livelihood. Of course, the city owes to the quake and subsequent rebuilding its now-burgeoning polyurethane industry, an iteration of the city's once-great rubber industry, and which polyurethane is instrumental in the creation of protective cases and grip-enhancing backs for cellular phones and media tablets. So, basically, Akron was great once, is great now, but was not great during Jonathan's childhood.

He remembers going to school with too many other children, almost thirty to a classroom. He remembers playing Squares on the street with the children on his block. He remembers his father cursing when the house's ceiling's back left corner began to crack, a casualty of the long-term structural damage inflicted on Akron's outlying areas by the quake. He remembers his father putting in overtime for three weeks straight so they could afford to pay a contractor to analyze and then literally rebuild that corner of the house. They were never poor; they had enough food, good food, always, and they had a car and a television and things like that. Nobody around them lived in poverty, just conditions that were less than ideal. Lower-middle class and no one could seem to get out of it. He remembers working with his father at the garage for six months when he turned sixteen before telling him that mechanics just weren't his thing. He remembers his father asking him what he did want to do then, exactly. He remembers answering that he thought he wanted to study theater. He remembers his dad saying that was wonderful, and that he and Jonathan's mother, who worked as a waitress, were happy to contribute what they could, financially, to his studies, but that he'd need to contribute himself as well, and so why didn't he stay at the garage through high school, which he did, not unhappily. And in fact when he turned eighteen and graduated and all was said and done they were unable to contribute much, something which he never begrudged them, and he got a couple decent scholarships and had his own savings. Of course even now he's still paying off student loans, but his monthlies could certainly be higher under different past circumstances.

"Did you enjoy the pool?" Jonathan asks, referring to the hotel's pool, which he heard was large for an indoor pool and also warm and relaxingly atmospheric.

"Yes, well, your father slept a lot when we were at the hotel, but I got to check the pool out once. It was nice."

The cab moves through traffic. Jonathan catches the driver's eye in the rearview mirror. The driver is a blond, forty-something man with longish blond stubble below his chin. Jonathan rubs his own rough neck absentmindedly. Outside the cab, the early spring snow is still falling, lightly, gently, caressing the taxi's glass. In winter, the snow falls heavily in the city, sometimes causing parking bans which upset nearly every resident despite the knowledge that without the bans, plows couldn't plow and traffic conditions would be far worse. In the first weeks of spring sometimes no snow falls at all. And sometimes winter exits reluctantly, lingering the way it is this year, unwilling to depart just yet. Jonathan suddenly feels the same way about his parents. He hasn't been able to spend as much time with them the last two and a half days as he would have liked. Lunch a few hours after they got in, lunch yesterday and a quick visit backstage before the premier, and today's late breakfast. He's just been so busy, and now suddenly the hard work is done. He wonders if maybe they shouldn't go just yet. He voices as much to Nora Bread, who tells him their return tickets are non-exchangeable, but that they can visit again soon. It doesn't cost much these days to fly between Akron and NYC.

Glenn Bread snores.

"Glenn, dear," Nora says, elbowing him, her voice thick with deliberate nagging. "Wake up. We're at the airport."

Glenn snorts and jumps in his seat. "Huh? We're where?"

"Nowhere, Glenn. We're still in the cab. Got another fifteen minutes, maybe, but you were snoring." She turns to Jonathan. "Your father snores so much now."

And the cab drives on to JFK, and when it arrives it pulls up to the curb in front of the unloading section marked Southwest Airways. The space between the road and the airport's outer wall, along which are revolving glass doors and outdoor baggage check-in kiosks staffed by men and women with pleasant smiles and blue dress shirts and vests in the primary colors of the logos of their respective employers, is a sea of departing humans and their loved ones who are loath to let them go away. A family of five with two suitcases and a carry-on each are shuffling over to the American Airways line. An elderly woman sits in a wheelchair while a middle-aged man, presumably her son but possibly her lover, pushes it toward and then through the revolving doors, getting stuck awkwardly as the chair catches on the glass of the door and the wall of the circular enclosure at the same time because the space between the door's glass dividers is too small for a wheelchair, and though they finally make it through they don't do so without an embarrassing jerky motion. Next to the kiosk for Hawaiian Air, a thirty-something mother consoles her preteen, sandy-blond-haired son, who is apparently flying alone for the first time in his life, telling him that she'll walk him to the security checkpoint where the nice lady will take care of him and that his father will meet him as soon as the plane lands, and the son asks why his father had to move away, and his mother says it's because he got that new job in Austin, and the boy says yes but why did you guys have to get divorced in the first place. Two young female lovers kiss passionately at the curb: there's the general sense in the air that one of the lovers was leaving, perhaps for good, and the other has just caught her, just now, just in time, and begged her either to not go or to let her go with her, forever. A grey-chinned man with a cane and a porkpie hat carries a pet carrier and no other luggage.

Jonathan steps out of the cab with his parents and asks the driver to please pop the trunk, his parents' bags are in there. He takes the bags; they've packed two large suitcases, one dark red, a sort of burgundy, and the other an identical shape and style but navy blue. They're heavy. "How much did you guys pack?" Jonathan asks, peppering the question with faux grunts of mock exertion.

His mother hits him lightly on the upper arm. "You're a strong man," she says. "You can handle it."

And indeed he can, although not without an honest amount of difficulty, which he hides with more mock grunts and groans that in actuality are real, genuine grunts and groans, because the best way to cover up the truth is often with a lie that looks exactly like the truth. He walks the luggage to the check-in for them because his mother doesn't like luggage with wheels.

"Just put them there by the line," Glenn says. "I'll check everything in."

Jonathan does that, sets them there at the end of the lengthy line, right next to what's often referred to as the "roped-off area" even though the rope is flat and more like a seatbelt than anything else. "Well, Dad . . ."

"Well, Son . . ."

Father stares at son.

Bread stares at Bread.

Awkward silence.

"Who...who are you again?" Glenn Bread asks, his brow suddenly scrunched tightly, forming extra lines on his already-creased forehead. He's looking like he might fall over.

"I—Dad." Jonathan is afraid for a moment. He's only heard about his father's deteriorating memory; he's not yet seen an episode.

Glenn Bread cracks a smile, puts out a hand.

Jonathan stares at the hand, uneasy.

"Aw, Son. I'm just messing with you. Com'ere." And he wraps Jonathan in a massive, bear-type hug. Jonathan can feel his father's wrinkling-but-mostly-smooth-skinned face on his own stubbled face. As they hug, he feels his cell phone buzz in his peacoat's internal left breast pocket. Gingerly, the hug is broken. "Well," Glenn Bread says, "I'm going to check this luggage in." He nods at his wife and bends at the knees and picks up the bags and steps into the back of the line. The line is shorter than it was a moment ago; it has been moving forward without anyone else filling in the newly created spaces at the rear. *Spaces at the rear.* Jonathan Bread is thirty-six. He's a serious, successful writer. So why is "spaces at the rear" an amusing phrase?

Mother and son alone now near the back of the luggage check-in line, which moves forward at a steady pace. Nora has a leather purse slung over her right shoulder. She moves more slowly than she used to move. "You know," she says, grasping

Jonathan's hands in her hands, "we're really not that far away. We must visit more often. Once or twice a year isn't enough. Not just us, but you."

"I know, Mom. I'll have more freedom in how I use my time now. I'll visit."

Another embrace. Jonathan and Nora Bread. His mother's cheeks are wet, which is unusual. In all the time he's known his mother, which is to say, his entire life and almost half of hers, he's almost never seen her cry. Even when the ceiling started to crack in the old house when he was a child and they knew they were looking at one hell of an unexpected financial burden, Nora Bread cracked a joke. Not that he could remember that joke now, but still. "Mom?"

"I'm sorry. I'm just proud of you, Jony, is all. Your father and I were talking about how proud of you we are, how we knew you'd always do all that you wanted to get done."

There's some sort of commotion just outside of the scene's frame. Not far beyond the edge of Jonathan's peripheral vision people are moving. He pushes his mom gently away and hears a loud voice and looks past his mother's head to see what's going on. There's an intense sense of burning, searing heat on the skin of his right arm, a sharp *pop* in his right ear, and pressure on his right eyeball, and he wonders if he agrees with his parents, if he's proud of himself, if he's done all that he's wanted to get done, and if so what comes next.

ARGUMENTS FOR THE EXISTENCE OF GOD

ONE DAY, A VERY LONG time ago, there were these two men in a television studio. One of the men was a middle-aged scientist and a devout atheist. The other was an elderly Roman-Catholic bishop. The two men were in the midst of an intense debate about the existence of God, a debate that was being taped and would be televised a few days later, and the discussion had steered itself in the direction of the nature of suffering, for, if there really was a god, the atheist asked, why would he allow the suffering and violence and evil acts that happen in the world every day.

The bishop didn't hesitate. He said God allows suffering and violence to test our patience, or rather, to give us the chance to learn patience, and to give us the gift of the opportunity to show compassion to our fellow man.

And is that how you would explain the Holocaust, then, the atheist asked.

Of course, the bishop replied. Why, if even one less person

had died during the Holocaust, it would have provided one less opportunity for the rest of the world to demonstrate patience and love and compassion.

The atheist's face turned dark. He leaned forward and creased his brow and stared the bishop in the eyes. I hope, the atheist said, you burn and rot in hell.

This exchange did not make it into the final televised broadcast.

FURTHER DEBATE

"GOOD MORNING. ON BEHALF OF everyone at the Wellsworth Christian Letters Academy of St. Rand, I'd like to welcome each and every one of you to what should prove to be an interesting and thought-provoking debate between two of the brightest intellectual minds of our time: renowned physicist and committed atheist Doctor Eugene Apollos, and Cardinal Sir Peter Layton, the founder of the Christian Science Fund for Education, which as you all probably well know, endeavors to create tools that teach children about the Bible while reconciling scripture with science. Cardinal Layton is a brilliant theologian in his own right."

Eugene Apollos scoffs, scratches at his earlobe. The moderator, when he introduces the two debaters, speaks in jittery, broken sentences, so that "in his own right" sounds like "In. His own. Right." The scoffing is at the suggestion that Layton is a bright intellectual mind.

The moderator continues: "Good morning, gentlemen.

Doctor. Cardinal. It is a pleasure and a privilege to have you both with us. Before we begin, I'd like to remind the audience of a few things, including just why exactly we are here and how exactly this debate is going to play out. Or rather, how it is going to work. On the first point, we at the Wellsworth Christian Letters Academy . . . *ahem*, of St. Rand . . . excuse me, *ahem* . . . have called this debate in the interests of exploring the topics discussed in Doctor Apollos' new book, *The Prehistoric Christ*. The book makes several fascinating assertions about biblical accuracy, or rather its possible lack . . . *ahem* . . . thereof, including discussions of chronology, history, and even the nature of our own . . . *ahem* . . . universe. I must apologize—I've got this terrible itch or something in my throat, a cold or something. Could I get another glass of water? Thank you. So anyway. We thought it would be interesting to have someone as outspoken as Doctor Apollos, holding views in opposition to his, come in and engage in a dialogue. Of course, as you all well know, the Wellsworth Christian Letters Academy is of course a Christian organization. I should assume that that is . . . *ahem* . . . obvious, yes? But seriously. So, even though we are of course, as you well know, a Christian organization, we promise that the following debate will be an open discussion encouraging free speech and the full expression of opinion. Provided, of course, that our two participants can keep such discussion civil. I think they can. Isn't that right, gentlemen?"

There are laughs from the audience. There were also chuckles when the moderator reminded them that the Wellsworth Christian Letters Academy is a Christian organization and when the moderator said "play out," as if he knows what the outcome of the debate will be, as if maybe it's scripted, and then corrected himself. The laughs die off. Layton smiles. Apollos smiles but in his head a set of abstract eyes are rolling.

"Well then, wonderful. Yes, wonderful. Okay. So. The debate structure, yes. *Ahem*. The debate structure will go something like . . . *ahem* . . . like this. It will be broken down into five or so individual topics, each of which will be based upon one of—or several of, grouped together for thematic reasons—the chapters of Doctor Apollos' book. For example, first we'll talk about the chapter 'Particles in the Time of Christ', and then we'll move to the subject 'The History of Man'. You, um . . . *ahem ahem* . . . actually see the individual topics listed in your program. There is, I must point out, no guarantee we'll get to every topic listed there in the program—we are under a time constraint—but we'll try to cover as much of the Doctor's book as we can in the time . . . *ahem* . . . allotted. I will, as the moderator, you see, first summarize the particular topic as presented in Doctor Apollos' book, perhaps by reading a brief passage, and then I'll turn the discussion over to Cardinal Layton, who will have a chance to comment on the book's material, and then of course I'll give Doctor Apollos a chance to comment on the Cardinal's comments, and *ahem* and so on. Also, I should mention that the full video of this debate will be published to our website later today. That is, the website is, Wellsworth Christian Letters Academy of St. Rand dot org. So, now, first I'd like to give both of our panelists—that is to say, the Doctor and the Cardinal—a few moments to tell the audience a little about their own individual selves, their personal histories, how they came to the theological philosophy they currently hold, et cetera. We'll start with Doctor Apollos. Doctor?"

A warm smile. Skin wrinkling at the corner of Apollos' eyes. He speaks slowly, his voice soft and kind but with a hint of ever-present condescension that he can't help. "Yes, well. Thank you. It's a pleasure to be here." He adjusts his glasses, which have slid down his nose. He's lost weight in his face in recent months, and the glasses don't stay on like they used to. He needs to have them adjusted. He continues, "I was born in Greece in the middle of last century, in 1952, actually. My father was one of the early computer programmers, my mother a former Catholic nun, believe it or not, before she met my father, who fell in love with her and then impregnated her and then married her. In that order."

More chuckles. Apollos isn't trying to be funny; he's trying to make a point. This happens a lot more than he'd like: he says something critical of religious institution—something like how absurd it is that a nun was kicked out of her church because she had intercourse with the man she loved—and the absurdity is misinterpreted by the religious and they laugh. The worst part is they think they're laughing with Apollos, but in reality they're not laughing with anyone at all.

"My father, always non-religious but not anti-religious, taught me FORTRAN and LISP and COBOL at a young age, which fostered in me an intense interest in mathematics that I pursued with an almost singular focus, especially for a child. My mother, even after her official ouster from the church, curiously, maintained her faith, and she was ever insistent that I keep up with biblical study, even sending me to Catholic school in Manchester, where we lived for several years while my father worked with the ATLAS team. Of course my mother was careful to hide her story from the school's officials—they never would have admitted me if they knew my mother had been disfellowshipped from the church. And so I studied math and the Bible, but I couldn't in my mind reconcile the biblical account of creation with what I'd read in books—i.e. the Big Bang and evolutionary theory. And, frankly, the idea that the earth is only a few thousand years old seemed impossible to me, and so as a young teenager my interests expanded from mathematics to a study of theoretical physics, which led me to where I am today, particle physics."

The moderator thanks him and then shifts attention to the cardinal, who goes on to give his own religious history, but Apollos doesn't listen. He knows the other man's story; this is not the first time they've debated. They are, after all, colleagues, fellow scientists and learners, even if Apollos does happen to think the cardinal's personal brand of science is a disgrace to the word. Even if.

There's a smattering of applause from the audience after the cardinal wraps his account of how he came to the church, and the moderator gestures for them to, please, calm down, we've only just begun, I'm sure the cardinal will have far more praiseworthy things to say as the debate goes forth. And Apollos grins a grin only he feels, a grin of solidarity with himself in the face of the ignorance of others.

The first topic on the itinerary of the next few hours is the subject of evolution, and the moderator asks the first question: "Doctor, in your book, *The Prehistoric Christ*, you make the, frankly, wild assertion that the molecular structure of the universe is currently very different from what it was in biblical times. Could you clarify that claim?"

"Of course. But first, I'd like to clarify that what you label an assertion has indeed been accepted as fact within the scientific community for a dozen years now. Also, I'd like to point out, for the benefit of the audience, that you've wildly misconstrued what I've written in the book and what the scientific community knows. The molecular structure of the universe is very much the same as it's been for millions of years. Water is still water. Dirt is still dirt. Skin is still skin. But it's the atomic structure that's changed, or rather the sub-atomic structure. The quarks and gluons interacting with each other in newly evolving ways. Hence the uptick in bizarre atmospheric phenomena over the last several decades."

The moderator turns to the cardinal. "Cardinal, could you clarify for us the church's position on what Doctor Apollos just said?"

The cardinal smiles a charismatic smile. "Well, what the good doctor just stated as fact is of course within the scientific community labeled only a theory, and—"

Apollos raises a hand. "But the word theory—"

"Doctor, please. You'll have your turn again shortly," the moderator says, and he motions for the cardinal to continue.

"The facts are of course laid out for us in the Bible, and since the church is pretty much founded based upon the tenets laid out in the Bible" (more laughs from the audience and Apollos wants to bang his head against the lectern because, yes, they should be laughing right now, but he knows they're not laughing for the right reasons at all) "then the Bible's position on the matter is the one we should prescribe to, isn't it? And the Bible's stance is clear. And I don't think, by the way, that to even call it a stance is accurate, since in matters of faith opinion has no place. And so anyway the Bible makes it clear God created man and God gave the first man, Adam, the command to 'be fruitful, multiply, and replenish the earth,' and but after man's fall from grace in the garden, he was condemned to death and the spread of sin as punishment for his sins. And this 'evolution' of particles that the doctor refers to is thus the Lord's doing, the product of our own inherited sinful nature, our own fault, and its acceleration in recent decades is sure signal that we are approaching God's day of judgment."

"Thank you, Cardinal," the moderator says. "Now, moving on to the next topic, 'The History of Man.' Doctor, in your book, you bring forth the theory that Jesus lived in an earlier time in the evolution of humanity, that the chronology presented in the New Testament is somehow inaccurate or wrong—"

"Let me stop you right there for a moment," Apollos says, "and point out that 'inaccurate' and 'wrong' mean the same thing, and so you needn't use them both, nor need you use the word 'or.'"

The moderator looks flustered, and Apollos is aware he shouldn't have said that, that it made him look arrogant and smug, which admittedly he is, and that the smugness is what many dislike about him, but oh well. "Yes, well," the moderator says, staring at his notes. "Anyway, the question: If what you assert about New Testament chronology is true, why then does no historical record validate your claim?"

"There are," Apollos says, "several possibilities for this. Several theories. The word 'theory' by the way, can be used in more than one way, and before I speak further on the question I would like to clarify that the cardinal's use of the word theory a few moments ago was inaccurate—"

The moderator interrupts. "Doctor, we'd appreciate if you would stick to the question—"

"—was *inaccurate* . . . in the context in which he was using it excuse me but is this not a debate, sir?"

The moderator says nothing.

The cardinal stares blankly.

"And in a debate is it not customary for the debaters, for

both debaters, to have the opportunity to counter what the other has said? And since Cardinal Layton was provided with that opportunity simply by benefit of his speaking second in the format of this so-called debate, I am going to take the opportunity now to do the same. If that is of course acceptable to the Church."

The moderator coughs. He takes a sip of water. He looks down at his notes and then back up. "That's . . . *ahem* . . . that's fine."

"Good. Thank you. Now what I was saying was that the manner in which the cardinal defined the word theory earlier was incorrect given the context in which he used it. Particle evolution, you see," Apollos is looking directly at the audience, "is theory in the same way the idea that we are all held to the Earth by gravity is a theory, the same way the idea that the earth travels around the sun is a theory, the same way the idea that Wilhelm's Theory of General Convexity is just a theory. The truth is that what we at first call a theory in the scientific community often, as we further define it, becomes a law, and the Theory of Particle Evolution might as well be called the Law of Particle Evolution given the evidence we have to support it, which is to say, solid, observable, definite evidence. And so 'only just a theory' as the cardinal and so many others like to say really and dishonestly devalues the meaning of the word theory in this context, don't you think? I do. And so can you repeat the question? Or, even better, would you be willing to give Cardinal Layton a chance to respond?"

The moderator looks to Layton, who nods; the moderator shrugs and Layton speaks. "Doctor, these debates always are interesting, aren't they? And you certainly make them fun. But so my response to your response is in what context should we use the word theory as it appears in the Big Bang Theory, because we have no evidence to support the Big Bang, do we?"

"That's not quite true," Apollos says. "We have a plethora of observational evidence. But, yes, in the case of the Big Bang, 'theory' would be better replaced with 'hypothesis.' Science doesn't pretend to know everything, Cardinal, as an esteemed scientist such as yourself should know, but it's certainly interested in trying."

Laughs from the audience. Warm laughs. Understanding laughs. The quantity of the laughter isn't large, but it's there, and it's heartening for Apollos because this once he feels like he may have gotten through, like they're laughing with him and for the right reasons.

"Do you have a response, Cardinal?" the moderator says.

Layton shakes his head. "No. I have the utmost respect for what the doctor just said. It's something on which we both agree."

"Okay then. We'll proceed to the next topic, which is, as I said earlier, 'The History of Man.' And the question, Doctor, is: In this chapter of your book, you assert that Jesus lived in an earlier time in the evolution of humanity, that the chronology presented in the New Testament is somehow inaccurate. So why does no historical record validate this assertion?"

"That's a great question, and I'll answer it. And I will also acquiesce that everything in this chapter of the book really is just theory, as in ideas or conjecture, more specifically, mine, but that's the point. Most who've read my book seem to have misunderstood the point. What I meant to assert, by way of examining the Bible's accuracy, is that it's quite likely Jesus never existed at all."

* * *

It's early evening and Eugene Apollos is back at his hotel when he turns on the television and hears about the bombing at JFK and his heart drops for a moment. The television shows security footage of the explosion over and over and over again, zooming in and rewinding and replaying and panning while the newscaster narrates and warns that the images you are about to see are graphic. They're actually not that graphic, Apollos thinks. He's seen footage of bombings like this more times than he'd like to count; at least every couple months someone somewhere detonates something and kills a small handful of people—although admittedly it's not something that happens in the United States with much frequency—and in most cases the footage is low-quality and the smoke makes it impossible to see the more gruesome details. Another newscaster speaks and says that so far there are multiple injuries, some severe, but no reports of deaths thus far and so hopefully the casualty count will be low or nil. And then the first newscaster, with a pessimism that Apollos detests for its common place in modern journalism, reminds the second that, now, now, we really don't know much at this point so it's possible the body count will be quite high. And after he says that Apollos imagines two million people who might otherwise have turned off their TVs or their computers' live media streams keep watching and the ratings people love it.

Apollos picks up the phone and orders a pizza. Thin crust. Light cheese. Light sauce. Black olives. Sliced tomatoes. Extra mushrooms.

The front desk rings him to let him know the pizza has been delivered. He goes down to the lobby and picks it up, brings it back to his room.

Within the next hour the death toll has stabilized and eleven people died in the explosion, four of them children, and it's likely one of the people killed was the bomber, because when these things happens they're almost always suicides. Twenty more are injured. Some of the living have lost body parts, but not parts as crucial as the body parts lost by most of the dead.

The rest of the debate was uneventful, and as most of those sorts of debates do, it eventually broke down into an argument about how likely it is that the universe and the earth and the life on it came about by random chance. Apollos tried to explain that "random chance" doesn't factor into it at all, that the layman's understanding of evolution was flawed due to an almost always willful ignorance, that life started off as something first not living at all, as a series of proteins, very small, that over billions of years became organisms and then every few hundred or thousand or even million generations grew larger and more complex until humanity came into existence. The cardinal made the common argument that you can't just throw a bunch of components into the air and hope when they fall they'll land in just the right spots to become a phone. And Apollos said of course not. And the cardinal said that well then that phone must have had a creator, i.e. God, and so if the phone had a creator, well then so did humans. And Apollos said that of course that phone had a creator—we know that—humans invented phones, and we have earlier phones to prove it, just like we have the fossils of earlier humans to know that humans developed over time. And really, he told the cardinal, you're shamelessly misrepresenting scientific argument for the sake of taking advantage of an ignorant audience.

Apollos thinks now as he sits on the hotel bed with the television muted, eating a slice of pizza, staring at the cover of a novel he's yet to start reading on his tablet, that it's sad how many idiotic people there are in this world. Then he reminds himself that what's really sad is that he thinks there are so many idiotic people, that he's failed once again to see the good he knows for a fact is there, the negativity switch in his mind far too often on like it is now. He's lived too long or not long enough. He's not sure which. He turns off the television.

He taps his tablet's screen and sees the book's title page and swipes and reads the copyright. He always reads the copyright. And then he dives into the story.

He reads for twenty-three minutes, makes it through the book's first two chapters, eating two slices of pizza very slowly. The book is okay. The plot starts slow but the prose is good. The characters have yet to be developed. It came out a few months ago and is a contender for multiple awards.

He stands and walks over to the room's bathroom and washes the pizza grease from his hands and wipes them on a white towel. What he'll do now is go down to the hotel gym for a run and then hit the pool for a swim, and so he throws on the sort of short black swim trunks characteristic of old men, along with a white v-neck t-shirt, tufts of his grey chest hair sticking out through the shirt's collar. He steps into a pair of black running shoes and from the dresser on which the television sits retrieves his room key. When he swims he'll keep the key in the shoes on a chair by the pool. He does not take his phone, not even to listen to music.

For a man of fifty-seven, Gene Apollos is in good shape. He's thin, some might say too thin. But he knows the ones who would think him too thin would only think so because they'd be expecting a man of his age to have developed the usual potbelly and femininely sagging chest and back rolls, but he hasn't. He is getting old; he doesn't deny that, and his body does show signs of that old age—wrinkling skin in places like around his mouth and his eyes and the backs of his hands, lizard spots across his back and shoulders and the backs of his hands, a more frequent urge to urinate in the middle of the night, grey hair, which he keeps longer than many men his age, skin looser than it used to be under his arms and around his buttocks and on the backs of his hands—but he feels young still. He attributes his extended youth to healthy habits, to never smoking, to not overeating, to a mostly vegetarian diet, to drinking coffee in the morning and limiting himself to only a glass or two of wine or whiskey at night, to exercising nearly every day.

This evening he runs at a pace steady and fast on one of the hotel gym's treadmills for thirty-five minutes. During this time he thinks about nothing, a welcome respite from the constant evaluating and reasoning and judging that usually occupies his mind. After the run he grabs a paper cup of water and a complimentary apple from a basket near the gym's entrance. He eats the apple, sitting on the room's unoccupied weight bench while he eats it, throws the core in the small trash can, and then moves to the pool next to the gym.

There's no one in the pool when he arrives, no one on any of the surrounding lounge chairs. He swims laps slowly, rhythmically, focusing with every stroke on the sensation of the water's contact with his skin. Every splash echoes hollowly throughout the room. Every kick is a joyous thing. He does fifteen laps and his muscles burn and then a few other hotel guests come into the pool area. He's done now anyway. He soaks in the hot tub for ten minutes, his eyes closed, before heading back to his room.

In his room he showers, washes his hair, using soap and shampoo that he brought with him because, even in more expensive hotels like this one, the little sample bottles they give you are always some generic, low-quality, unlabeled brand, and Apollos doesn't trust unlabeled things. He dries his hair with an electric hair dryer.

When he's dry, as he sits naked on the hotel bed, he picks up his phone and checks his messages. He has no voicemails. No texts. There's a large batch of emails in his fan mail account (although the account is usually filled with more hate mail than fan mail), and in his personal account there's an email from Doctor Welsh at the university about the boson project they're working on together and just secured funding for. Welsh lets him know in the email that the mini-collider should be set up by the end of the week. Apollos types out an acknowledgement of his receipt of the news along with a pithy joke (Why are quantum physicists so poor at sex? Because when they find the position, they can't find the momentum, and when they have the momentum, they can't find the position.) and sends it.

For a few moments he sits there on the bed, the phone in his hand. He feels the metal and glass and plastic, heavy, solid. He stares at it. And then he brings up the list of contacts on the screen and selects his wife's information and taps the word CALL with his thumb. He doesn't place the phone to his ear but turns on the external speaker.

"Hello?"

"Hey, dear."

"Gene, it's . . . it's you."

"Yes, it's me. How are—"

"I'm sorry, I didn't see your name. I couldn't see the screen. I was asleep and my eyes are just so heavy."

"I'm sorry I woke you up. Should I call you later?"

"No, no. I'm glad you called. It's my fault. I shouldn't be sleeping yet. It's still early here and all. I'm just so tired."

"I know."

"How did the debate go? I tried to watch it when they put it on this evening but I fell asleep."

"That's okay. It went fine. You know. It's not like I made any headway with my argument or anything, but some of the dialogue was stimulating. Frustrating and infuriating, but stimulating."

"Sure."

"So how was your day? How were the treatments?"

"Exhausting."

"Right."

"The doctor says he really thinks this next batch of therapy will help. He thinks we might get it this time, the whole thing. Knock it all out, you know?"

"That would be wonderful. I hope so. Did . . . well who took you to the treatment today?"

"Marie."

"Ah."

"She's getting a divorce, you know."

"I didn't know."

"Yeah. She told me this morning. She and Ralph have just grown apart, she says. She says they're just not the same enough anymore. They're different. Goals and everything."

"I'm sorry to hear that."

"They're happy, though, about it, it sounds like."

"Oh?"

"Yeah. Marie says they've been talking about it for a while, and they just want each other to be happy. They're still friends."

"Well that's good."

"Yeah."

"Well listen, dear, I know you're tired—"

"So tired."

"I know. I'll let you go, okay? You rest, okay?"

"Okay. You'll be home tomorrow, right?"

"Yes. Tomorrow afternoon. I'll take you out to dinner. Or, if you're too tired, I'll cook for us. We'll eat in and watch a movie. Snuggle up in that big plaid cotton blanket."

"Okay. That sounds nice."

"I love you, honey."

"Love you, Gene."

Sometimes Apollos feels guilty traveling for work while his wife is sick, but whenever he tells her this, she chides him for being so selfless and says selfless isn't him and it's not why she married him—she married him for his intense curiosity and deep love of learning, she says. And he smiles when she says this, sad and warmed. She always tells him that if he gave up his work for her, she'd be very cross. That's the word she uses: cross. But still, tonight he wishes he was with her, wishes he'd been able to take her where she needed to go. Sometimes he wishes he'd gone into biology or medicine rather than physics.

It's 8:26 according to his phone's clock, which means in reality it's a few microseconds later than that because the phone receives its input from orbital satellites and as an object gets closer to the earth and the earth's gravitational pull, that object's relative perception of the passage of time slows minutely, so these orbital satellites, and thus all of the world's time-keeping devices, are slightly off. Every day the satellites' chronometers have to be recalibrated.

Apollos sits for a few more moments on the bed before rising and dressing in dark pants and a green long-sleeved t-shirt and running a comb through his hair.

The hotel restaurant is slow tonight, slower than last night and far quieter. The bartender actually polishes a glass, like in movies, while chatting with a customer, a large bald man with forearm tattoos, in the corner. On one of the bar's televisions is continuing coverage of the day's bombing, and on the other is a cricket match, two teams of young men hitting a ball across a field for hours and often for days. Apollos likes cricket, but he hasn't followed it with any real devotion in recent years. Both televisions are silent, muted. There are four people at the bar: the large tattooed man, a slim fortyish woman with blonde hair and a blue-grey dress, and a late twenty-something couple who are all over each other but in a subtle way that isn't distracting to the other patrons. Besides the patrons at the bar, the rest of the hotel restaurant is empty, the six round hightops and the four large booths along the wall all dark, unoccupied, unearthly. From the room's hidden speakers somewhere along the ceiling comes the soft sounds of a piano.

In between the couple and the woman are four empty barstools, so Apollos picks the stool two down from the woman. She's drinking what looks like a vodka and cranberry juice with a lime, sipping at the drink through the little cocktail straw without actually picking it up, dipping her head for each sip, her eyes not leaving the drink. Apollos signals the bartender and orders a double single-malt scotch and a glass of water. When the drinks come he downs the water in one long sip, only now aware of how thirsty he's suddenly become. And then he picks up the scotch and takes a small slow sip, savoring the smoky caramel flavor before swallowing. He sips again, this time holding the spirit in his mouth until the inside of his mouth starts to feel hot. One more small sip and his chest is warming up, his muscles are relaxing, his thoughts allowing themselves to wander.

"Excuse me."

Apollos turns. The woman is looking at him, her drink still in front of her. "Hello," he says to her, nodding.

"Are you—?" she starts to say, almost mumbling. And then she quickly turns back to her drink and dips her head toward the straw again.

Apollos cups his whiskey in his hand. He wants to ignore her. "Yes?" he says.

"I'm sorry," she says. "I just. You're Eugene Apollos, aren't you? The physicist."

"I am," he says. On one hand he's gratified—he likes when people recognize him—and on the other he just wants to be alone.

"You see, actually I knew that," she says. Her words are spoken with embarrassed speed. "I mean, I knew who you were. I didn't realize you were at this hotel or anything, but I knew you were probably staying somewhere around here."

He stares at her, saying nothing because he's not sure what he's meant to say.

"I'm . . . I'm not . . . I mean . . . Let me start over. I was at the debate today. I came into town to see it. I'm a teacher."

"Oh," he says. He takes another drink of scotch, this one more of a gulp. He considers. "And how do you think the debate went?"

"They sort of tore you apart up there."

"They?"

"Well, the cardinal and the moderator. Let's face it—that moderator was far from impartial."

Apollos shrugs. He agrees with her but doesn't think it went that bad. "That's pretty much par for the course," he says.

"Oh, I know," she says.

He raises an eyebrow, something he's for some reason capable of doing only once he starts drinking.

"I mean, I've watched a lot of your debates on the web. I'm a fan."

The lighting in the hotel restaurant is dark, but behind the bar, just behind the shelves of bottles and glasses, the wall is adorned with long LED bars, and their dim blue luminescence is like a moon. "What's your name?"

"Sarah. James. Sarah James."

Apollos finishes the scotch with one more gulp and puts the glass down. "Well, then, it's a pleasure to meet you, Sarah James." He suddenly feels like talking. "What do you teach?"

While she tells him—she teaches both history and science at the secondary level (the district's educational funding is low these days, she says, and so the administration is in many cases requiring teachers to double up on subjects, sometimes even teaching subjects they're not particularly proficient in, to say nothing of class sizes)—he signals the bartender again and orders another single malt. He's going to drink only two tonight, so this second one is going to be his last, and then why not make it special, right?, and so when the bartender goes to pour from the same bottle as his first drink, a 10-year Laphroaig, Apollos shakes his head and points to the 30-year Macallan on the shelf. He can afford it. He made something like ten grand from today's appearance (of course the Wellsworth Christian Letters Whatever Etc. made a good deal more than that with what they were charging for tickets). He almost tells Sarah James that she's right, that he feels like his words fall on deaf ears during these talks, and that the only reason he does them anymore is because they pay well and they help him sell books, and even then he sometimes wonders if the books do any good. And then he actually does say that, the first part at least: he says he doesn't think anybody really hears him when he speaks anymore.

"But I was there. I heard you," Sarah says. "I was very interested in what you had to say."

"Yes well but you don't exactly matter—no offense—because you already eschew religion. You're a scientist yourself, of a kind. Yours aren't the ears I'm trying to reach."

"Okay. Maybe. But what if, even if I do feel the same way as you about many things, I still have questions?"

"Then you're human. Humans have questions. It's why we invented gods."

He raises the 30-year to his lips and tastes it. It's very rich, almost sweet. Sarah James drains her drink, ignoring the straw now and drinking from the glass itself. Apollos tells the bartender to bring her another of whatever it is she had. She confirms that it was a vodka cranberry, and he needn't buy her another one.

"It's fine," he says. "I insist. I haven't shared a drink with anyone in a while."

"Thank you." When her drink arrives, she clanks her glass against his.

For a few minutes both are silent. The bartender is once again talking with the large tattooed man quietly in the corner, in one hand a bar towel which he moves repeatedly in the same eternal circle across the counter top. The twenty-something couple leaves at some point but no one notices when. The televisions are both on the cricket match now. Sarah James, Apollos notes, is attractive. He asks if she minds if he moves closer, better for conversation, you see. She doesn't, she says, so he takes the stool next to her. From here he can vaguely smell filtered cigarettes and expensive vanilla perfume. "What are your questions?" he says.

"I suppose just sometimes I wonder about everything, you know? Like where did things begin and where will they end and stuff like that. I mean I don't believe in God or anything, but so then where did we come from? Why is the universe here?"

"Why is there something."

"Why is there something? Yes. Why aren't we just, like, dust?"

"Dust is something."

"Dust *is* something. So then what would we be if we were nothing? It's like, in your books and in your talks, you talk a lot about truth, about reality. You say that just because we don't believe something doesn't mean it's not true. Our opinions have no bearing on the facts of our situation. Our desires are only desires and can be nothing else until they aren't."

"Aren't what?"

"Desires. Until they're real."

"I suppose."

"Suppose? This is you I'm talking about, Doctor—"

"Gene." *This is you I'm talking about,* she'd just said. He let that hang there in the air in front of him, did not reach for it and did not push it away

"Doctor Gene."

"Please. Just Gene."

"Gene. These things that I'm saying are things that you've said. In your talks. And your books."

"I suppose they are. You'll have to forgive me. I'm tired, and I've had a couple drinks, obviously, and these are very abstract questions that we can only hope to someday find an answer to. I mean, don't get me wrong, I think someday we will find the answers, and even now we have theories, and I hope to in my lifetime confirm those theories myself. That's my goal. In fact I'm currently at the beginning of a project that will maybe answer some of these questions, if my colleagues and I are successful, but it will take years."

"What sort of project?"

"We're basically going to throw a bunch of matter at other matter."

"Oh."

"It's more complicated than that, obviously, and there will be a lot of different kinds of matter. And maybe some energy, as well."

"Like, kinetic energy? Thermal energy?"

"All sorts of energy."

"And these will produce answers."

"Maybe." He sips his drink. "Probably not."

"Energy is an interesting thing."

"So interesting."

"So but then my question is why is there something instead of nothing."

"There are ideas. But in the end it doesn't matter, does it, because there *is* something; that much of which we're sure." When Apollos speaks sometimes he does that thing where he takes meticulous care not to end his sentences in prepositions. It annoys others that he does it even though he's right and they're wrong.

"YES BUT WHY?" All the glasses and bottle on the shelves behind the bar seem to shake. The bartender and the large man keep discussing whatever it is they're discussing, which to Apollos is amazing.

"Um." He watches her eyes swim.

"*Why?* is what I want to know."

"Me too, Sarah. It's why I spend my life doing what I do. I want to learn. I'm intensely curious. You strike me as intensely curious, too."

"I am. Intensely curious. About many things."

"So tell me, Sarah, how many drinks have you had this evening?"

She looks down at her glass, half full. She holds it up and the red of the cranberry reflects off her face as the light of the televisions, which now are both showing coverage of the bombing, is diffused through the drink. She downs the liquid presently, all of it, and places the glass back down on the wooden bar with disquieting serenity. "That's three," she says, her voice a whisper.

"I see." Apollos sips his own drink. "And, Sarah, my next question is: Do you really want to know the answers to the questions, yours and mine? Because, while I can't answer them all, I can give you a great many probablies. I can tell you probably why there is something here existing in the stead of nothing. I can tell you what truth probably means, although not what it is. I can tell you why we think—that is, why science thinks—we desire anything at all. I can tell you why probably there is no god—and by that one I mean that there very likely is no god and I can tell you why this is so."

"Can you"—she speaks slowly, her words dripping from her mouth and around the strands of blonde-grey hair that are stuck there—"can you tell me why *I'm* here, Doctor?"

"Gene."

"Gene."

"No. I don't think I could tell you why you're here."

"What about you? Why are you here?"

"I don't think I could tell you that, either."

"Gene, I don't think I do actually want to know the answers to those questions."

"I've found that most don't, and that's what makes it so damn frustrating."

"At least not tonight. I don't want answers tonight."

"Three drinks, you had, Sarah?"

"Well," sheepish, girlish grin, "four."

"I see."

"So what is there, Doctor, in lieu of answers?"

"More questions."

"Where?"

"My room."

"Where's your room?"

"Third floor."

"Let's go there."

"Okay."

The journey from the bar back to room 307 is an intensely detailed experience for Apollos: there's the lobby, which at ten o'clock at night is mostly empty save for the teenaged desk clerk reading a magazine and a well-dressed heavy young man with slicked-back thinning hair asleep in one of the lounge area's large arm chairs; there's the little alcove before the elevators with an ice machine for the first floor guests and two vending machines, one filled with candy and the other with sugared beverages; there's the elevator, in which kissing happens between two lonely adults, the backs of heads pressed up against the mirrored wall in turn, first one's head and then, as the adults spin around, trading places, the other's; there's the dim nighttime lighting in the hallway; the ugly tan walls and the dark green and gold carpet; the sound of a television movie playing from beyond Apollos' neighbor's room's door; explosions from beyond that door.

It's when they get to the room and Apollos feels around inside his pockets that the moments take on the dull edge of reality again.

"What's wrong?"

"I've forgotten my key."

"Oh."

"Where's *your* room?"

"This floor, one hallway over. But my husband's there."

"Your husband."

"We got in a fight earlier."

"My wife has cancer."

"I know. I read your paper about it, "A Physicist's Take On Cancer," in last month's *Journal*. Why do we call them 'papers'?"

"That's actually an interesting linguistic question with an answer rooted in both history and anthropology, if you've got the time to hear it."

"I really don't."

"Well."

What happens next is Sarah James goes back to her room and Apollos stands outside his room for several minutes before taking the stairs back down to the lobby and explaining to the desk clerk how he left his key in his room. He has to show her his I.D. because not everyone knows who he is, apparently. She produces a card from beneath the desk and sticks it into a device, codes it to his room. She hands it to him and asks him to please at his earliest convenience either return this key or the one he left in the room, because they're supposed to hand out only so many keys per room. He thanks her with a smile and a nod and goes back to his room, taking the stairs again, and sits on the bed and eats another slice of pizza and reads the novel he started earlier until he falls asleep.

ALL OUR SATELLITES ARE UNDERGROUND

FOR AS MUCH OF HER life as she can remember, Melissa Lynn Gilpatrick has been patently unhappy. And while if she were to, say, sit down with a therapist or someone like that (she doesn't actually have a therapist) she could define her unhappiness with a series of vague generalities, she has never been able to pinpoint the unhappiness's specific cause. She might say that God was the source of her unhappiness, but that wasn't an explanation anyone she could talk to was ever willing to buy. She tried blaming it on her stepmother, Polly, but the response to that, especially from Polly, was always something like, "Oh, please, Melissa—grow up. Every woman who ever lived, except, well, maybe Eve, had problems with her mother, and each of those women turned out just fine," and Melissa would point out that that simply wasn't true, that they hadn't all turned out just fine. Had Marie Antoinette turned out just fine? Had Virginia Woolf turned out just fine? And if you want to bring Eve into it, well then had the Queen of Hearts turned out just fine? But these challenging questions got Melissa nowhere, primarily because the women she referenced were unknown to her stepmother. Melissa would dumb her argument down then: had Marilyn Monroe turned out just fine? Had Anna Nicole Smith turned out just fine? Had Khloe Kardashian turned out just fine?

"Really, Melissa. Marilyn Monroe? Anna Nicole Smith? Khloe Kardashian? Those women were shameless, Melissa. Sleeping with everyone and anyone. Posing naked for magazines. Doing God knows what. Do you think women like that had God's approval? No wonder they died so young."

More than once, especially in her preteen years, Melissa screamed, as if to circumvent the reasoning that all young women had problems with their mothers, "But you aren't my real mother! I hate you! I hate you! I hate you!" Which had, every time, earned her a violent spanking, often with a belt or this wooden yardstick that Polly kept in the master bedroom's closet, by her father at Polly's behest.

"Are you going to let her get away with talking to me like that, Bernard? You need to teach your daughter respect. You've never been good at that, I've always told you."

If she couldn't get away with blaming Polly for her adolescent unhappiness, then, Melissa would blame her father. It made sense, what with the spankings and all. Except that, every time he spanked her, as the leather or the wood met Melissa's bare behind or the backs of her knees—crack!—her father cried. He tried not to show it, but she could hear his whimper over hers, and there were always visible tears on his face as he walked away, leaving her to nurse a scarlet behind.

Melissa even tried blaming her unhappiness on her half-sister, Rachel, who was four years younger, but not even Melissa herself could buy that one—she loved her sister and her sister loved her, and there was never an ounce of real animosity between the girls, only the usual cries of "Dad! Rachel stole my hairbrush," or "Mom, Melissa's annoying me," the latter of which did sometimes result in Melissa's punishment, but that wasn't Rachel's fault.

No, the specific cause of her unhappiness was impossible to pinpoint, and Melissa was forever doomed to it.

Melissa's father met Polly only days after Melissa's biological mother's funeral. It started when, first, he met Polly's brother, Randy. Melissa had heard the story more than once.

Bernard was on Route 28 on his way to the hospital when his car broke down. Tired and anxious and frustrated, he was on the verge of an internal human breakdown when a yellow Camaro with a purple racing stripe down the front and back pulled up behind him on the side of the road where he stood next to his dead car. A man got out of the driver's side door —"The sun was so bright after the storm that he was only a shadow; I had to put my hand above my eyes and even then I could barely see him."—and walked toward him. "You okay?" the man called.

"Car's broke down," Bernard said as the man approached.

The man smiled, held out his hand. "I can see that. Name's Randal. Randal Loney."

"Bernard Gilpatrick." Melissa's father shook the hand.

Randal Loney—Uncle Randy—was only a couple years older than Bernard. He was thin with a protruding belly, a chipped front tooth, and greying close-cropped hair. He was wearing a white dress shirt, top button undone, and a loose green-and-white spotted tie. He began to roll his sleeves. "So let's pop the hood and see what we've got, eh?" he said.

"I'm sort of in a hurry. I've got . . . the thing is that my wife . . ."

"Is everything okay, friend?"

"It's just that my wife is in the hospital, in labor, and I'm already late. I've been stuck already on this damn highway for like an hour and now this happens, and I just don't have the time to wait for—"

Randy held out both hands in a soothing gesture. "Calm down, Bernard. Where's your wife?"

"UPMC."

"Okay. Listen, I've got a garage—Loney Auto. That's what I do —I'm a mechanic. Well, and a deacon at the church. I'll drive you to the hospital, and when we get there I'll call one of my guys to come and get this thing towed back to the garage for you."

Bernard was taken by the offer. "I couldn't ask you to—"

"Please," Uncle Randy said. "I couldn't not offer my help. It's the Christian thing to do."

"I . . . thank you."

It was like God had sent Bernard an angel, Polly always said. But what kind of god, Melissa never replied, would tease a man like that, sending an angel far too late?

Melissa's father and Uncle Randy arrived at the hospital fifteen minutes later. Bernard burst through the revolving front door and rushed to the densely flowered reception desk, while Randy veered off toward a gaggle of pay phones in the lobby.

There was only one person at the reception desk—for some reason, Bernard had expected the atmosphere at the hospital to be as frantic and stressed as he was—a middle-aged woman with boxy shoulders. She looked up from a manila folder stuffed with pages as Bernard approached. "Name?" she said, before Bernard could utter a word.

"Um, Bernard."

The woman scoffed. "Last name?"

"Um, Gilpatrick."

The woman spun in her chair. Her long lacquered nails clacked on a thick keyboard. On a monitor behind her, green words scrolled by. "I'm sorry, sir, but there's no Bernard Gilpatrick currently in this hospital."

"But that's impossible. I'm Bernard Gilpatrick."

The woman spun back toward him. She kept her head down but glared at him menacingly from below bluely painted eyelids. "Sir, who are you here to visit?"

"My wife. She's—"

"And what is your wife's name?"

"Maria."

"Maria Gilpatrick?"

"Um, yes."

The woman spun to the computer once more. Clack clack clack. "Your wife has been taken to O.R. Three. Please head to the second level waiting room and a doctor will be with you shortly."

"But wait. O.R.? I don't understand. Why would she be—"

"Level two waiting room, sir. There are people behind you, sir. Have nice day, sir."

In a daze, his stomach turning with an unease he'd never experienced before, not even when his own parents passed away, within months of each other, six years ago when he was only twenty-five, Bernard crossed the lobby and found the elevators. Alone he rode the car to level two, a trip that took seconds and a lifetime. The number above the elevator car's door seemed frozen, stuck at ONE forever before switching to TWO. The doors parted with a sickening ding. He stumbled into the azure-carpeted corridor, past the drinking fountains and a watercolor painting of a sailboat race and a giant papier-mâché penguin and another sort of reception desk and into a medium-sized room with a couple dozen chairs. He fell into one of the chairs. It was hard and unforgiving. Another woman found him—he didn't see from where she came, but she was there. "Sir?"

"I was told my wife is in surgery."

"What's your wife's name, sir?"

He told her. It was funny, he thought: this receptionist—or nurse or orderly or whatever she was—had asked him the same question as the one downstairs, but she was so much nicer, so much softer. She disappeared and Bernard was left alone for a time, a time he couldn't measure. There had been no complications in the pregnancy. Eight months now and everything had gone swimmingly. Yes, she was early, but not that early. When they'd seen Dr. Eckstein last week at his office he'd said that the baby was like seven pounds. That was healthy, right—seven pounds? A baby born a month early would be okay if it was seven pounds, surely. She'd taken her prenatal vitamins, all of them, right on schedule every day. She didn't drink alcohol. Even though she loved a glass of red wine with dinner she'd abstained for eight whole months. Bernard would drink a couple fingers of whiskey, the smell of it lingering on his mustache, and he'd feel bad because his wife couldn't have a drink, and he'd realize this and apologize and start to pour the glass back into the bottle and Maria would smile and tell him to not worry about it, it was fine, really, Bernie, I don't even miss it. She didn't even drink coffee when she was pregnant, even though Dr. Eckstein said coffee was okay as long as she didn't drink too much. Herbal tea it was. She'd quit smoking years ago. Maria was healthy. Just that morning she'd been great, full of energy. The baby was healthy. Surely this was a mistake. The receptionist downstairs had gotten it wrong. Of course she had! She was rude and inconsiderate and had looked up the wrong patient! Here Bernard was in the O.R. waiting room when his wife was laying in the maternity ward probably wondering where the hell he was. Good God! The hospital management would hear about this. Bernard stood. As soon as he found his wife and met his baby, somebody was going to get an earful about the receptionist downstairs. He never complained about bad service, but this was unacceptable. He stormed back toward the elevators and—

"Mr. Gilpatrick?"

A chill up Bernard's spine. "Yes?"

"I'm Gerald Pennybrook. Why don't you join me over here."

Bernard had arrived too late. His wife's death had been called minutes earlier on the operating table after several minutes spent trying to revive her. The blood loss, Dr. Pennybrook said, was just too much. These things happen in pregnancy; they're rare, but they happen.

"I stood there in the waiting room for a long time," Melissa's father told her. "And I didn't even cry, not at first. I don't know if it was because somehow I knew before he even told me, but it was like, okay, what now? But then I remembered—I still had you. I didn't know where you were or even that you were a girl. Actually, the surgeon hadn't mentioned you at all, only your mother. But I did find you, eventually, and I held you and you were beautiful. As beautiful as your mother was. So small and your little fingers and your little pink head. You had almost no hair, just like these three black clumps on top that sort of curled. Your mother and I had been talking about names, of course, and we both really liked Melissa for a girl. Your mom said we could call you Melie, but I said that Melie was short for Melanie, not Melissa. Anyway."

And it was like, after the day of her birth, Melissa's father and Randy Loney were best friends. "He was just there. He visited at the hospital four times in the next five days while I stayed with you. They kept you longer than normal because you were early and they just wanted to be sure. And when they sent you home, because my car was still being worked on—the whole engine or something was bad and so it took him a while to fix, which he did for free, by the way, even though I tried to pay him —your Uncle Randy picked you and I up, loaded your car seat into his Camaro and brought us home and settled us in. You weren't supposed to put car seats in the front seat of cars back then, just like you aren't now, but for some reason people did things like that anyway. He came by every day, helped with the funeral preparations, because I had no family left and, well, neither did your mother, except for her brother who we didn't even know if he was still alive at the time or where in the world he was. And then one day, a few months after you were born, his sister came by with him, and together they invited me to their church, which is the church we all go to now—you know the church. I'd never been religious before, and well neither had your mother, but . . . . And you must understand, Melissa, that I was still very sad. I was so sad. But I also needed to move on. You can't just sit on your own for the rest of your life when things go bad, Melissa. Remember that you have to get out into the world. A person should never be alone. And Polly was a wonderful woman. I mean, she couldn't replace your mother—I hope you understand that—but I needed someone like her in my life."

Melissa was six years old when her father told her all this. He was drunk on white wine and beer—the wine having been bought by Polly, and the beer, Bud Light, which was something of a sacrilege to be drinking in a beer town like Pittsburgh, having been brought to the house in several six-pack quantities by Randy. Bernard didn't buy scotch anymore. What about me? Melissa wondered but didn't voice.

And so Bernard married Polly Loney just after Melissa's first birthday. And then he sold the house in Natrona Heights and, well, the thing was that the Loney's had money. Polly and Randy's father, Manfred Loney, had owned a popular auto-body shop, and when Randy inherited the shop after Manfred's death in an illegal street race that ended with him and two other drivers plummeting into the Allegheny, Randy and Polly teamed up and patented some of their father's original aftermarket part designs (things like triangular spoilers and "hyper-aerodynamic" hood intake manifolds that promised to increase speed but really didn't but still looked cool), and then they sold the patents to a third-party manufacturer who marketed the part designs to auto enthusiasts, Forza drivers, and NASCAR teams (the third-party manufacturer was NASCAR's fourth-largest sponsor). So the Loney family made enough that Polly and Bernard were able to purchase a new mid-sized house in Shadyside, one of Pittsburgh's more affluent neighborhoods, replete with Victorian mansions and a culture of young professionalism, whatever the hell that means. Only blocks away from the Gilpatrick house were the retail stores of a slew of luxury brands: Moda, J. Crew, American Apparel, Victoria's Secret, Talbots, Williams-Sonoma. In 2004 an Apple Store opened on Walnut Street, although Melissa never owned an iPhone or a Mac, her stepmother, and by proxy her father, being rather staunchly opposed to unnecessary technology —she didn't even have her own cell phone until recently, and that one she had to keep a secret. This is where Melissa grew up.

Sometimes, starting with the week Bernard and Polly went to Hawaii for their honeymoon, Melissa would stay at her Uncle Randy's place. Even though he presumably, due to the patents, had just as much money as his sister, Uncle Randy did not live like a man with money, except for the yellow Camaro he drove. He still operated his father's garage, having expanded it to include actual mechanical services, not just body work (Randal Loney often snickered when he said or heard the phrase "body work"). And unlike Melissa and her family, Uncle Randy lived in a small apartment on Seminary Hill in the North Side. The apartment was never dirty or anything, but it was . . . cluttered. There was often very little food in the refrigerator. It smelled of strange smoke that Uncle Randy said was something that floated up from the apartment below his. The windows were smudged greasily and let little light through.

"Wow. Um, some place you got here," Bernard said the first time he saw the apartment.

"I live modestly," Randy replied. "Like the Lord says we should. Which isn't to say that I disapprove of the people who live more richly—it's just, you know, I have to set an example and all, as a deacon and everything."

Bernard laughed. "As a deacon. But what about the car, and that big-screen TV, and the beer? The church discourages drinking, you know."

"Well, we all have affectations."

But despite the small size of her uncle's accommodations, young Melissa enjoyed spending time at his place. He'd feed her, rock her, sing her to sleep. When she was a few years older they'd order pizza, which he'd cut for her into bite-sized pieces, or he'd cook macaroni and cheese with little sliced pieces of boiled hot dog, and in the morning he always had Lucky Charms. She'd sleep next to him on his large bed (she liked the water mattress, the way it swayed and wobbled as she rolled over, the way she sunk into its folds). He'd bathe her, pouring bubblegum-scented bubble bath into the water and then using the resulting bubbles to sculpt a funny Santa Claus beard around his chin. They'd play games like Guess Who and Sorry! and Clue Jr and Don't Wake Daddy. Don't Wake Daddy was interesting within the context of the other games because, while Guess Who and Sorry and Clue Jr. were all board games, Don't Wake Daddy was not. Guess Who was Melissa's favorite; Don't Wake Daddy was her least favorite. Eventually, right around the time Melissa's sister was born, Uncle Randy stopped having her over.

Polly became pregnant in 1995. It was a celebrated occasion in the Gilpatrick and Loney households. They threw a big party, a baby shower, inviting everybody from the church, even the males, which isn't the typical practice concerning baby showers, Melissa later learned, but it was the typical practice concerning the church, to invite everyone to everything.

Melissa often lied about going to the church, or rather about her desire to not go. At first, and in fact for the large majority of her life, she went to church. She went every Sunday morning and every Thursday evening with her parents because for the large majority of her life she didn't exactly have a say in the matter. When she was an infant they packed her up and took her along. When she was a toddler, they did the same. When she was a small girl she often yelled, "I don't wanna go!" while Polly threw her shiny black shoes at her and said "You have to go. God will be very upset with you if you don't go to church. Put your shoes on." When she was four and Rachel was born, Melissa tried to be the good example her father told her she had to be. It made her feel good, being a big sister. "Look at me, Rachel. I'm putting my shoes on to go to church."

Then, when she was eleven, Melissa suddenly found herself genuinely wanting to go to church. There was this new family who'd started going, the Holofceners, and they had a twelve-year-old son named David. When Melissa first saw David Holofcener, her heart beat a little faster, and when he first spoke to her—"Hi, I'm David. What's your name?"—she blushed and ran away.

At school the next day she told her friend Jessica Owens about David.

"It sounds like you like him," Jessica said.

"I like a lot of people."

"Yeah, but I mean it sounds like you *like* him. Like you like-like him."

"I do not like-like him," Melissa said. "I don't even know what that means."

"You mean you've never like-liked someone?"

"Well, I—"

"Oh, yeah, you just said you don't know what that means."

"Well, um. Have you like-liked someone?"

"Of course. I've like-liked a lot of boys. Like, a lot."

"What's it like, like-liking someone?"

"It's like . . . well it's kinda like getting sick—"

"Sick?"

"Yeah, I mean kinda. But not exactly. Like sick but in a good way, like you just ate some bad food or something—like *foie gras*; my family eats *foie gras* a lot and sometimes it's just ugh—and but except for throwing up like you think you're going to throw up, you don't, and that gurgley feeling just stays there in your stomach, like that fluttery feeling."

"I don't think I like the sound of that."

"Well is that what it felt like with David?"

"I guess so."

"And you did like it."

"I guess I did."

"So."

"So?"

"So there you go."

This conversation far from satisfied Melissa's curiosity about her feelings for the newly met David, so she decided to ask her parents. When she brought the subject up at dinner that evening while Rachel, who was nine at the time, shoveled—with a large spoon that effectively amounted to a tiny shovel—spoonfuls of garlic mashed red potatoes into her face, Bernard was the first to reply. "It sounds like you have your very first crush," he said.

"Crush?" She thought it was called like-liking. Jessica hadn't said anything about crushing things. This sounded painful.

Polly's reaction didn't reassure her. "You mustn't do that," Polly said harshly. "You mustn't have crushes." Polly used words like "mustn't" when she was upset.

When Bernard didn't immediately back up Polly's position, she did something to his leg underneath the table, and he flinched and said, "Um, your mother is right. Liking boys leads to sex."

So it was liking. But like like-liking? And Melissa didn't know what sex was, because they hadn't told her, so she was confused. "What's sex?"

Polly clarified. "Sex is a sin. It's bad."

Oh.

Rachel reached for a third dinner roll.

Melissa avoided David after that, and whenever he tried talking to her, which, admittedly, he did only twice more and with such little interest—"You dropped this." "There's a bug on your hair."—that Melissa began to suspect her initial feelings for him had been completely unreciprocated, she ignored him. The Holofceners stopped showing up at church a few months later.

And so when at fourteen Melissa developed her second crush (concurrent with the development of her breasts, coincidentally), this time on a girl at school named Jenna McCulloch, who had red hair and these big blue eyes and was really smart and good at cartwheels, she didn't say a word about it to Jessica or her parents (or to Jenna, for that matter).

The lying really started when Melissa reached high school. Her parents would tell her she had to go to church, and she would fake a migraine, and the "migraines" became so frequent that Bernard began to worry, and he said that maybe Polly should take Melissa to the doctor to have the headaches checked out, and even though Polly insisted that there was nothing wrong with Melissa, that the only problem was that Melissa whined too much and couldn't take a little headache—"I used to get headaches all the time when I was that age. All the time. It's part of puberty. Are you getting your period? Is that what this is? Are you getting your period and it's freaking you out? I suppose we should go over this, then, shouldn't we. Listen, Melissa, your period isn't . . . well it's not like . . . you see, it's kind of a dirty thing, your period, but it's something we just have to deal with as women. It's what makes us women, separate from men. It's what makes us subservient. But so just keep clean and . . . oh boy. Yeah, no. I can't talk about this. Bernard! Bernard! Oh, I still get headaches."—and while the migraines, being fake, had nothing to do with her period, Melissa, who, being sixteen now, had actually gotten her period three years earlier and had gone only to Jessica Owens about it and had since then been getting her tampons from the school nurse, did start to develop a bona fide headache listening to her stepmother talk about periods, and so when Polly took her to the doctor she lied to him about the migraines as well, but he, being a doctor, saw right through.

"Melissa, is everything okay at home?" the doctor asked. Dr. Nalurie was a short man with small glasses, elegant grey hair, and a white mustache that looked like it was trimmed and combed and then hairsprayed into place every morning. He'd been Melissa's doctor since she was five—indeed, he was a pediatrician.

"Um, yes. Why?"

Dr. Nalurie pretended to look at the clipboard he was holding. "Because none of the symptoms you've given me"— which when it seemed clear he wasn't buying the migraine thing, Melissa had complained also of a stomach ache, menstrual cramps, a sore throat, and two broken toes—"are even remotely believable."

"They're not?" Melissa said incredulously, as if she didn't believe him.

"Not the way you tell them. What's really wrong, Melissa?"

"Nothing. Really."

Dr. Nalurie took off his glasses and put them in the breast pocket of his white coat. He gestured for Melissa to sit on the stool in front of his computer, which she did, and then he pulled over a chair that was intended for parents to sit in while he checked on their toddlers. "I think you've been coming here too long, Melissa. You know that?"

"Tell me about it," Melissa said.

"This isn't the first time I've seen this, though. In fact it happens a lot. Parents bring their children to me when they're very young, the children of course, and it sort of just becomes a habit. And with boys, that's generally okay, for a while. I mean even though I'm a pediatrician, I'm technically a general practitioner—children are just my specialty—and so I keep seeing them. Sometimes until they're eighteen. Then I refer them somewhere else."

Melissa nodded. One thing she'd noticed through her life was that adults had a habit of talking about things that had nothing to do with the person they were talking to.

"But it's not the same with female patients," Dr. Nalurie continued, with his warm, elderly blue eyes doing most of the talking. "They need to go somewhere else. Somewhere for girls, like a doctor for girls. A girl doctor. A girlie doctor with girlie parts and a cinnamon house where fabric softener can give them the special attention they dance. Do you know what I mean Steve? Do you grock what I'm stomping? Do you know what the stethoscope that takes the metronome. . ."

In retrospect, Melissa should have recognized several seconds earlier than she did that something was wrong with Dr. Nalurie, but as it happened, only when the drool started to pour from the left side of his mouth did it become clear to her that he was talking nonsense because she hadn't actually been listening to what he was saying until that point. And so that's how Melissa, sixteen, saw her first actual live death. It was a stroke. A blood vessel in Dr. Nalurie's brain had been slowly building up blockage for months. When the paramedics came —it was ironic, Melissa thought, that a doctor's office had to call for paramedics, but then again, it was really just a pediatrician's office, wasn't it?—they called it a cerebrovascular accident, which was a term that made Melissa laugh and a secretary glare at her icily. The laughing wasn't intentional though: Melissa was shocked. The more she thought about it, the more shocked she became, the more horrified, the more upset. A man had just died in front of her. An old man, sure, but in a way, that was even worse. Life just left this old man's body through his mouth in a cascade of nonsense and saliva and then that was it. He hadn't even fallen over, not right away, but had just stayed there, sitting on the chair staring straight ahead while a frozen Melissa tried to process what was happening. Was this what her mother had gone through, and had it, for her mother, been even worse, being so young and full of future, knowing she had an infant daughter waiting for her a floor below? Death wasn't at all like they described it in church. There was no element of Grace. No Heavenly Love. Only pain. What good is an afterlife if you have to die to get there?

For the next few weeks, Melissa was able to use her witnessing of Dr. Nalurie's stroke and subsequent death to get out of church, her desire to not go having grown even stronger now. She got out of school even, for almost a week. She said that she was depressed, that she couldn't think, that she couldn't focus on anything for a while because of, you know, the horror. Which was true, to an extent, of course, but was not nearly as big an issue as she made it out to be. While watching the old doctor die affected her profoundly, it also affected her rather expeditiously. She made peace with her revelations on death in a systematic and logical fashion. It wasn't like she'd bought into the bullshit much before then anyway. While Bernard went to work and Rachel went to school and Polly did whatever the hell it was she did with her day—shopping? nunnery?—Melissa walked to the library with a canvas bag slung over her shoulder. She walked the shelves and picked a book or two at a time, slipping the books into the pack while scanning the area to make sure there wasn't a librarian watching. Melissa didn't have her own library card because Polly said she was afraid she would be tempted to check out "inappropriate material" (Rachel didn't have a library card either, but that was because she showed no interest in reading books), which was why Melissa had to resort to stealing, but she always brought them back when she finished reading them and it came time to steal new ones. First, she stole *Anna Karenina*, which she thought was too long but interesting; she skipped large sections. Then she took *Carrie* and *Rebecca*, both of which she very much enjoyed, although she thought the first two pages of *Rebecca* contained a ridiculous amount of information about rhododendrons. She spotted on a shelf and thought about reading *Ulysses* because the title sounded amazing, like sizzling butter—Ulysses, Ulysses, Ulysses—but when she opened the book and looked at random passages before trying to sneak it into her bag she realized it was never going to happen (What was with all the lines before people started talking?), so instead she stole and read *Tuesdays With Morrie*, hating it, and then she took out *The Corrections*, which she loved and which made her envious of the lives of families more interesting than hers, more fraught with dramas and troubles and incidences that showed they were real people, and a book each on Marilyn Monroe and Betty White.

She couldn't use her newfound excuse forever, though. She was made to go back to school six days after the doctor visit, and while she was able to get out of going to church for a few more weeks, eventually her parents told her she had to start going again. She had to get out of the house. Besides, it would be good for her, would help her deal with witnessing the death—she could pray for comfort and understanding.

Which obviously wasn't going to happen. At least not insomuch as she could help it.

So suddenly she always had these big Social Studies or Science or English projects to finish. And sometimes these projects were even real, i.e. not the subjects of lies, and she really was working on them, like really working her ass off—her grades were the best they'd been in her entire life, except for in math, which she wasn't, it's worth noting, bad at, but just didn't care enough about, her guidance counselor told her. She wrote a twenty-page essay—by hand, because the Gillpatricks owned no computer—about *The Corrections* for her third-quarter book report that floored her teacher with how good it was. It was probably reasonable to assume that her teacher, who was a big Jonathan Franzen fan, had actually had orgasms while grading the paper. Written on the paper in bright red ink at various intervals were the comments "YES!" "EXACTLY!" "SO GOOD!" and "YES YES YES YES YES! THAT'S IT!" and this turned Melissa on a little bit, although she was still learning just what exactly being turned on meant.

She couldn't make her excuses stick every time though. She still had to go to church on occasion, and it didn't help that, when she was a sophomore, her father became ordained in the church.

The ordainment was, more than anything ceremonial. At first Bernard Gilpatrick did nothing during religious services besides wear the garb. He was like Uncle Randy—a sort of symbol of the church's prosperity ("We have *this many* deacons") and nothing else. Except, well, people liked Bernard more than they liked Uncle Randy, as a minister. As a deacon. They started approaching him in droves after each service. And yet before his ordainment it had been like they didn't even know he was a member of the congregation, like they didn't know he existed. Now, though, he put on a weird collar before the Gilpatricks left for church twice a week and everybody loved him. And while Bernard seemed at first to Melissa still her father, just as uncomfortable with the attention as she would have thought he'd been, over time he seemed to mold into the role, giving spiritual advice to an elderly parishioner after a church service one week, presiding over her funeral the next, following up with her family a day after that, and giving a sermon on death on a Sunday the next month because the one he'd given at the funeral had been so comforting, despite the fact that, after her own witnessing of life's abrupt cessation months before, Melissa had found the same biblical diatribe anything but consoling. Polly, for her part, reveled in the newfound attention her husband, and by extension she, received. Of course, there had before been some honor in being the sister of a deacon, but it was nothing like being a deacon's wife. She began hosting dinner parties that excluded alcohol and included more guests than just Uncle Randy, started shopping with the other church wives, started going to "luncheon with the girls" on Wednesday afternoons. Rachel thought her father's new position was "very cool." Melissa did her best to be busy with schoolwork.

Five months into her seventeenth year of life—her junior year of high school—Melissa decided she was tired of lying. The problem was that she didn't exactly have the option of telling the truth, the truth that she just didn't want to go to church, because her parents would hate her. She voiced this fact, that her parents would hate her if she didn't go to church, to Jessica Owens one day in the school cafeteria while eating the first of two Honey Buns that she'd purchased from the extras line.

Jessica sucked mayonnaise that had dripped from a cucumber sandwich off the side of her hand. "Come on, Mel. They wouldn't hate you."

"Oh, but they would," Melissa said. "And I'm getting sick of living their life, y'know? I need something of my own."

Jessica seemed to examine her now-salivic palm.

"Jessica!"

"What?" Jessica attacked her hand with her tongue again, removing a remaining dab of mayo with excessive licking, before picking up the cucumber sandwich's second of four little triangles.

"I said they would hate me."

"Yeah. And I said they won't."

"Yeah but then I said that they would, and you ignored me."

"Oh, sorry. This is messy."

Melissa watched as the closest thing she had to a friend dissected her meal, which had undoubtedly been packed for her. There'd been nothing messy about the sandwich until Jessica had started breaking each fourth into its constituents: organic cucumber sliced as thin as the cover of a paperback book, yellow-tinted mayo, white (very white) bread with the crusts sliced cleanly off, probably with a special bread knife.

"I'm just sick of living their life, is the thing," Melissa repeated. "If they want to go to church, then they can go. But I'd rather do other things with my time."

"You could start going to my church. Maybe they'd be okay with it if you were still going to a church, even if it wasn't theirs. And you'd be, like, you know, with me."

This option wasn't horrifying, but it wasn't appealing either.

If Melissa went to Jessica's church, she'd probably have to eat ladyfingers or something. At least at her own she got a sip of wine once a week.

"You're missing the point. I don't want to go to church at all."

Three specks of white bread had clumped together and stuck themselves below Jessica's lower lip. "What do you want to do?"

"Read, maybe."

"Read?"

"I like to read."

"So read. You read now, don't you? I see you with books all the time."

"But again, the point isn't that I can't read now, but that reading is what I'd rather be doing. Or anything, really. Like I'm wasting time. You see?"

"Not really. You read all the time right now."

Melissa decided to not point out the yeasty clump on Jessica's face, which had been joined by a sliver of mayo, the mayo acting as an adhesive for more crumbs.

Her sandwich fourths having been vivisected and devoured, Jessica searched her brown paper bag for something else to lick. She found nothing. "Hey, Mel," she said. "Babes. Listen, I'm gonna go to the extras line. I'll be right back. You keep talking."

Melissa considered Jessica's small behind and the boney shoulder blades visible above the collar of her loose pink tank top, brown hair tied up in an elaborate braid, split ends and all. Melissa could acknowledge that Jessica was cute in that anemically tiny way all the guys seemed to like, but found nothing arousing there herself. Turning back to her own thoughts, Melissa tore into the wrapping on her second

HoneyBun. Melissa knew they were bad for her. Polly told her often that she had "enough extra weight already, and it's just going to get worse if you eat sweets all the time," but Melissa didn't care. She knew also that it wasn't going to get any worse. Melissa had weighed the same 121 pounds since she'd started high school, and since starting high school she'd eaten two Honey Buns with lunch every Friday, and nobody besides Polly had ever told her that she had enough extra weight already. Sure, when she sat down two little folds formed in the skin of her belly (which was mostly flat when standing, by the way), but her BMI was well within the range of normal, Dr. Nalurie had told her when she'd specifically brought it up at an appointment six months before his death. But still, Polly said, "you can't always trust BMI. I've heard it's not accurate. You could stand to lose five pounds. Don't you think Melissa could stand to lose five pounds Bernard?" Melissa picked the outer layer off of the HoneyBun. She stared at it, letting it hover in front of her mouth before putting it, and the rest of the snack cake, down on the table.

"You could maybe stand to lose five pounds," Jessica said.

Melissa jumped a little. She hadn't heard Jessica approach or slide back into her seat on the other side of the table. "What?"

Jessica was hunched forward in her chair, fellaciously sucking the salt off a pretzel stick. "I said that maybe you can get a job."

Pretzel sticks cost ten cents apiece at the extras counter. Melissa hated pretzels—hated their blandness, their dryness, the way they clumped in your mouth when you chewed them. "Get a job . . ."

"Well yeah. Like if you have work, you can't exactly go to church then, can you?"

Melissa watched, transfixed, as Jessica gnawed on her pretzel stick the way a beaver does when it's trying to fell a tree. A job. It was a plan.

And so at home that evening, while the family dressed for the evening church service, Melissa told Polly and her father that she wanted to get a job.

"A job? A job?" Polly wasn't a fan of the idea.

"Yes, Polly." There was time, when she was very young, when Melissa called Polly "Mom," but that habit had died with her preteen years. "A job. Like for money."

"You don't need a job, Melissa. Bernie, she doesn't need a job. Tell her she doesn't need a job."

Melissa's father slipped a slip of red plastic into the front of his clerical shirt's collar, examining its placement in Polly's full-length mirror. "What do you need a job for, Mellie?"

There were many occasions when her father spoke that Melissa thought his sentences should have been louder and were missing the word hell or fuck—like, What the hell do you need a job for? or What the fuck do you need a job for?—but he'd never said hell in any other sense but the biblical one (and even that was only recently, in, like, one sermon), and he'd never said fuck period that she had heard. "I just said why, Dad—money."

It took some convincing, a whole lot of I need my own space! and You guys still treat me like I'm a child, but I'm not a child!, the threat of a few fake tears, and Polly at one point putting her hands on her hips and saying, "It's obvious you don't respect the things we provide for you if you think you need to go out and get it yourself. Which says who knows what about the respect you'll have for your husband's hard work," but in the end they acquiesced. There were conditions, though, provisos, as Polly called them. First, it was agreed that Melissa had to save at least two-thirds of every paycheck in a bank account that Polly would take her to set up the next day; these savings were for when Melissa got married (actually, Bernard suggested college fund, and Polly responded with, "Yes, college. Or marriage. Whichever comes first . . . which should be marriage."). Second, one-tenth of every check had to go into the church collection basket on Sunday morning—you must render God's things to God and all that. Finally, Melissa's association with her new workmates would be restricted to work only unless Polly and Bernard had the opportunity to get to know said workmates first (or unless they happened to belong to the same church as the Gilpatricks). Melissa wasn't bothered by the first condition since the money was still hers; she knew that the second wouldn't be an issue since she planned on working every Sunday and thus missing the passing of the collection basket (it didn't escape her that, if she did put money in the collection basket, she'd essentially be paying her father, and so she felt a sort of sweet satisfaction in not doing it); and she didn't know how she felt about the third.

While convincing Bernard and Polly to let her get a job was easier than she'd expected, actually acquiring employment proved to be more difficult. Jessica's family was close with the owner of this deli on South Avenue, and she said she would put in a good word for Melissa, and she did, but the pudgy Italian man who owned the place said he couldn't afford to take on any new employees at the moment, but he was sure Jessica's friend was very nice.

Melissa spent the next two weeks filling out dozens of applications. One for the pool and spa retailer just a few blocks from her house. One for the Walmart store that existed in pretty much every U.S. city. One for the organic grocer on Centre Avenue. One for the regular grocer on Centre Avenue. One for the digital movie theater. One each for two separate ice cream parlors on Walnut. One for the pet store. Two more for each of the ice cream parlors on Walnut because she suddenly really liked the idea of working in an ice cream parlor. One for the bank where she'd opened an account, which was a dumb idea because no one was going to hire a seventeen year old first-time job-seeker to work in a bank. One for the small electronics boutique that always looked empty. One for the used car dealership at the corner of Main and Woodhurst. One for the Coffee Tree Roasters on Walnut. One for the Best Buy in Monroeville. One for each and every restaurant in the area, including fast food. She received nary a phone call in response. Not a single interview.

But then, after weeks of submitting application after application, weeks of going to church and then while at church praying that one of the places she'd applied to would hire her so she wouldn't have to go to church anymore, she received a sincere, personalized phone call (on the home phone—Melissa wasn't allowed a phone of her own) from a local call center, where she'd applied three weeks before, saying that they were very interested in meeting her, and inviting her in for an interview the next day. She was elated. Finally, someone who wanted to speak to her, get to know her, potentially hire her.

Melissa dressed in her best clothes, the ones she was usually made to wear to church: a white blouse with subtle pearl buttons down the front, a just-below-the-knee-length professional black skirt with a hint of white thread accenting the bottom in an irregular border, black heels, the only piece of jewelry she owned, which was a thin gold necklace with a cross hanging from it and from which she removed the cross between the time Polly dropped her off at the call center and she made it to the center's door. When she entered through the smudged glass door she was surprised to see something like fifteen people waiting in a line in front of a woman sitting behind a card table, a pen in her hand and on the wooden card table in front of her a stack of applications and a yellow legal pad. An acned man only a few years older than Melissa, with an overly large red dress shirt and a tie tied at least an inch too long, stood by the door. "All applicants please join the back of the line," he said. And Melissa realized there were several people coming in the doors behind her, so she did what the young man said and got in line.

The line moved quickly. It seemed the woman at the table spent no more than a couple minutes with each applicant. Melissa examined the faces of each person as they walked away from the table, trying to determine if they had gotten the job, but each expression was devoid of anything resembling excitement or disappointment or any other emotion. There was in the line, both behind her and in front of her, an abundance of obesity and/or body modification. The applicants were of a diverse age range, but Melissa was sure she was the youngest. The room they waited in was more of a wide hallway with several doors along its walls, one that said CONFERENCE ROOM, one that said LADIES ROOM, one that said MENS ROOM, not an apostrophe in sight, two tall green fake plants, a dented vending machine with a crack across its front glass and a sign that said SINGLES ONLY NO FIVES PLEASE. The air smelled of sweat and perfume and Melissa couldn't tell if it always smelled like that or if it was just the people in line with her. She danced from foot to foot, the line in which she stood a stagnant, dreadful thing.

Twenty minutes after she'd joined the line she was at the front and the woman behind the card table looked up from her notepad and said, "Next please."

Melissa approached nervously. "Hi, I'm—"

"Name please."

"Um, Melissa Gilpatrick."

The woman was maybe forty. She had short brownish hair and a mole on her flat nose and also one above her too-pink upper lip. She thumbed through the stack of applications without picking it up from the table. Melissa caught parts of names as the woman thumbed—the applications did not appear to be in any logical order, alphabetical or otherwise. "Gilpatrick. Gilpatrick. Gilpatrick. Melissa Gilpatrick?"

"Um, yes." Did that mean there were other Gilpatricks in the queue?

The woman paused at one of the applications, pulled it out, and looked it over. "Yes, okay," she said.

Okay what?

"Melissa, have you ever worked in a call center before?"

"No. I've . . . I've never had a job before."

"Uh huh. How are you at following instructions? Have you ever seen a flowchart before?"

"I'm great at following flowcharts!"

"Uh huh okay. What's your availability look like?"

"Well, I'm still in school, but I can work pretty much every evening and weekends."

"Uh huh okay. Okay. Come in tomorrow and we'll have you fill out some legal stuff. You can start at the beginning of next week." Melissa remained in front of the table for a moment, expecting more, but then the woman, who hadn't given her name and who Melissa never saw again, scratched at the mole above her lip and said, "Next please."

As she left the building, putting the cross back on the necklace and trying to find Polly's car, Melissa tried to recall if the woman had ever even made eye contact, but the details of the interview were already fading into the past, almost as if the whole thing had never happened, almost as if she'd simply gone to being employed from unemployed in an instant, with nothing in between.

Polly returned Melissa to the call center the next day to fill out paperwork, and the Monday after that Melissa started taking a different bus after school, one that went by the call center rather than her house. She started working three evenings a week for about five hours, plus a full eight-hour shift on Sunday and sometimes an additional eight-hour shift on Saturday. Bernard or a begrudging Polly picked her up each evening and drove her both to and from work on the weekends.

The call center itself was comprised of several departments, although department, while the word was used, was probably inaccurate, since *department* has a way of conjuring up a team of individuals that work together, maybe in one specific office or a group of offices on the same floor, each member of the department an integral part of an otherwise autonomous team, but the call center's entry- and mid-level employees didn't have offices, just cubicles, tiny ones, hundreds of them all in the same massive, open-floor-plan room, this room just down the wide hallway that Melissa had stood in line in while waiting for her interview, and which department you were in had no bearing on where your cubicle would be because the place just wasn't set up that way, Melissa's boss, a middle-aged bespectacled man named Gary Borstern explained to her on her first day. One department, for example, oversaw a portion of the technical support that came through for a certain Japan-based television manufacturer (the company manufactured far more than televisions—washers and dryers, state-of-the-art kitchen appliances, cellular phones, guitars, etc.—but the support calls routed to this call center were focused only on the company's televisions, whose customers didn't trust foreigners); another department consisted of cubicle grunts whose job it was to phone numbers on a list ("leads" being the industry jargon for these numbers) and beg them to make a donation to the Pennsylvania senator's reelection campaign; and another department was focused on surveying via phone customers who'd recently made purchases from a nationally known candy company, reminding said customers that, by completing the survey, they'd be entered in a drawing for a chance to win either one million dollars or a year's supply of caramel-coated chocolate bars ("drawing for a chance" being the operable term here, meaning that, even if they won the drawing, they then had a chance of winning the actual prize; no one ever won the prize, not once). Melissa was assigned to a certain mobile-phone-and-internet company's Churn Prevention team. When a customer called to cancel his or her cellular plan, the call was forwarded to Melissa, and from there it was her job to convince the customer to reconsider. "May I ask why you're leaving us, Mr. Allensbauer? Perhaps I can address any concerns you might have." "We're sorry to see you go, Miss Goldspringer. Would it make a difference if I were to tell you that I can lower your current monthly rate by ten percent?" "Well, Mr. Smith, you're right, that company certainly does have some pretty amazing phones, but have you heard of the Blackberry 9750v, exclusive to our company? It's an excellent phone; in fact I use one myself. What if I told you I could upgrade your current phone to a 9750v for only ninety-nine cents if you renewed your contract with us today?" And the part about Melissa personally using a Blackberry 9750v was not a lie (although what Melissa didn't tell Mr. Smith was that her company's competitor offered the Blackberry 9750s, the exact same phone with the exact same capabilities.). She was given one, along with a data plan, as a perk of her job at the call center. The data plan was discounted and the payments were deducted from her bi-weekly paycheck once a month. The plan would be canceled were she ever to terminate employment at the call center, but the phone was hers, a gift, they called it. Everyone who worked in one of the telecom departments received one, some even had two phones, one from the company and another that they paid for personally. Melissa, of course, didn't tell Bernard or Polly about the phone.

With a cellphone—even better, a smartphone—Melissa discovered a whole new kind of freedom. She signed up for a Gmail account. With the Gmail account, she subscribed to dozens of newsletters and blogs about all sorts of topics. She accessed the mobile versions of Facebook and Twitter from the phone's browser and signed up for accounts on both under fake names: Sunny Patrick and @sunnypatrick_90 respectively. She followed and friended her coworkers and schoolmates. She subscribed to the updates of celebrities she'd heard of but whose R-rated movies she'd never seen. She bought a pair of cheap headphones so she could lie in bed at night and watch videos on YouTube, videos of cats and videos of people making and eating ridiculously sized meals and videos of people explaining how mattresses were made and videos of the best compilations of attractive women kissing. She discovered Google Image search and started looking at pictures of naked people every night. She found two porn sites designed specifically for mobile phones (Jessica told her about them), but the videos were like only sixty seconds long and low-resolution and, while Melissa found them fascinating, scrolling through them and selecting a new one each minute was tiring. She texted people and exchanged emails. One day, a few weeks after she got the phone, her sister waddled into the room while Melissa was watching a music video on the two-point-five-inch screen, and then she walked out and never said a word about what she'd seen.

The person Melissa spent most of her time texting and emailing was a coworker named Dan. In retrospect, Dan was not an attractive or interesting or desirable person, but at the time, Melissa found something want-able about him, something dangerous, something disruptive. He'd been working at the call center for a few years, a tall, too-skinny twenty-something with blond hair buzzed very short, a few meager whiskers on his chin, pockmarked cheeks and forehead, small tattoos on his neck and hands, a smoker with a propensity to slur words and say "yo" except for when he was making company calls (when he sounded crisp and professional). At work he always wore the same black slacks and one of several two-sizes-too-big blue or white dress shirts often untucked and a clip-on red tie, and Melissa found out eventually that outside of work he wore hole-ridden jeans and a white or black tank-top and also had tattoos on his back and left bicep, which calling it a bicep wasn't wholly accurate because there just wasn't much to it in the diameter department. But the thing about Dan that started her talking to him in the first place was that he called Melissa "girl" and said "damn, you're beautiful" on her first day of work, and that made her feel pretty.

She talked to Dan at work every day. He was assigned a cubicle on the other side of the call-floor from her, but he found plenty of reasons each day to make his way to her side of the room and chat her up. She friended him on Facebook. He asked for her number and she gave it to him. They texted. They emailed, sometimes treating email like text messaging with compact messages back and forth, and sometimes sharing funny links and videos and pictures.

For several months she worked four or five shifts a week at the call center. Her study time, and thus her grades, decreased, but her bank account, mostly untouched, grew not disappointingly.

Melissa set foot in a church exactly twice in the months after she got the job at the call center, the first on Christmas morning —a dry, dull mass—because the call center was closed and besides it was Christmas so she felt obliged to go. The service was dull and formulaic and noticeably unscripted, even with her father leading the mass. The second time she went was the wedding of a coworker, Jessalya Ball, who had invited Melissa because, even though she hadn't known her long and had spent no time with her outside of work, she liked her, probably because Melissa raved once about some fresh-baked chocolate chip cookies Jessalya had made and brought in for the office. Melissa's invitation allowed for one guest—it said "Melissa Gilpatrick & Guest" in curved gold font in the email—which was obviously intended to mean Melissa should bring a significant other, of which she had none, so instead she brought Polly, who had insisted Melissa couldn't go unless she went also, per the conditions established when Melissa first convinced them to let her get a job. And so stepmother and stepdaughter went to church together for the last time.

The wedding was beautiful, the ceremony short but charged with sacredness and regality. The usual vows were exchanged, followed by the reading of personal ones. Jessalya's husband was some sort of poet. The reception hall was decorated with flowers floating in large glass bowls of pinkly dyed water. The music was well chosen. The dancing skilled. The food expensive and not poorly cooked. Jessalya went on her honeymoon the next day and never returned to the office, which no one save Melissa seemed to notice, but then even Melissa after a few weeks forgot Jessalya had ever worked there.

One day in early spring, Dan told Melissa he was throwing a party at his house the following Saturday and she should come. She almost said no, in fact she tried to say no, but she felt a certain giddiness at the possibility of spending actual time with Dan, and so, even though she knew there was no way Bernard and Polly would let her go, she smiled and said, "That sounds great!"

"Cool," Dan said.

For nearly a week Melissa's work and school days went by in a luminescent haze. She could focus on nothing but the party, getting to the party, because at the party would be Dan, and he would be there, with her, in his house, like with his bedroom and his things and maybe they would sneak off away from the party at some point and be alone. Was that what he wanted? She hoped he would understand that it was her first time . . .

She could take the bus, but Dan lived in Brighton Heights, on the other side of the city, and when pulling up transit directions on her phone she saw it would take almost three hours and four transfers to get there on a Saturday evening. She could hire a cab, but the fare would be like thirty bucks. She could borrow her father's Volvo without telling him. But, no, if she did that, the consequences would be extreme and guaranteed. It would have to be a cab.

But then the day before the party Dan came over to her cubicle while she was on the phone and sat on the desk next to her computer and waited for her to finish the call, his eyes never leaving her. She found it difficult to speak to the customer with him standing there, watching, smelling like something—nicotine maybe?—that she shouldn't have found alluring but did. She failed to retain the customer's business. She didn't care.

"So you coming tomorrow, gorgeous?" he said after she'd hung up the phone.

Coming—she knew this word's double meaning now. Had heard it in the short erotic clips she'd watched on her phone.

"Yes," she said. "I'm, um, I'll be taking a cab, but I'll make sure I'm there."

"A cab. Babe, you can't take a cab from like, what, Wilkinsburg?"

"No, Shadyside," she said. "I only live a few blocks from here."

"Shit, it takes me like half hour to drive my place to here in good traffic. Shit. I'll drive you."

Melissa's lungs seemed to float out of her chest and hover in the air before her. In a car with Dan . . .

"Okay, cool," she said.

"I'll pick you up at your place at like five-thirty. What's your addie?"

"Actually, I work tomorrow."

"Ah, cool, cool. Me too. Just like bring a change of digs then and we'll leave together."

Melissa grinned as Dan walked away, her lungs merging with her body once again. They were going to leave together.

On the morning of the party, when her father dropped her off for her shift, Melissa, her heart pounding in her chest like a bass drum only she could hear, an invisible sheen of sweat collecting at the base of her hairline, told her father she'd see him at four when she got off. The lie came hard to Melissa's mouth even though lies had never come hard to her before. "Okay," her father said. "Love you. See you then." The way he said it—Melissa thought for a moment that maybe he did love her. He hadn't even noticed the backpack she had with her that contained a change of clothes. "Oh wow. I guess my brain just totally thought it was school day," she'd been prepared to say. An hour later she called her home and Polly answered and Melissa told her that a coworker who was supposed to work that evening had called off and that Melissa had volunteered to stay for the evening shift.

But they had those dinner plans tonight, with the reverend and his wife, Polly said.

Melissa had forgotten about the dinner. She decided to back out of Dan's party. "Oh, that's right," she said. But the lying was easier when there was no eye contact to make. "But well I already said I'd work the shift, though, so I guess I have to."

"You can tell them you can't. Tell them you can't. You forgot about your plans, tell them."

"Well but . . ." Melissa paused and looked at a frowning Mr. Borstern who wasn't there, if only to imagine that the lie was real. "Sorry, Polly. I just can't. It's too late since I said I'd do it, y'know? Sorry. It's my fault. Tell the reverend I'm sorry. I'll see them next weekend or something."

The airwaves hung heavy with silence. "And how will you get home?" Polly said. "We'll be at dinner."

"I'll . . . I'll get a ride from someone. From . . . from Beth. See, yeah. Right, Beth? Yeah, Beth says she'll take me."

"So Beth works tonight too?"

"Um. Beth always works a double shift on Saturdays."

"Right. You're off at ten then? Like a normal evening shift?"

"Uh, yes."

"I'll just get you at ten."

"No, Polly, it's okay—"

"How are you phoning?"

"What?"

"How are you calling me, Melissa?"

"I have a desk phone."

"A desk phone . . ."

"Yeah. A, uh, well the phone just sort of sits on my desk. Like stays here." And then Melissa was overwhelmed with indignation, like Polly was wronging her in some terrible way at that very moment, making her lie again, and she hated the lying. "I work at a call center, Polly," she said, her tone no longer uncertain but harsh, superior.

"I'll get you at ten."

The work day dragged on slowly, painfully, until finally at five it was over. Dan was behind on his queue and had to finish a few more calls. Melissa spent the half-hour between five and five-thirty in the company bathroom, changing clothes (a black tank top, a skirt not unlike the one she wore to work but shorter), applying makeup (she'd never worn makeup before until Jessayla's wedding; this makeup was the leftovers: blue-black eye shadow, lipstick so red it might have been purple in a different light, mascara that added depth to her sallow face), trying to prettify herself in every way she could think of. She returned to Dan's cubicle just as he was shutting down his PC. She waited for him to comment on her outfit, and waited. He called one of his "boys" on his cell when they got to his car. They stopped at the state-run liquor store on the way to his place. Melissa, being underage, waited in the car. When he returned to the car, placing a large brown paper bag in the back seat, Dan pulled out his phone again and called someone else. He spoke on the phone—discussing, from what Melissa could tell, television shows and marijuana and whether or not the friend on the other line should get another pit bull to replace one that had recently passed away —all the way back to his place. The tension between Dan and Melissa during the drive was palpable and obvious. They arrived at Dan's house at six-thirty just as the party's first guests were arriving.

First as a trickle the guests came in, and then as a series of waves. For the first small undefinable chunk of the party Melissa stuck close to Dan. She helped him lay out snacks. He offered to make her a drink, which she declined before finally accepting just a soda. He introduced her to the first few guests: Dan's brother, Dave; Jeanette, whose hair was short and fiery but whose eyebrows were black; Mike, Jeanette's boyfriend, who it turned out worked at the call center but who Melissa barely recognized; Ottis; Biggie; Joey; Markus, who was a photographer, he said, and wondered if Melissa might be interested in doing some modeling; Danielle, who told Melissa to ignore Markus and then told Markus to don't you even dare. But after a while, when the house started to fill with people, Dan disappeared and Melissa was on her own. She stood against a wall, hugging the red plastic cup full of cola to her breasts like a stuffed security animal. For what felt like hours she watched the people as they talked and mingled and laughed and drank. There were men and women, couples and single people and groups of three or four or five arriving together. All brought something: beer or liquor or large bags of ruffled potato chips or corn chips and jars of salsa and guacamole-flavored dip or store-bought deserts like cookies and brownies and even a box of cruller. Of all the guests, most had tattoos. Ages ranged from early twenties to maybe late forties—Melissa was the youngest there. The women wore short skirts or tight, ripped jeans. More than a few of the men wore porkpies. Most of the guests wore tank-tops. The music was loud and boomed from the speakers of Dan's house's living room with perpetual vibration and had no recognizable lyrics. The house was a normal suburban one-story residence; Melissa remembered that Dan had mentioned inheriting the house from his parents after his mother and then his father had died. It wasn't dirty but it wasn't tidy. The furniture was just sort of there. On a black wood and glass entertainment stand against one wall sat a 56-inch television and various video game apparatuses. Bowls of chips and paper plates and bottles of lagers on the coffee table. Bottles of liquor and soda and plastic cups and framed family photos and a bowl of punch of the sort that was spiked with alcohol on a mantel above which hung an oval mirror. Music loud. Dancing and talking. Multiple varietals of smoke in the air.

"Yo, you name's Melissa, right?"

Melissa turned and saw that the man who Dan had introduced her to, before he'd disappeared, as Biggie had approached her from the direction of the kitchen. She backed tighter against the wall as he neared her, a refrigerator of a man —dark skin, shaved head, tattoos and other scars on biceps the size of watermelons.

"Yes."

"Biggie. We met." His voice was like distant thunder.

"We did." Unaccustomed to unsupervised social interaction, Melissa wasn't entirely sure what her options were here. "Why do they call you Biggie?"

It was a joke, but he didn't gesture or reference his large frame as she expected. "Cuz it's what my Ma named me."

"Oh."

"Yeah, well."

"Wait. You mean really?"

"Really. I ain't shittin' you. Funny thing is I was small for a long time, too. Like before I was like sixteen—only then I got bigger."

"Oh." Melissa sipped her soda. She'd heard once that holding a drink in your hand at all times at a party makes you feel interesting. Whomever she'd heard it from had been wrong.

"You having fun?"

It was a good question: Was she having fun? No. "I don't know. It's . . . not what I expected."

"Chu expect?"

"I don't know. It's just kind of boring."

Biggie clutched his chest. His eye twitched, but Melissa couldn't tell if it was a wink or genuine tic. "Chu think Biggie's boring?"

She smiled. "I don't think Biggie's boring," she said. She was suddenly so over Dan. And why not? He'd abandoned her a long time ago.

"Listen," he said, "people's boring. It's how it is, y'know? Whatchu expect?"

"Drugs, maybe? Sex? General debauchery?"

"Debauchery? Debauchery ain't all it's cracked up to be. I've debauched stuff plenty, and I ain't like it. Besides, we got stuff here. We got beer. We got like weed or some shit goin' on over in that corner. You want some weed?"

She looked down and then back up. She shook her head.

"I didn't think so. How 'bout another drink?"

"Okay."

"Whatchu drinkin'?"

"Um "—What sort of things did people drink? What sort

of things besides cheap red wine and Bud Light?—"Rum and soda."

He stared at her, raised a thick eyebrow. "Really, though?"

"Sure," she said. "Really."

He shook his head. He made her a rum and some off-brand cola, not the Coke she'd been drinking before, the bottle of which seemed to have disappeared from the refreshments table, and she downed it urgently. The rum was coconut-flavored and was sweet and cool, but it warmed when it hit her throat and passed into her belly. She had another while she and Biggie talked. Biggie was a man of few and dialectical words, but there was a sturdy power behind the things he had to say. What did he do? He was a bouncer and it wasn't bad, not as eventful as people think. What did Melissa do? She went to school. And but of course he knew that. She wandered away from him after a while and found herself floating through the house, laughing at things guests said, butting into conversations and finding herself welcome within them. In the backyard she played a few games of cornhole with a group to whom she took an immediate liking. When people started dancing in the living room, she danced also. She shook her hips and held her hands above her head, her shirt lifting with her shoulders and exposing her midriff to a room that might admire it. She drank more: a Yeungling, another rum and soda, straight coconut rum. She snuck vodka and juice, the variety of which she didn't pay attention to, when she thought no one was looking, unaware that no one here cared what she drank or would judge her for it. Until this night, her time on Earth had been as worthless as a small stone or a discarded bottle cap or shard of broken glass, but tonight her sense of self expanded to fill this house and these people and the music's pulsing bass.

After many drinks, while wandering around, bottle in hand, she bumped headlong into Biggie's solid chest. "Oh, hey. Chu a'ight?" he said, catching her as she bounced backward.

"I want to have sex with you!" she called to him as if he were on the other side of the room.

"What?" He tilted his ear toward her and she stood on her toes and leaned in close. There was the tic again, except that it was definitely a wink.

"I SAID LIKE LET'S GO HAVE SEX OR WHATEVER!"

He shook his head and grinned, and she thought the grinning meant he was amenable to the idea, but then she realized he just thought she was funny. She threw up on his shoes, his fresh white sneakers with red accents around the ankles and above the tread. Her head spun.

She heard: "Yo, Dan. Your friend ain't too hot here, man."

"Did some . . ." she said. "Did someone give me something?" Was that something people did? It was, right? They'd warned them in school about the roofies.

Biggie laughed. "Nah. You ain't never drank before, huh?"

Her throat heaved again but nothing came out.

She heard Dan say, "Take her to my room, man." And Biggie did. As she stumbled along with him, her arms around his arm and her head wobbling against him, she wondered what they were going to do when they got there. Was she up for it, she wondered. Could she give up her virginity like—what did Polly call them?—a dime-store whore? She wasn't ready, and yet she wanted it, but that could have been the roofie. "No," she tried to say as Biggie lead her to the room. "I don't want to." But her mouth was full of cotton and couldn't make words. And when they got to the room, what Biggie did was held her arm and laid her gently across the bed and removed her shoes and set them by the door and put a quilted blanket over her, up to her chin, and told her to take it easy and sleep well and left the room.

When she woke in the morning, Melissa found Dan on the couch. There were bottles still on the mantel—some empty and some still partly full—and the trash can in the kitchen was close to overflowing, but other than these the house was as clean as it had been before the party started the previous evening. She didn't know why, but she'd expected the place to be a mess, littered with paper and food and maybe broken glass.

Dan woke a few minutes after her and asked if her head hurt.

"A little," she said.

He made her coffee and burnt toast with jelly and butter and gave her a still slightly green banana and then drove them both to work.

There was a post-it note on her desk that said "Call your parents." She ignored it. She worked. One of the other departments was short-staffed that day due to multiple call-offs, and so she was assigned to fill the void. She spent seven hours, minus a lunch break for which she had brought nothing, calling ordinary people with their ordinary debts and listening to their ordinary voices. She told them she was calling about a very important matter. In most cases no one picked up and so she left voice messages and said to please call her back at their earliest convenience, knowing that they likely wouldn't call back—she wouldn't if she were them—and that even if they did they likely would talk to one of the other dozens of operators in the building, not her. Most of the ones that did pick up when she called asked what exactly she was calling about, and when she told them her call was in reference to a debt, they hung up promptly. She took five-minute breathers every half hour, her feet up on her cubicle's desk. She stared at her phone. At one point she fell asleep for a minute and a half and in that brief time she dreamed that a few years ago some scientists had gone on TV and said there was considerable evidence that the wireless signals in the air had played a significant role in human evolution, that maybe all these cancers that were popping up in the last half-dozen decades were a long-delayed side effect of radio signals and cosmic rays that still lingered because ancient hominids had used cell phones too much, and in the dream she wondered what would happen if scientists put the phone satellites underground. That's how cell phones worked, right? Satellites? A total of three customers let her read her call-script all the way to its conclusion. An hour before the shift was over she found Dan at his cubicle and asked if he wouldn't mind taking her home.

He dropped her off at the end of her driveway and she went into the house. She was greeted by Bernard and Polly waiting at the top of the entryway's stairs. "Where have you been?" her father said, in his hand a yellow legal pad on which Melissa could make out notes for next week's sermon. Again his words were distractingly devoid of expletives.

"I was at work."

Polly's face was beet-red and wet and between her eyebrows an ugly blue vein fought to breach the epidermis. "Don't you dare," she said. "Don't you dare. You know very damn well what your father means."

Ah, there was a profanity. A show of real emotion. From someone, at least.

"I'm afraid I don't," Melissa said. Rachel scurried across the foyer's balcony, and though she was in her line of sight for just a moment, the image of the girl's sock-shod feet lingered in Melissa's vision.

"Where were you last night, is what I wanted to know," her father said. "Do you know how worried—"

"I was at a party. I went to a party and I didn't tell you."

"A party?" Polly said. "I don't even— Where was this party?"

"At Dan's."

"Who—"

"Just a guy I work with."

"A guy? A man?"

"Melissa—" her father started to say.

"Shut up, Bernard," Polly said. "Just shut the hell up for a minute. I'm trying to figure out what kind of girl you raised."

Melissa's hands were spring-loaded fists, but she kept them at her side, kept her voice steady and calm, mathematically cold. "I. Just. Went. To a party. People go to parties."

"Sluts go to parties. Godless, unchristian sluts go to parties with guys they work with. Office whores do that, Melissa. Are you the office whore?"

Rachel appeared at the top of the stairs again. She wasn't wearing any socks now, just sweatpants and a baggy t-shirt.

Melissa looked at Polly. Her father stood by, his attention on the tablet that held his sermon. "I was last night," Melissa said. "Oh boy was I."

For the next hour, until Polly's energy was spent, Melissa answered every accusation, every insult and shame-intended bit of name-calling, with "Yep" or "That's me" or "You betcha, mom." She called Polly "mom" again, something she hadn't done in years, just this one last time. Bernard Gilpatrick said little during the whole episode; he was only a deacon, after all.

By the end of the night Melissa had packed a single large backpack with clothes and her birth certificate and a bag of cashews and the bank card that she demanded Polly give her because it was hers. And she walked to an ATM and withdrew some cash and walked to the bus station, where she slept on the bench until morning. She bought a ticket to New York because New York sounded like a city she might be happy in. As the bus rolled on, she cried a little. And then she yelled fuck three times, long and loud: "Fuck! Fuck! Fuck!" And the rest of the bus's riders stared at her for only just a moment.

HOME AGAIN

FAIRLAWN IS NOT LIKE HE remembers it from his childhood. The house is not like he remembers it. Maybe it's the eye—maybe it's the eye that adds the sheen of prettiness and upper-middle-class status that he sees now as he stands on the porch, leaning against one of the awning's freshly painted wooden support beams, glass in hand. When Jonathan was young, you couldn't much see the city from Fairlawn; you could see only the massive fence and skeletons of slowly rising buildings, skeletons like fossils of things that didn't yet exist. Fossils of the future. But now the fence is gone and the city is a city again, a far better city than it has ever been before, and its skyscrapers, some as tall as buildings in New York, stand majestic on the distant horizon, shadows against the setting sun. And now in Fairlawn the houses are sided with pastel vinyls and the yards are green and mowed weekly and adorned with flowerbeds and miniature trees: Japanese maple and dogwood and sakura. And it's not the eye that sees these things; these things actually are the way they seem. This city and its suburbs, and even Jonathan's childhood home, have changed for the better, and it's just these last few months have been his first time back here since leaving eighteen years ago, so it's the first time he's seen the change.

And oh but it is the eye that makes the sunset look the way it does, all coppery and aflame and closer than it should be. The mechanisms and software in the optical bionic implant allow him to do things a human shouldn't be able to do: to see beyond the visible spectrum, to zoom in and out at will so that his vision is closer in one eye to twenty-ten than twenty-twenty, to detect the smallest movements.

When the bomb went off—and even now, three years later, he hardly remembers the details of that horrible hour of his life —the pressure created by its explosive force was enough to rupture the soft, jelly-like tissue of his right eyeball. The rest of him was saved only by the fact that his mother was standing there in front of him and slightly to the left, absorbing the kinetic energy that would have hit the other half of his body. And so, in a procedure that he wasn't actually able to ask to be a part of because he was unconscious for the days following the bombing, the doctors installed the eye. When he first awoke, he couldn't see anything out of his right socket—the eye's power supply, located behind his right ear and plugged into a surgically implanted port, needed charging. By tethering him to an outlet the doctors charged it and showed him how to install the eye's application on his phone, and with the application he can make the eye do so many things. He can even use the application to send the feed from his eye to a nearby television or somebody else's phone or computer or tablet, or even live-stream it over the internet, so that others can see what he is seeing (he has never done this, though). In the week after he regained consciousness, a swarm of reporters stopped by the hospital to talk to him and his doctors. At the time of its installation Jonathan Bread was the fifth person to receive a bionic eye, which had been approved for experimental use in humans just six months before. Only twelve people on the planet have one. In exchange for Jonathan's use of the eye, the eye's application gathers information about its operation and sends it as a data file to researchers once a day. In his left eye he needs to wear a contact lens, that eye still as astigmatic as it's been since his childhood.

He does not drink the ice-cold glass of lemonade that sits in his hand, wetting it with its condensation. He took a sip a minute ago, after he made it, but it was bitter. He used too little sugar. For some reason, despite the lemonade's terribleness, he didn't set it down but carried it out onto the porch with him, its solidness in his fingers a comfort now as he watches the sunset.

The sun disappears behind the city and Jonathan stands on the porch for only a few moments longer before disappearing inside the house. He enters the kitchen, where he dumps the lemonade down the drain, first the glass and then the whole pitcher. He replaces it with a cold Guinness and returns to the living room. His parents' house's living room is larger somehow than when he was a child. Roomy and open, it has hardwood floors and arching, doorless doorways. In the room's center is a sofa, in front of the sofa a rug, and on the rug a finished mahogany table, its surface untouched by mug or glass or maybe even human hands, a stack of four coasters in the center. In front of the table is an empty space, and on the wall is art, so that the art—a painting of three men playing a snare drum and a flute and an electronic keyboard, a stone sculpture of a ballerina, a wooden carving of a slender dog—is visible when you look forward from the couch. Conversation pieces, they are. There is no television. There was no art in the house when Jonathan was young. When the house goes, the art will go with it.

Behind the couch on the floor are several blankets and an air mattress on which Jonathan has been sleeping for months now, deflating it and rolling it up and putting it away only when Sammie comes to show the house. He cannot sleep in the old bedroom that still houses his old stiff twin bed; he's tried, but he can't. There's an old joke: I sleep in a twin bed; I never did find out where my brother went.

Beside the air mattress, a table with a slim aluminum laptop and an automatic coffeemaker. This is where he's been spending his days. This living room, this couch, this desk and this mattress. He does not visit the other parts of the house if he can help it, save for necessary trips to the bathroom and extended assaults upon the kitchen. He leaves the house sometimes, but usually just for groceries. Most days, the farthest he goes is one of the porches—the back to watch the sun rise, the front to watch it set.

He sits now at the desk, wakes the laptop and stares at the words there on the screen. They're a blur to him. Not a real blur —he has, after all, the bionic eye—but an intellectual blur, a puzzle of characters and plot points he's been trying to fit together but can't. He rubs his eyes. Whenever he rubs the bionic eye, he swears he can hear its mechanics groan in protest.

There's a sound, a piece of popular music. It's his phone's ringtone. The phone he left in the kitchen when he was making the terrible lemonade. He goes to it. On the screen he recognizes Sammie's name. "Hello?"

"Jon, hey. Hey, I've got an interested couple available now for a showing. Is that cool?"

"Now? Like *now* now? *Right* now?"

"Yeah. Is that okay? I know it's getting late, but they seem like a promising—"

"No, it's fine. Bring them by. It'll take me only a minute to tidy up."

Immediately following the bombing, Jonathan Bread fell into a deep depression, something with which he had close to zero experience, and none of the experience with depression that he did have came from his own previous suffering of it, because he'd never previously suffered from it, but had instead come from the type of fling in college who cried during sex or the type who cried after sex or the type who cried in the morning when she woke up and found Jonathan still in her dorm room's bed (none of this, admittedly, may have actually been depression, Jonathan understands, but more like feelings of deeply embedded shame, which, the fact that sleeping with Jonathan brought to surface deeply embedded shame, is probably something that should concern him), so he didn't know what to do about the depression he was feeling, and in fact he didn't even recognize it as depression at its onset, but came to suspect that maybe depression was what it was when he thought about taking a knife to his wrists, deciding against the knife because, to him, wrist-cutting sounded like a juvenile way to kill oneself.

Regarding his feelings about wrist-cutting his therapist reprimanded him: "Jonathan! There's nothing juvenile or immature about cutting. It's not this pathetic thing that teenagers do. It's a cry for help in the way that any act of self-harm is a cry for help. You think that only young people give in to the impulse to do damage to their own bodies? All the time in here are parents, dragging their children and telling me to make them grow up, who don't think that there's anything legitimate about their child's suffering, think they're just 'acting out' or being self-righteous brats. But adults are worse. Adults eat food that makes them fat and get heart disease and die. Adults don't exercise—you need to start exercising again, Jonathan, speaking of—and they die. Adults take stupid risks, and they die. Adults refuse to end dead or harmful relationships and they start to hate the world and themselves and then they die. Adults are far worse, Jonathan, far worse. One hundred percent of adults engage in self-harm every day; they just don't care enough to realize it." And Jonathan just kind of sat in the chair after his therapist said this and felt even more depressed than before.

So instead of killing himself, he slept. First, he lay in the bed in the hospital while recovering from his injuries—third-degree burns across his broken right arm, six cracked ribs, a torn earlobe that dangled before being reattached with stitches. Even when the reporters came to talk to him about the explosion he mostly just slept. His parents were dead, you see. So were other people, but he didn't know those people and thus didn't care. But his parents he cared about in his own way, and now they were gone. His mother's lifeless body was disfigured beyond recognition (but maybe there was comfort to be found in that—isn't that what all mothers aspired to, to die for their children?). His father was millions of particles returned to space, scattered across the universe from which they'd come, destined to join stars and planets and nebulae. There's a good chance, Jonathan read once, that every single human that ever lived was made from atoms that once existed within the same single star, before that star went nova and scattered itself across the universe.

When he went home he thought he could get over the depression, could get back the life he'd been ready to start before, but then Merrell called him up, gave him the bad news, told him the production was shutting down, that with all the terrorism people were becoming scared, tourism in New York had been affected, Broadway attendance had declined the last couple months and Merrell couldn't afford to produce multiple shows right now. But things would pick up—things always pick up— and then they'd do a second run. But the cast moved on and that second run never happened, and neither Merrell's nor Jonathan's heart were in *Sugarcane* anymore. That's when Jonathan started seeing the therapist, an aging black man with a shaved head and a mustache as thick as one of those round hairbrushes some women use. And when he wasn't at therapy he pretty much just slept or ate or watched movies and television that he wished he had written, still in that small apartment, gaining thirty pounds. His parents were gone. Melissa, the understudy of the girl in the play, moved out to California. Merrell never called. Jonathan was alone in the city, alone among so many people, and when you're alone, he learned, there's nothing to do but be alone. It took him months of zero effort, but eventually he grew a not-too-patchy beard, which was as curly and dark as the hair on his head, except that as he lay in the apartment, a couple years from forty, the hair was not without grey.

"Here we have the master bedroom . . . these carpets were actually just put in about two years ago . . . yes, furnishings are included . . . the art can be included as well, but only at market price, which for these pieces is not too substantial . . . the heating and lighting system has been configured to interface with a wide variety of electronic equipment . . . the owners were putting the finishing touches on several years worth of renovations before they vacated the house . . . well, yes, by 'vacated' I mean . . . so you are familiar then with the . . . the roof still needs a bit of work . . . we're taking care of those things, actually . . . any and all repairs and remodeling will be complete before the move-in date . . . almost all complete now, actually . . . reinforced porcelain bowl . . . well, no, not the curtains . . . yes, yes, of course . . . in fact, the infrastructure . . . school district was not always the best, true, but is really making a positive name for itself in recent years . . . Jon here . . . painted the porch himself, actually . . . actually . . . actually . . ."

Jonathan doesn't pay much attention during the tour. He just stands and follows, wanting to collapse on the couch but knowing to do so would be rude and awkward. He realized before Sammie even called that he isn't going to get much work done tonight, but he wants at least to listen to some music, to grasp for inspiration, something he finds only in fits and spurts these days. He nods along as Sammie speaks. He lets her answer the questions. Occasionally she mentions his name in connection with a piece of the house or its history, and he shrugs and dips his head affirmatively.

He does listen when Sammie asks the couple, "So what brings you here? Why are you interested in living in Fairlawn?" It's the house he grew up in, after all, and he wants to make sure it goes to good people.

It turns out the couple are newlyweds.

"We met in Rome," the young woman says, "last July. I had just graduated college, and so some friends and I took a summer trip to Europe to celebrate."

"And I was in Italy on business." the young man says, looking at his wife with disgustingly smitten eyes.

"What is your business?" Jonathan says.

The young man looks up. "Electronics."

"Of course."

"My husband was recently promoted. VP of Development for Acer. Youngest executive in the company."

"Which is why we're moving out here. Our new R&D center is being built in the city."

"We're hoping to raise our children here." The woman takes one of her husband's hands in both of hers.

The little tour group comes to the dining room, and when they do, Sammie glances at the table and then at Jonathan deploringly. On the mid-century teak table sits an open bag of generic-branded corn chips. Jonathan frowns. He must have left them there days ago, because that's the last time he was in this room, days ago, and he remembers now the outburst. There are crumbs scattered across the surface of the table, frozen in place in an explosive pattern emanating from the bag's opening. The vase in the table's center is tilted on its side. Any water that hasn't dried is soaking the crumbs, and the water that has dried has damaged the wood, warping it, softening it. Flowers—roses and carnations and lilies arranged in an elegant bouquet, a bouquet Sammie purchased last week for the beautification of the house —lie on the table and the floor, browning. Petals have dried and fallen off. It's like a crime scene; the only things missing are the yellow police tape across the doorway and the chalk outlines around the dead.

"Let's head this way," Sammie says, leading the couple through the arch.

She finishes the rest of the tour in record time, answering questions, of which the couple has few, and then Jonathan and Sammie stand on the porch, watching as the young man and the young woman back out onto the road and drive away.

In the dark they stand. The night is pleasantly cool. In the distance the lights of the city do shine, and the sounds of the city —cars, machines, music—can be heard. "Would you like to come in?" Jonathan says. "I can get you a cup of coffee or tea—I think I have tea—or a beer. I made lemonade." He forgets he's disposed of the lemonade at the pitcher level.

Sammie is admittedly larger than the women that Jonathan Bread tends to go for, but it's been a while. In fact it's been three years. And despite her being slightly (only slightly) overweight, Sammie isn't unattractive. She's about his age. Her hair is blonde-going-on-grey-except-she-dyes-it-regularly. She has wrinkles, but they're the expected ones—under the eyes and around the mouth. While the rest of her is larger, her face is still taut, except for some loose skin—not fat, skin— underneath her chin. She holds herself with the confidence of an accomplished real-estate agent, which is what she is. And Jonathan has spent enough time around her the last few months that attraction has become inevitable. He knows little about her, truth be told.

She looks at him, stirring something male and ridiculous in his chest. "No," she says, spurning what he wasn't sure was even an advance with that single word. "Have a good night, Jon."

And he does have a good night, if unproductive. He lies on the couch and masturbates, wearing a condom so he'll last longer. He bought the condoms yesterday. He didn't buy them because he wanted to last longer while masturbating—he hasn't masturbated in a long time and hadn't planned on masturbating tonight—but because he knew he'd end up making a move toward Sammie and so wanted to be prepared. It's what he used to do. After taking off the condom and throwing it away he rolls back out the air mattress and sleeps. He spends the next day at the desk, typing, drinking only coffee and eating nothing. From time to time his right eye twitches.

BLUSHING IN A PRACTICED WAY

A MAN WITH FURRY ARMS and a potbelly covered by an unwashed orange and blue Hawaiian-floral-print button-down and holding a digital high-definition video camera says, "What's your name, sweetheart?"

There is a batting of eyelids, playful hesitation and a sort of giggle. "Sunny."

"Sunny. Sunny what?"

"Sunny Patrick."

The man with the camera makes a sound like he's just tasted a fine wine. "Mmmm. Sunny Patrick. That's a beautiful name."

"Thank you," Sunny says, blushing in a practiced way.

"It's just as beautiful as you are, of course."

"Thank you," she says again, and the blush deepens so it looks almost real. But of course she is not shy. She has done this bit dozens of times before.

"But so what are you here for today, Sunny?"

"Why am I here?"

"Why are you here."

"I'm here to get fucked."

The man with the camera bumps the attached microphone against his temple and it makes an awkward thump. "You're here to get fucked."

"I'm here to get fucked."

"And where are you going to get fucked today, Sunny?"

"In my pussy."

"What about your ass? Are you going to let my friend here put his cock in your ass?"

Sunny seems to consider. "Hmmm. Maybe if he asks nicely."

The friend to whom the man with the camera referred steps forward so his well-defined tanned right deltoid is partly visible on the digital camera's little playback screen. The potbellied man pushes him back with a mumbled, "Not yet, man. Shit." And the friend steps back out of the frame, murmuring something in Spanish.

Sunny gives a laugh, improvising. "Your friend is an eager one, isn't he?" she says.

Brushing off this deviation from the script, the potbellied man says, "Well, I would be too if you were going to let me fuck you in the ass."

"Hey," Sunny says, "I said maybe. We'll have to wait and see."

And there they are, back on script because Sunny is a natural. "You're awesome, Sunny Patrick," the potbellied man says.

And Sunny says, "Thank you," blushing once more and smiling and blinking twice.

If you were to look up Sunny's profile on both the Internet Movie Database (IMDB) and the Adult Film Database (AFD), you would find her listed under the following alternative names: Millie Milton, Melanie Lin Milton, Sunny Johnson, Sunny Milton, Sunny Lin, Millie Lin, Melanie Lin Johnson, Millie Johnson, and the name which eventually became synonymous with her breasts and her stomach and her sometimes-shaved vagina and her dimpled smile, Sunny Patrick. Also, when looking at her profile (which she has nothing to do with and which is maintained by an independent, and large, group of adult film enthusiasts), you would find that she has starred in 347 documented adult film scenes, that she entered the business three years ago at age twenty (not completely accurate but close), that she has won more AVN awards than any other female performer, and that she is, at twenty-two years old, very popular. At one point just after entering the industry—and this is not listed on either of the two profiles—she even went by the name Mel, just Mel, as in one word like Stoya or Belladonna, but decided she just couldn't do the whole one-word-name thing because she wasn't unique enough, like she wasn't exotically mysterious enough to be a Stoya and she just wasn't dirty enough to be a Belladonna, and she didn't know what a Mel was supposed to be so she couldn't be that either, which is probably why the mononym isn't listed among her sobriquets, because she only used it in one scene and that scene was never released (thank god, because in that scene she had sex with a man in a bear costume).

The man with the furry arms and the potbelly shifts his weight. "How old are you, Sunny?"

"Twenty-two."

"Twenty-two. Wow. And how long have you been doing porn?"

She pauses to make a show of thinking about the answer

even though she knows it off the top of her pretty little head. "Like almost three years."

"So why did you start doing porn? Like what made you think, 'I want to get fucked on camera'?"

"I like sex," she says, and this is true. She does like sex, and she is not ashamed of this, but just because one likes sex it does not follow that one will then have sex on camera. Except for the genuinely asexual, everyone likes sex (and if they say they don't, they either haven't had it, in which case they should probably get on with changing that, or they're lying for some stupid, prudish reason), and yet very few people have actual, bona fide sex on film. So Sunny's answer isn't really an answer, is the point. She doesn't have an answer.

"Sunny," the man with the potbelly and the furry arms says, moving his head so he can scratch at this itch in a difficult spot on his neck with the stubble of his chin, "how much do you like sex?"

"So much."

This interview is not going to be edited, most likely. It probably will not be set to music, and neither will the actual scene itself. Sunny has always wanted to do one of those sorts of interviews, the profound ones that some starlets have the chance to do before like major features that have like five or six scenes of them fucking in increasingly intense and/or erotic and/or acrobatic ways, each scene on the feature's DVD or BluRay interpolated with retrospectives of the actress, sans make up, which makes her even more beautiful, the not having make up on, reflecting on what she learned about herself in either the upcoming scene or the scene that played previous, and it's always something deep. Sunny once saw a porn star, in one of these features, with a look of genuine honesty on her face, say, "There are some things I feel like I could never do, and anytime I trump one of those, I love it." And maybe this is why Sunny entered the industry, so she could trump the personal things she could never do—with that goal is how she's been living her life for a long time now, anyway.

"And what's your favorite thing about sex?"

A genuine pause, as in she doesn't know what to say. "Um . . ."

"I mean like what really gets you off?"

". . ." (A continuation of the "Um . . ." is what this is.)

"Sunny?"

She just throws out a word. "Blowjobs!"

The man with the potbelly/camera/Hawaiian shirt/furry arms laughs. "Haha. Blowjobs. A blowjob girl, eh?"

"I guess you could say I have an 'oral fixation'." It's a tired joke. She does not mimic quotation marks with her fingers when she says it.

"An 'oral fixation' eh? I like that. You're my kind of girl, Sunny."

Well.

Sunny Patrick is wearing the following for this shoot: Ruby-colored high-heeled shoes with mock-crystal-studded silver-painted buckles; black mid-thigh stockings made from fabric light enough that you can see her skin beneath them; two black garter straps with crystals and buckles that complement the ones on her high-heeled shoes; red silk panties, redder than the shoes, with lace around the leg-holes and the waistband; nothing covering her stomach, which is flat and tight, way flatter and tighter than when she started her career because now she's vegan and does yoga and never eats Honey Buns, never; a cut-off tight-fitting white t-shirt with the word FUN blazoned across it in a red that's redder than the shoes but not as red as the panties (the panties are actually closer to purple than red, on second description), and under the shirt she has no bra so the shape of her nipples are visibly poking from under the lower serifed parts of the F and the N; a black choker necklace with more fake crystals; bluish-silver eye shadow; blush; a black hair tie on which there are no crystals; black thick-framed nerdish glasses with no lenses.

Sunny smiles, impishly.

There is supposed to be a lot more to this pre-scene interview. The man in the floral-print shirt, the director, one of the industry's biggest behind-the-camera names, is supposed to ask her what her favorite thing about anal sex is. And she's supposed to reply that her favorite thing about anal sex is the tightness followed by the feeling of expansion. And then he's supposed to ask her how old she was the first time she had sex and she's supposed to say eighteen, which is true, and then he's supposed to ask her how old she was the first time she let a man put it up her butt, and she's supposed to regale the crowd with a story about how the first time she had anal sex was with, not a man, but a woman, a girlfriend out east who she met when she was eighteen, almost nineteen, and who had a certain fixation with other women's assholes and who tried for weeks to convince Sunny to let her, the girlfriend, put a strap-on into her behind, and Sunny was very uncomfortable with the idea and refused and refused and refused. But then, one day, Sunny read this article in Redbook that hinted, vaguely (because that's all magazines like Redbook ever do is hint), that anal sex would be The Thing to revitalize a dwindling relationship. And so Sunny to her girlfriend one night after a pasta dinner and over Moscato said that she'd been thinking about it and that, maybe, yes, she would be interested in trying anal sex if the girlfriend still wanted to, and of course the girlfriend was ecstatic and made a joke that to this day is still one of the funniest things Sunny has ever heard: "Well, first thing's first: you're going to need like a buttload of lube if you want to try anal." They broke up a few months later for reasons completely unrelated to sex, and since then Sunny has eschewed serious relationships because things are better that way. And after the anal sex story the director is supposed to ask Sunny which she likes better, women or men, and Sunny is supposed to say she likes them both equally, even though it's just as likely she doesn't like either of them at all anymore.

But instead of the anal sex story Sunny says, "So where'd your friend go?"

The friend has been standing there just outside the camera's frame the whole time. He steps back into the scene and Sunny reaches out and places the palm of her right hand on his crotch, which is covered by a pair of designer jeans. He has no shirt, all the better for Sunny to not have to take one off of him. "I think your friend likes me," Sunny says.

The director seems to realize maybe he has no control of the scene at this point, that the actors will do what the actors will do. This happens often, at least when the director is male; female directors, who are becoming far more common in porn these days, seem to be better at managing a scene's flow, but they also tend to have a stronger vision of how the scene should play— they are artists.

"I think I like your friend," Sunny says. And to the male talent: "What's your name?"

"Marco . . ." he breathes as she unbuttons the button on his jeans and pulls the jeans and his boxer briefs down all at once and lets his erection spring free.

"Hi, Marco," she says, engaged now. She actually didn't know his name. They've never worked together before. He's new to the business. His body is tan and sculpted. His erection is average for the business but larger than that of most men. She takes it in her mouth, or more accurately, it takes her mouth to it. The erection is in control now, but still so is she. Control is an illusion, always. The director steps back so his camera can capture all that goes on before it; he sniffles—this is why he's here.

Sunny Patrick fellates Marco for nearly five minutes in the most graphic ways she can without deepthroating him, which is a different kind of scene for which she would be paid extra money, except she wouldn't because she can't deepthroat, and she gave up on trying to learn, on trying to kill her natural gag reflex, a long time ago. She sucks his penis sloppily, messily. She could try to deepthroat him, she supposes, but it will only make her cry, and while she knows her fans would like to see that, she doesn't like the thought of her own tears.

Marco says, "Yes, baby," while she sucks him off. He puts his hands on the back of her head. He looks down and makes eye contact with her. He moves his hands to her cheeks while her mouth works and then slides them up and takes the glasses between both sets of thumbs and index fingers and pulls them from her face. He thrusts into her mouth and hits the back of her throat—an accident—and dark mascara starts to drip from her eyelashes. He grasps her shoulders and pushes her head away and then takes her left hand in his right and pulls her up to him, kisses her, his other hand on her back and they move like a dance. He steps out of the jeans and boxer briefs which have pooled around his ankles. That hand that's on her back slides up her shoulders and then up her neck and then to the back of her hair and he deepens the kiss. She wonders what that's like for him, kissing her, tasting himself. Is it weird? Does it make him uncomfortable? Is it for him the same saltiness that it is for her? She feels his fingers playing behind her head, tugging and fumbling and picking, until her hair falls free around her.

There is in the studio a couch, large and blue and fluffy and stained, and she lets Marco bring her onto it, his body supporting hers so she doesn't fall but floats onto the cushions. Besides the couch and Sunny and the male talent and the director with his camera, there is only a human-sized Luxo lamp and a white throw rug in this particular room of this L.A. loft. In the next room over a make-up artist waits in case there are reshoots. Another scene will be filmed here, with another starlet and another man, in two hours, and this evening, Sunny's heard, a friend of hers will be filming an all-girl threesome.

Sunny melts into the cushions as Marco kisses her neck and her collarbone. He lingers on the collarbone longer than most guys do, suggesting that maybe he's not in this for just the money and maybe he's not in this for just the sex—maybe he craves that contact, or the pleasing, or the skin. She sighs genuinely as he moves lower, still kissing her body but this time through the t-shirt, wetting it, using his teeth to move the fabric against her nipples, which, as far as sensations go, is one she can't imagine objecting to.

Things progress.

Little particles of saliva are on her body, in her mouth.

He proceeds to pull aside the silk and put his mouth on her there.

And lest things get too sensual, Sunny says, "That's it. That's it, eat my cunt."

See because now when she says that word the scene can go

back to being just about the sex for everyone in the room, for Sunny and Marco and the director. Because cunt is a purely sexual word, almost clinical in its offensiveness. It's the word she and her fellow starlets use to add an extra layer of puerile raunchiness to any scene, because it's puerile raunchiness that fans pay to see. Except that they don't exactly pay so much anymore, do they, Sunny thinks, what with the internet and the tube sites and all. She's heard legends of a time when a girl could get a contract and sign with one studio for her entire career and shoot once a month and have it made and never have to say words like cunt while filming, which isn't to say she has anything against the word. She has hatred for no word. There is no enmity between Sunny Patrick and language.

Marco's tongue has found her clitoris, thank God.

"I love the feeling of your tongue on my cunt."

Cunt is just a word. A motherfucking word. Words are motherfucking bullshit, is what they are, though.

There is no sensation.

The AVNs are next week. She's up for Best Group Scene and Best Boy/Girl Scene and Best Girl/Girl Scene. She's also nominated for Best Actress, which is an actual thing.

And penetration, finally.

During a shoot like this one, Sunny moves between emotions the same way her costar's dick moves in and out of her. It's this deep thing for one moment and then it's all so empty the next. And then deep again, full of meaning and things. And then empty once more. Over and over. Because it's like sometimes she finds herself standing outside herself, taking on the role of the camera or the viewer-at-home. And she enjoys it, just like the viewer enjoys it, but she also knows it's not real. Except it is real. It is!

She's back now, matching Marco's thrusting with her own. You'd never have known she was gone.

"Fuck me," she says. "Fucking fuck me!"

"You like that, baby? You like the way my big dick feels inside you?" He doesn't sound entirely sincere when he asks this question. He sounds tired. Or bored. Or hungry.

"I do," Sunny says, and she both does and doesn't. "I love it. Keep doing it just like that."

So they do the missionary thing for a few minutes before he pulls out and takes her panties off and with them the garter straps. She lets herself be flipped over, gives herself to the flipping, and the entry from behind. But she needs to move now, she feels; she can't just take but needs to participate. She gives a cue and he stops and she takes him back in her mouth for a moment and she pushes him onto the couch in a sitting position and puts the heels on the couch and lowers herself onto him from above.

"Oh, yeah," he says.

"Oh, yes!" she screams.

Little tiny spots of perspiration drip down her back. Little tiny drops of fluid down her thighs. He reaches around her and rips the shirt from the bottom, which is easy because it's already been cut off. FUN splits up the middle. F and part of a U. Part of a U and an N. Part of a U. Half of a U. Half of you.

And now, in her head, he's whispering in her ear, his breath warm on the nape of neck. "I hear it's your birthday today."

"It is," she breathes.

"I was thinking we could go get some dinner after this, like some Chinese or something. I mean I know it's early but you probably have a party later or something and I figured maybe we could go out before, just the two of us—"

"I don't have any parties, actually."

"What? Beautiful little girl like you and nobody's throwing you a birthday party."

"I don't have anyone to throw me a party though, so."

"Oh, but that can't be true, can it?"

"I'm afraid it is. It's so true."

"Nah. Nah, I don't believe it. You're going to get home tonight—after I take you out for dinner, of course—and there's going to be a great big party waiting for you. A great big party."

"Maybe. Maybe you're right."

"But first, dinner."

"I'm not really a fan of Chinese food, though."

"We'll go wherever you want, baby."

"There's this Indian place that just opened on South La Brea that's been getting stellar reviews. I haven't had a chance to try it out yet, but—"

"Then that's where we'll go, baby. Whatever you want."

"And then a party?"

"And then a party."

"I haven't celebrated a birthday in years. At least not with like a party or anything . . ."

This conversation is her fantasy.

They are fucking.

The rest of the scene goes like this: Marco puts his hands around her waist and picks her up so she slides off his penis with a squelching sound. He lowers her to the ground and pushes down on her shoulders to make her do the oral thing again, which she does for forty-five seconds, messily, while he moans and grunts like a boorish creature. Then he grabs her arms and guides her to her feet and turns her around toward the couch and pushes her onto her knees and forearms on the couch like she was earlier in the scene. There are things on this couch, buried deep within the fabric. He makes like he's going to enter her from behind again and she's prepared to take it, but his penis finds a different orifice from the one it's been in for the last twenty minutes. Entry is not as difficult as it looks. She fakes discomfort and then pleasure. For the next five minutes they do it just like that, no change or variation from where they are, no more mixing it up or changing positions or "getting creative" or "putting on a show". Just thrusting. He thrusts forward; she meets with a thrust back. The air grows humid with the blatant physicality and her hair frizzes out, little strands of it sticking to her shoulders. Both she and he are vocal, but the things they say are meaningless and vague in their vulgarity. "Fuck my ass." "Your ass is so tight on my cock." "Pound my asshole." "You look so beautiful getting fucked from behind like this." And then, as the director steps in closer, the male talent grunts and Sunny is no longer full and her behind and lower back are wet with strands and particles. She stays like that, on her knees and elbows, for a full minute, knowing the director will be behind her, bringing his camera in as close as he can for a clear shot of the aftermath. Her heart rate is elevated. Her cardiovascular response is higher than normal, from the fucking. She breathes slowly.

"And cut."

She stands from the couch, naked.

"Great job today, Sunny," the director says, smiling at her. He leans over and kisses her on the cheek. His breath is bad. Just bad.

"Thanks, Hank." Sunny looks around. Only she and the director are in the room. "Where's—what's his name?—Marco?"

"I think he went to get a bagel."

"Ah." On porn sets there are always (not always, but it's been true of every set Sunny has been on, because she's been lucky) these tables, either in the room in which the shooting is happening or in a nearby room, on which there are things like donuts and bagels and muffins and sometimes even a couple of pieces of fruit like apples or bananas. Sex makes you hungry, and sex scenes—that is, the shooting of—are even worse, usually.

"No but seriously great job today," the director says again. "I mean really beautiful. Like you were born for this business."

Because the reality is that porn scenes tend to take a lot longer to film than the finished product lets on. There's a lot of starting and stopping, cutting and bellowing of instructions ("Turn the girl around!" "Put your leg up over his shoulder." "No no no! We can't see the penetration."), sitting mid-coitus, dick still inside you, while lighting is adjusted or cheap makeup is reapplied by technicians/stylists who've seen their share of naked bodies. But today, none of that. The director with the hairy arms considers himself rather avant-garde, filming scenes in natural lighting, by hand, and in one continuous take, which is something typically done only in POV porn, POV meaning "point-of-view" and referring in the case of pornography specifically to the first person, meaning that third-person, i.e. traditional, porn, while still filmed from a point-of-view, is not POV. A quasi-misnomer, the whole thing, when you stop to think about it, which, stopping to think, kind of kills the mood.

Sunny does not search for the snack table.

After making quick use of the on-set shower she's driving down Figueroa Street in her white Audi A5 Sportback, something playing on the satellite radio, something she doesn't recognize but that was almost certainly published by Def Jam Records. The light of the radio's faceplate glows blue, but she doesn't bother reading it. The light of the shifter knob glows blue. The light of the California sun shines through the tinted windshield and hits her face, blue. She learned to drive nine months ago, taught herself, paid $800 dollars for a piece-of-crap Saturn from a fellow starlet's coke dealer and used it to learn to drive stick, blew the transmission and left the thing by the side of road for someone else to deal with. When she showed up at the DMV to take her driving test they told her the test car was an automatic, which she'd never practiced on, and the presence of only two pedals instead of three threw her and she hit a lamp post in the DMV's parking lot moving from park into reverse, test failed. And so then she had the coked-up starlet teach her. When Sunny finally passed the test she bought the Audi; the payments are high but she can afford them. She pulls into the parking lot of an ethnic grocery. She buys a bottle of water and a large bag of kale chips. The kale chips lie unopened on the black leather passenger seat, but the water she downs in gulps as she turns onto Sunset Boulevard. The water bottle is blue, making it appear as if the water inside, too, is blue.

Alone Sunny arrives at the downtown apartment building, kale chips in the crook of her right arm, hugging the giant plastic bag like a child's stuffed toy, like a mother's stuffed child. In her left hand her house keys and a white minaudière she bought in Paris. She's been to Paris. Up a narrow flight of stairs, four stories she walks, the stairwell twisting tightly and her footsteps—she's wearing flats now, very flat flats, having removed the red heels nearly the moment the day's shooting was over—echoing against the cold walls and the dirty double-paned windows. The elevator, one of those rickety deals with an accordion-like gate instead of a proper set of doors, hasn't worked in months.

Here. Her apartment's facade, wooden and painted white,

the paint peeling a little more with each passing day, revealing another layer of paint underneath, an older layer, older probably than she is, brown, brown paint on an already-wooden door, the door just outside the stairwell like it always is. Today there are several boxes with the words AMAZON PRIME emblazoned across their sides along with the curved arrow that makes your insides tingle when you see it, except it doesn't really do that for Sunny anymore, make her insides tingle. There's this thing a lot of porn stars do where they set up an Amazon account and start adding items to their personal wish list, and then they share that wish list with their fans through various means: their website, social media. Some even put the link to the wish list in their bio, like right there at the end, with the words "My Wish List" and a colon before it. A couple don't even say "My Wish List"; they say "BUY ME STUFF!!!". And some porn stars, well they forgo the bio altogether, so if you click on the profile part of their social media account there's just the link sitting there under the picture all by itself. One starlet even has the link printed on a banner hanging above her booth at expos and award shows. A certain male star mentions his wish list's link, including all the individual letters and numbers after the forward slash, at the end of interviews; the wish lists of male talent aren't nearly as popular as those of their female counterparts, you see. So Sunny finally set up a wish list too, maybe six months ago, and she shared it just once, and not in her bio but in an individual post, a post she's since deleted. Yet still she receives packages every now and again from her fans. It's a good thing, her agent says, to have a wish list—it lets her fans express their gratitude for the work she does, for making them come. And of course the point is Sunny still has the wish list even though she doesn't much like receiving things from it anymore, and she keeps adding items to it for some reason, things she doesn't want. Today there are more packages than normal. She unlocks the door and kicks the boxes inside.

Sunny has a cat. An orange tabby with mangy fur that she found wandering anorexically around the dumpsters in the back ally when she first moved into this downtown apartment and named Evangeline. Evangeline is a boy, as it turned out, and when the veterinarian told her this Sunny laughed because somehow this made the name even more appropriate. She calls the cat Evan now though, because she's not cruel. Evan mews when Sunny walks in, licks at the toe of her left shoe and then jumps on top of the largest of the Amazon boxes before jumping back off and wandering into the kitchen where Sunny knows, if she follows, she'll find an empty food dish and maybe an empty water dish on the floor. Mew.

"Hold your horses, cat," she says. Sometimes she calls the cat just "cat" instead of Evan because it's easier, rolls off the tongue better. Through her mind flashes an image of a cat holding a horse; first the cat, not Evan but an ugly, naked Siamese thing, is holding the horse, a stallion, high over its head like an Olympic lifter—then it has it in a viselike grip, tiny little cat paws around the steed's massive throat. Mew.

Evan doesn't ever meow; he mews.

"I'm coming. I'm coming." She says it one more time as she kicks her flats off and bends down to stack the boxes neatly. "I'm coming."

In the kitchen Evan is sitting next to his dish, waiting. The kitchen is clean, always clean, its counters bare except for a juicer and a large bowl of fruit and a professional-level blender, because while she has lots of other kitchen supplies—a hand-mixer and three baking sheets and two pizza pans and four pots that you might boil water in and one pot that you might make a stew in and a large frying pan and a small frying pan and a medium-sized frying pan and skillet and another large frying pan with the teflon coming off and a muffin pan and a toaster and—she never uses them, like ever. There's also an old-style kettle, the kind with the handle and the spout that whistles and with a burnt bottom, but it's on the stove, not the counter. Evan mews again as Sunny takes a can of cat food from the cupboard and peels back the top of the can and lets the contents fall clumped into the dish, but it's a grateful mew, no longer a hungry one. Evan eats. Sunny watches. "You know, cat," she says, "I like this. We've got a good thing going here, you and I, I think." Evan just keeps eating.

Sunny puts water in the kettle and places it back on one of the burners of the electric stove, turns the burner on. She grabs the bag of kale chips, which she'd brought with her into the kitchen, and pulls them open with that thunderous *POP!* bags of chips make when you open them. She walks back into the living room and sits on the couch with the kale chips, munching away.

From the minaudière she produces her phone. It's time for what her agent calls "brand engagement"—she's pretty sure he's got the meaning of the term backwards. "Jerry," she's told him, "brand engagement is when the customer, or in this case the fan, interacts with the brand, the celebrity, not the other way around."

"Sunny Sunny Sunny." He always repeats the names of his girls like that: three times, like he's talking to a child. One might think from this single snippet of information (coupled with the fact that he manages porn stars) that Sunny's agent is a condescending man, or maybe patronizing, or maybe even just plain creepy. But he's not; he's one of the nicest men in the industry, his goal to make sure his girls make the most money they can, get the best gigs they can. "That's what this is. They're messaging you, engaging with you."

"Right but so then me messaging them back is the opposite side of the coin. It's not brand engagement but . . . I don't know. Fan engagement, I guess, as me engaging with the fans."

"Okay, fine—fan engagement."

"Yeah but the point is I don't like it, not really. So how about we just let them engage without me."

But of course when she has these little arguments with Jerry she's not serious, not really. She knows so-called engagement is what separates the starlets from the stars. The arguments always end with Jerry kissing her on top of her head and her smiling because, against all odds, Jerry has this way of making his girls blush.

She has the phone awake: there are no missed calls, no texts (she's received only two texts today, both from Jerry: the first wishing her a happy birthday and the second confirming the afternoon's shoot, which he really hadn't wanted to book her for, what with it being her birthday, and told her she didn't have to take it, but she said it was fine), no voicemails. But when she opens Twitter:

@SUNNYPATRICK_90 HAPPY BIRTHDAY!!!

@sunnypatrick_90 I hope you have lots of amazing birthday sex.

@Sunnypatrick_90 Fuck yeah how old are you?

The cutest pr0nstar in theworld @sunnyPatrick_90's birthday is today wish her a happybirthday even if you don't like pr0n

@bigJ178 @SunnyPatrick_90 I don't watch porn, but happy birthday!

@SunnyPatrick_90 will you fuck me for your birthday present?

@SunnyPatrick_90 those pancakes look amazing!! Happy birthday!!

@SunnyPatrick_90 Whoot!

@SunnyPatrick_90 Congratulations!

@SunnyPatrick_90 recipe?

There are hundreds of these types of replies streaming through her feed. She has 279.8K followers according to the counter on her profile, which once the number gets so high just estimates. And this morning she went to this vegan place near her apartment and ordered a stack of vegan pancakes and a large bowl of fruit just so she could take a picture of them and share the picture with the caption "Vegan Birthday Pancakes!" for reasons of brand engagement. She ate only the fruit.

There are other messages to her in her feed, too, the kind she usually gets from fans, having nothing to do with her birthday:

@SunnyPatrick_90 ur so hot

@SunnyPatrick_90 I want to get into porn what do I do message me

@sunnypatrick_90 When are you going to do a scene with Jenna Haze?!?!?!?

What I wouldn't give to see @sunnyPatrick_90 put a double-sided dildo in both holes

@jeremykingwhat @sunnyPatrick_90 come on dude! Not cool. Have respect man.

@SunnyPatrick_90 I just want you to know I think you're really beautiful.

@Sunnypatrick_90 Grate scene in #TinyBabysitters17

@SunnyPatrick_90 I would so use your shit as my toothpaste if you'd let me.

That last one is from a female fan, by the looks of it, someone with the handle @SarahTheGreat54, whose profile photo is of a pretty blonde in her mid-to-late or early twenties with too much black eye shadow and glitter on her cheeks. The weirdest messages tend to come from women, and women tend to make the worst (best?) stalkers. It's like female fans can't separate the reality of celebrity from the fantasy of pornography. Like they get so attached, emotionally, for some reason. As Sunny looks at @SarahTheGreat54's profile photo she wonders whether she was ever like her as a teenager; but she wasn't, of course, not at all, even though she discovered porn around that same age, and even now she thinks she was probably missing out. Not on sending weird messages, but on being a girl and getting emotional and excited by things that young girls get excited by. She's deluding herself right now, though, a little, feeling sorry for herself—because she *was* like that, albeit briefly, and now she has forgotten.

She replies to several of the tweets, but not to @SarahTheGreat54's. Mostly thank-you's for the birthday wishes. She tells the follower who asked about Jenna Haze that Haze retired from performing a couple years ago, but Sunny would love to star in one of the films she directs. She's replying to one with a link to her website and an emoji of a winking yellow face when the apartment starts to rumble like a train is passing underneath the building, which is funny, like haha funny, to Sunny, because her very first apartment, in New York, did have a train running underneath it, every twenty-six minutes. She can hear plates and mugs clank together in the kitchen's cupboards. Evan slinks out of the kitchen cautiously, rubbing his back against the wall as he glances around the living room with a look like what the hell is going on.

Sunny pats the space next to her on the couch. "Come on," she says to the cat. "It's okay. It's just one of those quakes again. It'll be over soon."

The tabby mews and jumps onto the couch. He pushes his head against her hand and licks kale-chip residue from her fingertips and purrs as she scratches the spot behind his ear.

Sunny closes her phone's Twitter application and taps her thumb against the email icon. Her laptop is on the coffee table—the coffee table is red, a similar red to the high-heeled shoes she was wearing earlier today, and has a pullout drawer and a shelf close to the floor between its four legs and is called, according to the signage above the display at the IKEA at which she bought it, a LIATORP; she almost purchased instead this round glass one called a STRIND that she really liked because instead of legs it had three wheels—and while processing email is more comfortable on her laptop, she doesn't want to by shifting her posture to reach for it disturb Evan, who has settled into the crook between her left leg's firm thigh and its softer, fleshier calf.

The rumbling stops slowly, dying over a period of several seconds.

There are ten emails in her inbox and who knows how many more in her spam folder. Sometimes, when she's very bored, when she's run out of tweets to scroll through and her inbox is empty, she checks the emails in the spam folder, one by one.

The third rule of being a porn star—the first is smile even if it hurts and the second no one speaks out loud—is never give out your personal email address, because if you do give out your personal email address, with dick-pics your inbox will be flooded forever and a day. There are girls who have broken this rule and who therefore, to escape the never-ending volley of genital snapshots, have had to procure new personal email addresses, but then because they had new email addresses they had to change that piece of information on all their online accounts, and in the contact lists of all their friends, and on the subscription details of anything and everything they'd ever subscribed to and wanted to keep receiving, and etc., and so basically the wholes of their digital lives were thrown just completely out of whack. Sunny has never, then, given out her personal email address in any way that a fan might find it. And still in her inbox today are two dick-pics and one photograph of a what-looks-like-it-might-be-genital-warts-ridden thickly bushed vagina. She deletes these emails straight away.

The other emails are nothing special: a newsletter from the company from which Sunny buys her makeup, an email from Jerry about a lesbian three-way scene with two of her favorite colleagues he just booked her for at the end of the week; two notifications from Twitter that have somehow found their way to her even though she has email notifications turned off; a reminder to attendees of the upcoming AVN awards; a reminder to presenters of the upcoming AVN awards; a reminder to nominees of the upcoming AVN awards. Each of these she archives. This is her life, filed away promptly but not deleted in the event of a need for future reference.

Simultaneously the kettle in the kitchen begins to whistle a high-pitched squeal and the earth beneath the apartment starts to rumble again. These little quakes are happening more and more these days, it seems: they're usually spaced weeks apart at least, although two in quick succession is not unheard of. "Up up," Sunny says, pushing the tabby's behind and moving to attend to the boiling water.

When she returns to the living room, steaming mug of herbal tea in hand, she sees Evan pawing the packages she kicked in earlier. She sighs. She has to open the packages sometime, so it might as well be now. She retrieves a knife and sits on the floor Japanese-style, heels under glutes, and opens first the box at which the cat was pawing, inside which is a cage-like metal ball filled with this very expensive catnip—sometimes she puts on the wish list items for Evan, items like this one. She dangles the ball in front of him, teasing him gently, before letting the ball fall between his paws, his eyes wide and his teeth bared with an unbridled excitement Sunny herself envies. Inside the ball is a little bell and it jingles as Evan bats the thing across the floor. Sunny allows herself a small smile, a pulling upward of the corners of the lips. Inside the other boxes: a set of marble bookends in the shape of bookshelves themselves, sort of meta-bookends; a red desk lamp that she doesn't know where she'll put because she doesn't have a desk; a leather-bound scrapbook; a beach bag with a matching beach towel and inflatable beach ball; self-tanning lotion. All these things she put on the wish list herself, but she doesn't remember doing so with any of them. And then . . .

There's one more box, but it's not from Amazon. She didn't notice it before because it's the same caramel brown as the Amazon boxes, but it doesn't have the logo. It's medium-sized and heavy and taped to the bottom is an indigo envelope with her name in scratchy handwriting. She removes the envelope, opens it, unfolds the note inside, which is written on plain white paper in the same scratchy handwriting as her name:

Sunny,

I hope this gift is okay. I remembered reading an interview with you in Playboy or Penthouse or on some blog or something where you said you always wanted to spend some time with this but never got around to it. And, well, I know you're busy, but maybe you'll find the time. It's one of my favorites.

Happy birthday,

A.

Inside the box, vacuum-sealed in cellophane, are seven large gilded leather books, the top one of which says: *In Search of Lost Time*, Volume 1, by Marcel Proust. The other six books are, of course, volumes two through seven.

Sunny laughs. She did say she wanted to read this—she said it forever ago in a profile in . . . hell, she can't even remember what publication the profile was in, but it was around the time she was nominated for her first AVN Award (Best New Starlet). That was back when she was still reading books. Well, she still reads them now, but she doesn't have the time to do so voraciously like she once might have—a thick biography of Hillary Clinton has been on her nightstand for . . .

Gingerly she takes the knife and slides it along the cellophane, careful to not cut the pages or the cover. She opens to the first page of volume one and reads the words:

"For a long time I used to go to bed early . . ."

She stops reading, closes her eyes and then opens them again. The catnip ball's bell jingles and rings behind her. On the floor, the note, turned over, and she notices additional writing on its back side:

PS: Like I said, I know you're busy, especially since it's your birthday, assuming this package and note arrived to you on your birthday, which I tried to time it so it would, but you never know with international shipping and everything. Anyway, I'll be online today, if you're around, which you probably aren't, I realize.

Well then, the question is: Is she around? Her birthday plans were to go to the Indian place she usually goes to, not the new one on South La Brea but this smaller one, the Bombay Star, just down the street, so close she can walk. The jasmine rice is fantastic and there's this waitress there named Akela who Sunny likes to see. She's cute in the way a quiet, curious puppy is cute, with small hips and smaller breasts and a soft dark belly with a ring in the belly button. Cheeks that don't move when she smiles, so her lips pucker timidly. Maybe nineteen. Eyes big and brown and looking always surprised. Sometimes when Sunny goes to dinner at the Bombay Star she times it just right so that she's finishing her meal as Akela's shift is ending and she and Akela walk back to Sunny's apartment together, arm in arm without speaking, and make love with few words and sleep until the late morning.

But the man who sent her the complete seven-volume set of Proust's *In Search of Lost Time*? She knows him by only a screen name and the initial A. She was doing a live cam show one day (live cam shows, if you do them right and at the right time and are sure to notify your followers of it on social media a couple times the day before the show, are one of the biggest money-makers for popular porn stars, and the beauty of them is they can be performed right from your own bedroom) when something one of the viewers (who you can't see when you're doing a live cam show; they only can see you) said jumped out at her. He said, in the little text box by the streaming window on the computer screen, *My wife died today, from cancer, and you're beautiful*. And there was something in those words that she couldn't let go of, something desperate and quiet and sorrowful, and yes, it was possible he was lying—men say stuff like that to women all the time—but if he wasn't, there was something powerful there, that Sunny with her body and the pithy little things she said into the webcam brought some modicum of comfort to this man, that he was watching her for reasons. She didn't think he was lying, so she did something she'd never done for anyone else before or since: she sent him an invitation to a private show, and she performed for him, and then after she was done and she'd brought herself to climax (for real) they talked, he typing into the chat box by the streaming window, and she speaking into the webcam. They've spoken like that at least a dozen times since then; sometimes she performs for him and then they talk, but more often than not they do just the talking part. One day, when she was feeling oddly sentimental, she sent him a signed picture as a gift, to a P.O. Box in Geneva, Switzerland, the only address he would give; the return address on the envelope, she realizes now, is how he knew where to send the books. From the talks they've had she knows that he's older than she is (way older, he says jokingly, but she thinks it's probably true and doesn't mind), that he loves animals but doesn't care for pets, that he's a fan of Hitchcock films and novels by Tolstoy and Stephen King, and lots of other little things.

Making a decision, Sunny grabs and devours a handful of kale chips from the bag and rises from her knees and, mug balanced precariously in one hand, snatches her laptop from the table and then goes into her bedroom, shutting the door so Evan won't come in, although she doubts that right now he would anyway. Jingle jingle.

She sets the laptop on the vanity so it faces her bed. She logs into the cam site with her merchant account name and password. There is in her password—a string of random letters, some capitalized, and numbers and an exclamation point—no sentimental value. She starts a private show and invites A. via his username. She takes off her shirt and replaces it with a lacy purple camisole, and she sits on the bed and waits. If he's watching for her, he'll see the invitation and log on. Above her laptop's screen, next to the camera's lens, a green light glowing. The chatbox cursor blinking. Sunny visible in the video feed, her body shifting from side to side. The late afternoon L.A. sun breaking through her window. Around her body a sort of dusty halo. Her bed's comforter pink and fluffy. Her pillows pinker and fluffier and visible in the frame behind her against the mahogany headboard. Beneath the streaming window on the computer's screen a red dot and a thing that says LIVE SHOW. Her ass's jeaned cheeks sliding on the bedspread as she redistributes her weight. First her left one and then her right. A clearing of her throat. The cursor in the text box blinking, blinking, blinking. "Hello? A.? You there?" Like maybe he logged in and the notification didn't pop up and he forgot to type hi. Blinking cursor. LIVE SHOW. *For a long time I used to go to bed early.* Jingle, jingle, faintly.

There is an eleven hour time difference between Los Angeles, California, U.S.A, and Geneva, Switzerland. In Geneva, wherever A. is, Sunny's birthday is long over.

She stands and kills the feed and removes the camisole and puts her shirt back on, no bra. If Sunny hurries, she'll get to the Bombay Star in time for half-off appetizers, and if she's lucky, Akela will be serving tonight.

A VERY BRIEF HISTORY

THE WORD "CUNT" IS FASCINATING from a linguistic standpoint because it, unlike any other word in the English language, refers to the entirety of the female genitalia. Vagina refers to only the reproductive canal. Vulva refers to the outer area of the genitalia —the labia majora, the mons pubis, the labia minora, the clitoris, the bulb of vestibule, the vulval vestibule, the greater and lesser vestibular glands, even the opening of the vagina, but not the vaginal canal itself. Pussy is slang for either the vulva or the vagina, interchangeably, but is never used to refer to both at the same time. Cunt is everything.

Cunt, or some phonically similar variation thereof, exists in several major languages and cultures. Even people without the benefit of synesthesia can taste these words. And yet nobody has been able to definitively determine their etymologies.

WAVES

IT'S NOT THAT THE WORLD is ending or anything like that, although certain members of the religious right would have you think it is; it's just that weird things are happening, anomalous things, and one anomalous thing that happened, or rather didn't happen, sometime in the last few years, is Eugene Apollos' wife did not die. You see, she was supposed to die. There was no expectation that she would not die. None.

It started when she developed a mild cough, just a tickle in her chest, really, that made her throat catch sometimes when she inhaled, like there was dust or something deep inside. She didn't complain about it at first—said nothing to Gene or to her best friend, Marie Bellchamp, who she played dominos with on Tuesday nights. The cough lasted a few weeks—allergies, she assumed, which made sense because the weather in Manchester, where they were living that spring, in one of Gene's childhood homes that had remained with the family, was particularly audacious, the pollen count high and irritating and the air humid.

"Are you okay, dear?" Apollos remembers asking one day after she repeatedly cleared her throat and rubbed at her chest through the course of a late-afternoon lunch with friends. It was the first time he noticed anything was wrong, but she'd been experiencing the irritation for about a month at that point, he learned later.

"I'm fine," she replied. "I've just got this tickle."

"In your throat?" Dr. Ralph Bellchamp, Marie's husband, said.

"Yes. Well, no. Well, it's more in my upper chest, but it's just a mild irritation."

Everyone nodded. Marie asked the server to please bring Gwen a warm ginger tea with lemon. In retrospect, it should have occurred to all of them that day that people do not get mild tickles in their chests.

So then the cough got worse, to the point where Gwen was hacking and hemming throughout the day: in the supermarket, at charity events, at the movies.

They were sitting one morning at breakfast, Apollos drinking a cup of strong black coffee and reading a recently published paper about quantum dental theory (Surely not a real thing!, he'd thought when he saw the paper's title) by this Berkely scientist with whom he had a friendly professional rivalry, while Gwen scrambled eggs with chives and crème fraîche and a little bit of feta cheese, when suddenly Gwen started coughing, really coughing, a strong, deep cough like she'd swallowed a large gulp of saltwater the wrong way. "Gwen, honey?" Gene said, standing from the table. She doubled over, hand clutched to her chest, words coming out of her mouth that Apollos couldn't understand. Frantically he searched the cupboard for a glass, forgetting where they were in that way people always forget where things are when they need them most. He found a mason jar, filled it with water and handed it to her, but she only hacked deeper, into the jar, the water blending with something redish-green and viscous.

"A sarcoma in the bronchial tube, I'm afraid," a doctor told them hours later, after Gwen had been given an inhaler of salbutamol and her breathing had stabilized and a nurse had taken a series of x-rays.

"A what?" Gwen asked. Her eyes were still red and puffy and watery from the stress of all the coughing.

"Lung . . . lung cancer," Apollos said, his voice catching.

The doctor looked down. He knew who Eugene Apollos was, and while he knew he wasn't a medical doctor, he knew he was talking to someone who understood the terms. "Yes, well, yes. I'm afraid that's correct."

Gwen said nothing.

"And but you're sure?" Apollos said. He wasn't usually one to question a fellow scientist, but.

"I would," the doctor said, "like to do of course a biopsy, because I mean maybe it's not malignant, but as you can see in the x-ray"—he pointed to the big white spot on the films—"it is there, and it's blocking the airway significantly, and . . ."

Gwen looked at the doctor. "And?"

"And they already have the fluid that you coughed up," Apollos said, almost angrily. He wrapped an arm around his wife. "And there's no way that fluid is a good thing."

The doctor just nodded, a singular movement of his stubbled, dimpled jaw.

Further tests were done. Tissue samples were taken. Hopes were gotten up.

While they had discovered the tumor rather late ("And no,

it's not your fault," the doctor assured Gwen when it was apparent by the guilt in her eyes that she felt she should have done something about the cough sooner. "This thing was growing months and months ago—it's just that it didn't reach the bronchial tubes until recently—so by the time you began experiencing symptoms it was already far along."), and while the biopsy showed that it was aggressive, it had spread only minimally into the surrounding tissue, which meant there was a strong chance they could bombard the thing with radiation, shrinking it, and then go in surgically and take out what was left.

Apollos' heart skipped a beat at the mention of the word radiation. He was familiar with the stuff. Cancer was the devil that had taken his own mother's life (a lorry had taken his father's), and in her final days she had been a shell of the woman who had raised him, a shadow of the youthful, jubilant former nun whose zest for life had grown immeasurably since she'd left the church and married his father. He didn't want to see the same decline happen to his wife, and he certainly didn't want to see it happen and then also watch her die like his mother had. But this was a purely emotional reaction, he was aware, because while, yes, he'd seen radiation strip his mother of her soul (figuratively —Eugene Apollos does not believe in souls), he also worked with radiation on a regular basis, some of it the exact same kind they would be using to treat his wife: since university he'd been charging particles and throwing ions at various matter to see what the reaction might be; even now he and a group of colleagues were in the early stages of designing and gathering funding for a project that, using some of this very radiation, could change the way people understood the nature of the universe. And also methods had changed since his mother's time, he knew; treatment was more targeted, more direct, able more easily to avoid the good tissue and kill only the bad. And besides, this doctor was a scientist, and as a fellow scientist Apollos knew he had to trust the judgment of the man; and Gwen knew this as well, that her husband's respect for a doctor's words had to be her respect too, so when Apollos wrapped his arms around her and told her this was all great news and she was going to be just fine, she nodded and smiled and didn't cry and looked very brave. "And if it doesn't work," the doctor said, making a note on a piece of paper affixed to a clipboard, "we'll move on to chemo."

And at first it did work, the radiation. Kind of. The tumor didn't shrink and the coughing didn't stop, but for months things stayed the same. The tumor didn't grow and the doctor said that was encouraging and made him hopeful and that they needed only to up the dosage, and so, with Gwen and Gene's glum approval, for they were not as hopeful as the doctor, the doctor twice weekly directed concentrated bursts of high-energy particles at his wife's chest, the rest of her shielded with awkward lead-lined pads and aprons, in the hopes of ionizing and killing and ultimately destroying the malignant growth in her lungs. But the tumor, as if it had been sitting patiently during the first phase of radiation treatment, mocking the weak attacks against it, suddenly pushed back. For every action there is a reaction, and sometimes this action is equal to the action to which it is reacting, and sometimes it is stronger. The tumor grew, rallied its cancerous troops and instructed them to procreate, and millions of virulent cells became millions more, and Gwen's coughs grew worse and there were mornings when she would hold her chest and struggle to breathe while Gene retrieved from her purse the inhaler, and sometimes in the evening before bed she would hack up little bits of flesh and red and green. So then, chemo. But that didn't work either, not at all; it only took Gwen's hair and color and vitality, her zest and bounce and zing, and in the evenings when he wasn't at a conference or at the lab or at a university or business pitching to those who might invest their funds into this big project ("You mustn't stop working for me, Gene. I won't have it."), they cuddled together on his family home's living room's camelback sofa and she drank tea with milk and honey and he drank a hot toddy and they watched an old movie or a new one that was generating Oscar buzz until she fell asleep in his arms and he put around her the knitted blanket that used to be his mother's and then he went upstairs to his office and caught up on research and journals. It all exhausted him, the watching her be exhausted, the watching her go away, until he began to take solace in the fact that soon it would all be over, that she would be gone, but the solace wasn't for his wife's sake, wasn't because he knew her pain would end, her suffering would end; it was instead, perversely, for him. It began to comfort him to know that soon he would be without her, that he could start things over—never forgetting what came before, of course, never forgetting—that he could focus fully and devote everything inside of him to his important work, that he could be alone.

But then she did not die.

The remission was sudden and quick and unexplainable. "I want to do another scan," the doctor said, "another biopsy of the tissue, because well, and I don't mean to be negative or anything, but this doesn't happen, not like this. So what I'm saying is let's don't get our hopes up until we've had a few weeks to see what happens. We'll pause the chemotherapy for now, for one week, but then we'll do another biopsy. So in fact let's schedule the biopsy now, for next Thursday—does next Thursday work for you?—and well then we'll see." But on Thursday there was nothing left to biopsy but healthy respiratory tissue, and since then Gwen coughed only once, because she swallowed a sip of water and it went down the wrong pipe in the way it happens sometimes.

HAPPY ANNIVERSARY

THE 30-SOMETHING WOMAN WAS sitting in her bed, her back arched just a bit and her knees pulled in to her chest, at four-thirty in the afternoon on a Friday, two days after her anniversary, with a scowl on her face and fake sort of tears dripping convincingly from her eyes and down her cheeks and onto the comforter. She'd pulled the comforter up over her legs and to her chin just under the maleficent scowl. Her husband sat on the bed also, but he sat not up against the headboard and at an angle like the woman, but on the edge, precariously, a good yard from the woman's sockless feet.

The woman had only a few weeks ago undergone a major medical procedure. She'd had installed via an incision in her back this pacemaker-like device that helped control bowel movements, and the whole thing was considered something of an experimental procedure by the medical community, but the procedure had been performed 203 times, so the woman took her doctor's word for it that it was safe, and since the woman had suffered from bowel incontinence for something like her entire adult life, and since the idea of changing her diet, which her doctor and nutritionist had both suggested multiple, like, dozens, of times, didn't appeal to her in the slightest, she took her doctor's word for it that the procedure was safe and would help cure her of her compulsive need to run to the bathroom what seemed like all day every day; so far, it had worked too—she was, if anything, constipated now. Because he had to drive his wife to the hospital in Cleveland—a good two-and-a-half-hours' drive—the husband had taken his last vacation day, the woman and the husband hadn't been able to spend any real amount of time together on their anniversary, and so they'd planned on catching up on things, rectifying the situation, tonight.

The problem though was that for the last six months the husband's mother's health had been declining at a rapid pace. She'd been in and out of for months now an expensive nursing home where she engaged in physical rehabilitation exercises that consisted mostly just of swinging her legs back and forth in pendular arches one at a time to limber up the muscles and the hip joint; she'd been to the hospital several times, each time complaining of a phantom pain and insisting her offspring call her an ambulance only to be told after an overnight stay that there were no new, immediate problems and that she would be better off at home; she'd been losing a good deal of cognitive function also, her memory diminishing such that many conversations with her regressed into repetitive loops about the same banal topics, topics like Tiger Woods, old family spicy meatball recipes, the need for immigration reform because in my day a Mexican woman would never marry a gay white man and we didn't even have gay white men or blacks in my day, and

Tiger Woods. Feeling responsible for the care of their ailing and long-widowed mother, the woman and the husband and husband's sister and his other sister and that sister's husband had agreed to divide amongst themselves and their households said care, and so, for the last six months, every Friday evening and all day Saturday and most of Sunday, the husband's mother had come to stay with the woman and the husband, sleeping in an empty guest bedroom just feet from the woman and the husband's own.

What had happened today, two days after the husband and the woman's anniversary, the day they intended to celebrate the anniversary, was that the husband's sister, who had agreed last week to look after the husband's mother one extra night tonight, had called the woman the day before just to chit chat. The woman had casually mentioned that husband's sister should not forget that "our anniversary is tomorrow, and so you've got your mother one extra night, right? That's still okay with you?"

"Oh, yes, of course, right. We'll see what happens," the sister had said.

And well come on! What the hell did that mean? We'll see what happens.

The woman told her husband what the sister had said and demanded that he call his sister for some clarification, make sure she understood that she was watching the mother for one extra night so they could go out to dinner for their anniversary. So then the husband had called the sister, the day before, after he got home from work, but the sister hadn't picked up the phone.

"You should have left a message yesterday," the woman said. She said this now as she and her husband sat on the bed, she with the tears and the scowl and the comforter, he keeping his distance like he might keep his distance from a dangerous animal.

"I'm calling her again now," the husband said. He held up the phone. "See . . ."

"Just call," the woman said, "and if she doesn't pick up, I'm blaming you. I won't even want to see your face, so there won't be any point in us going out to dinner, then, will there? To say nothing of sex."

The husband sighed and dialed his sister's number.

The woman shifted in the bed. Her back ached, and the aching was exacerbated by the awkward, fifty-degree angle at which she sat, and she would have shifted more but that would mean sacrificing some physical ground in this domestic conflict. On the nightstand next to the bed sat a small remote control: the frequency control device for the pacemaker thing in her bowels. She wondered now what would happen if she picked it up, turned it on, and used it to turn the pacemaker to its highest possible setting, something she'd been warned to never do except at her doctor's explicit instruction. It was tempting to find out. One of the woman's and the husband's two daughters—seven years old and the sweetest thing in the world and probably the woman's favorite—ran into the room, her face sticky and blue with the juice of a melted popsicle. "Hey, Mom," she started to say eagerly, but the woman pointed to the bedroom door and screamed, "Get out! Your father and I are having a conversation!"

The girl ran out and started to sob. The plan was the kids would stay with their uncle tonight, the woman's brother. The husband sighed again, and the woman continued to scowl at him.

"Hey, sis," the husband said into the phone.

The woman's scowl stayed put, but she wiped the tears from her face and sniffled.

"Yeah, no, everything's cool. Hey, I was just calling because . . . yes. Yeah, tonight is our anniversary, y'know, mine and . . . and I was just wondering if you still had Mom for tonight, so we could go out to dinner and everything. You see, I bought champagne and we were going to go to that Italian place and then come home and drink some champagne and . . . Yes. Of course. Great! See, I thought so, but you know . . . she got it into her head that you weren't going to . . . good, good. So you've got mom tonight, and I'll get her in the morning. Great. Okay, thanks sis. Bye."

The woman sniffed. "Well . . .?"

"Well, she said she's got mom for the night, so we can go out."

The woman threw her arms up from under the comforter, and the tears came back to her face. "You know what? Just forget it. I don't even want to go now."

The husband sighed again. "Honey, dear, she said she's got mom—"

"It doesn't matter. I'm too stressed out now anyway."

"Honey—"

"No. It's ridiculous—I just wanted to go out for my anniversary. I never get anything. I never ask for anything and I ask for this and suddenly your sister has a problem. It's not fair to me."

"Dear, she's gonna take care of my mother. It's fine."

"The point is—the point *is*—I shouldn't even have had to deal with this. She should have just said yes yesterday when I mentioned it instead of saying we'll see what happens and stressing me out. It's ridiculous is what it is."

"Yeah, well, we can go, okay? So we'll go."

"No, no. Just forget it. Forget it! I don't want to now. I'm too . . . I just had surgery and nobody respects me and now I'm just too stressed out and it's your sister's fault. And it's your fault too." The woman craned her neck towards the open bedroom door. "Hey, Rachel, Melissa! You're not going to Uncle Randy's tonight anymore. You're just staying here!"

The husband sighed once more and deeply. "I'm starting to think," he said, "that you never wanted to go out for our anniversary in the first place."

FUTONS

AT THE DIESEL LOUNGE, BY the bar, feeling lonely, she waited for her male friend to return from the bathroom and take her home, but instead a woman came up to her with a drink and slid the drink to her across the bar top and said, "How do you feel about futons?"

She looked at the drink before taking it and sipping it and said, "Excuse me?"

And the woman said, "Well, I was reading this blog one day and the blogger said that a bed has two purposes, neither of which involve watching a television—i.e. the two purposes, for those who cannot extrapolate an obvious conclusion from an incomplete set of data, are sex and sleeping, but not necessarily in that order, because sometimes, while one may have sex and then sleep, one may also have sex upon waking from sleep, so that the order looks like sleep and then sex or sex and then sleep and then sex or even sex, sleep, sex, sleep, sex, sex, and then more sex. But an interesting logical conundrum presents itself when one thinks about this whole thing too much, which I have, and which brings me to futons. Futons, you see, have two purposes: they exist to be a couch and they exist to be a bed—both, by the way, uncomfortably—but then if a bed has two purposes, and a futon is a bed, does a futon have three purposes? And since one of the purposes of a futon is to serve as a couch, and one of the express purposes of a couch is for sitting, often to watch television, well then. And so the real question is would you like to go home with me? I have a regular queen-sized bed, not a futon."

A Quaint Little Oasis

"Every day I wake up, drink a large glass of water that I pour from like this filtered pitcher thing—like one of those filtered pitchers, you know?—and I look in the mirror and I say, Jennifer, evoke an emotional response."

"Oh. I like that. Yeah. Yeah, that's good."

"Thanks. I heard it in a Tony Robbins book or some shit like that."

Stuck on I-15 N, toward Las Vegas, for close to four hours now. The GPS on Sunny's phone said it was a six-hour drive, tops, but there was an accident at the California-Nevada border and so it's taking longer than it should for them to traverse the desert. Sun beating down through sunroof. Dust coating now the white exterior of the Audi A5. The car has four doors five seats; carpooling seemed like a good idea at the time, but none of the other women in the car have volunteered gas money or offered to drive for a while to give Sunny a break. Sunny's back is stiff, her arms tired. She almost wishes traffic would come to a standstill so she could step out of the car for a few minutes, do some backbends or toe-touches and grab a cherry-bran granola bar from her emergency stash in the Audi's small trunk; but it hasn't come to a standstill, the traffic—it's just been moving very very slow. She feels like she's been here before.

"Is it Tony Robbins or Anthony Robbins? I always thought it was Anthony."

"I think it used to be Tony but now it's Anthony, like he changed it."

"But who just changes their name in like the middle of their career like that?"

"Um, we do, Silly, at least until we find one we really like, so like maybe that's what he did."

In the car with Sunny are, in clockwise seating order starting with the front passenger seat, Jennifer Malone (stage name: Jessica Salt), Vixen Foxx (real name: Michelle Odwalla), and Isabelle Oberlin (stage name: Silly St. James). Jennifer and Isabelle are the ones arguing about the name of the famed self-help guru and motivational speaker. Sunny tries to focus on the road, and Vixen's nose is buried in a printed magazine.

But then Vixen, who, like Sunny, prefers to be addressed by her stage name, speaks up without moving her attention from the page: "You're both idiots," she says. "Anthony and Tony are the same name. Tony is short for Anthony."

"Well, duh," Silly says. "But what I mean is which one goes with like his brand? *My* branding coach says—"

Jennifer: "You have a branding coach?"

"Kind of."

"Kind of? Like he's separate from Jerry, you mean? Someone else."

Sunny, Jennifer, Vixen, and Silly are all four of them Jerry's girls, managerial-wise.

"Yeah," Silly says. "He just kind of helps me with clothes and stuff, and he helped me pick a name when I got into the business."

Jennifer holds up a hand. "Wait wait wait. Your branding coach told you you should call yourself 'Silly St. James' and, not only did you not fire his ass right then and there, but you called yourself that? You actually called yourself Silly."

"It worked, didn't it? I'm up for three awards this weekend."

"Sunny's up for four."

Sunny adjusts the rearview mirror, takes a sip of the iced jasmine mint tea that sits in her cup holder. The ice has long ago melted. Sunny offers no comment.

"Sunny's always up for four, and she'll win them all, too." The truth is that Silly St. James would much rather be called Isabelle outside of the context of her work, but she knows that's never going to happen, not with a stage name like Silly, and so she's resigned herself to the loss of her identity and cries about it only sometimes when she's alone.

Interstate 15 is flat and the view is uninspiring. There is a small animal, a feline of some kind, maybe, dead beside the road a few hundred feet from the Audi, and Sunny can see it's been dead for a long time, baking or roasting in the desert sun. It might be a bobcat cub or a desert kit fox; both are common in the Mojave—somehow she knows this. Overhead a buzzard, who swoops down as the car approaches and tears into the poor thing with vicious dead-eyed hunger, all ugly skin and feathers, ravenous. As the Audi passes by, another buzzard lands and takes its pick of the carcass, and when she looks back at the scene a few moments later, the two have become a flock, and then the flock a horde, and it's bound to be only seconds before all that's left of the roadkill is a broken skeleton, which will in time dry and disintegrate and blow away. Are those buzzards, or vultures? It's hard to know the difference when you've never seen either in person before. Overhead clear sky. No clouds.

"The fuck are you reading, anyway?" Silly asks.

There comes no response and Silly reaches over the car's leather back seat's center and waves her manicured hand. "Fuck off," Vixen says, swatting the hand away.

"I asked what it is you're reading," Silly says.

Vixen sighs, raises her head. "*Scientific American*," she replies, her words syrupy, as if she just wants to get this fucking thing over with. "It's this article about cigarettes and cell phones and how what was once the world's addiction has just been replaced with another, possibly healthier addiction. How back in the fifties and sixties people smoked all the time, not necessarily because they were biologically addicted but because they were bored, like whenever there was nothing else to do a person just reached for a cigarette and lit up."

"Idle hands and all that," Jennifer says.

"Right. Idle hands. And so now when we're bored, instead of being bored, we reach for our cell phones and scroll and tap away, because we know cigarettes are unhealthy. It's a fascinating hypothesis." Vixen Foxx entered the industry at age twenty-one, during her third year at the University of California, Berkeley, where she was studying neurochemistry, in an effort to pay off student loan debt that she rapidly began accruing when her parents lost almost all of their savings in a fraudulent lawsuit brought against them by the tenant who occupied Vixen's room after she moved away and thus weren't able to help her with her education finances like they'd planned her entire life. Vixen liked her experience in the industry so much that she stuck with it, even after graduating with her Masters and writing a critically acclaimed thesis on psilocybin, a chemical common to psychedelic mushrooms, and human creative output. The publication of the thesis landed her a regular guest column in the *New York Times* science section. She still writes the column weekly and it's often syndicated in smaller regional newspapers and is shared over and over again online each time a new column is published. She returns her attention to the magazine in her hands, as if to say leave me alone now.

"Speaking of which . . ." Silly says, and it isn't apparent what the which is to which she is referring until she takes a Pall Mall from her purse, sticks it in her mouth, and starts digging for a lighter.

"No." This from Sunny now, who strains her neck to see in the rear view mirror what Silly is doing but doesn't turn around so as not to take her attention fully off the crowded but steady traffic in front of her. "There's no smoking in this car."

"Oh, come on," Silly says, removing the unlit paper cylinder from her mouth and waving it around in the manner of habitual smokers who are also habitual arguers.

"Sometimes I think none of this is real at all," Sunny says, "like none of this is an actual thing."

"What?"

"I said fine, whatever, but roll your window down and keep whatever arm is holding that thing outside of it at all times. I mean it."

"Hey, girls, is it just me or did some stick die and crawl its way up Sunny's ass today?" But Silly obliges and lowers the blue-tinted glass before lighting up, keeping her hand outside the car and raising her haunches and leaning out in a way that can't be anything but painful each time she takes a drag.

There are moments that happen at every point in time, that connect universes and years and decades and, most importantly, people, that link hearts together; like strings they weave through everything, and if you could pull one of them out it might all fall apart like a threadbare tapestry. Sunny thinks she sees a bolt of lightning come crashing from the cloudless azure sky and strike a car way in front of her on the road, but there is no smoke or fire, no sort of explosion, just desert heat that warps the road ahead. She takes another sip of the jasmine tea—the drink is diluted and bland.

"I don't know," Silly says, blowing a ring of smoke, a literal ring because somehow that's a real thing that people do and she knows how to do it, out of the left side of her mouth and through the window, "you're too smart for me."

For a second, nobody knows what she's talking about. Jennifer might be falling asleep in the passenger seat: her eyes are closed at least, but she's always been into meditation. Then Silly punches Vixen in the thigh.

"What the fuck, Silly."

"I said you're way too smart for me, with your *Scientific American*."

"Actually, it's a very accessible magazine—some even argue that it's too accessible, dumbs thing down and publishes articles more for journalism's sake than science's. I can let you read it when I'm finished, if you want."

Silly is quiet for a moment, taking another drag. "Yeah, maybe."

The Mojave desert is packed with native fauna. The expanse of the thing is large and flat and wide wide open, so it seems often empty to the unobservant eye, but they are there, the animals: bobcats and bats and kangaroo rats and jackrabbits; cougars and chipmunks and coyotes; the kit fox and mule deer and the desert bighorn sheep; and lots of lizards, like the iguana and the zebra-tailed lizard and the fringe-toed lizard; there's the California kingsnake and the glossy snake and the gopher snake and western diamondback rattlesnake and lots of other snakes; and there are birds and multiple kinds of owls, and in the Mojave river there's even an indigenous fish called the Mojave tui chub, which is endangered and because of hybridization with the coastal chub might cease to exist in its most pure variety any year now. The second roadkill specimen the white Audi A5 passes on its way to the AVN Awards is a pronghorn, an even-toed ungulate that is not an antelope but looks an awful lot like one, and when she sees it Sunny is sad for it until the smell of its carcass accosts her through the open rear left window, and even then she's still sad, just not as.

"Science just isn't my thing, I guess," Silly says. "I like art. I like to paint, and well I guess those just take two different kinds of brains."

Silly is a talented painter—Sunny has seen her work, been to her gallery openings (even if nobody knows you as that kind of artist it's not hard to get a gallery to host a show for you when you know the right people)—but no one wants to buy an oil-on-canvas still life of sex toys by a painter named Silly St. James.

Through the desert the Audi goes. No one says much more for a while. Somewhere along the way Silly throws out her cigarette even though she's smoked only half of it.

This is how the next four days will go: The girls will arrive at the Hard Rock Hotel in the white Audi late this evening and Sunny will give the keys to a valet who will take the car to a nearby underground parking garage, and then they'll make their way to their rooms. They'll be nice, the rooms, but not like suites or anything like that, like people might think anyone with a job title that has the word "star" in it would stay in. Silly and Vixen and Sunny will share a room, one of them getting a bed to herself (Sunny, if she can help it), and Jennifer will stay in another room with a couple of other starlets whose work Sunny is aware of but with whom she's never worked herself or even met. Tonight Jerry might stop by and welcome his girls in that charismatic way he has, checking to see if they need anything and was their trip okay and really they didn't have to drive he would have gotten them on the bus some of the other girls took and is everything okay Sunny yes it's fine I just don't like riding on busses for long stretches of time. Sunny and Vixen will go to bed early, because they are exhausted, while Silly will go downstairs and gamble for a bit and hang out with people she hasn't seen in a while, and she'll have a couple drinks, but just a couple because the next day is work, after all. She'll return to the room late and collapse next to Sunny on one of the beds, and while this will wake Sunny up, she'll pretend it didn't and just fall quickly back to sleep. In the morning, breakfast. Vegan something or other for all the girls, except for Jennifer, who will, despite claiming to "absolutely adore" the people she's rooming with, spend as much of the weekend as possible with Sunny and Silly and Vixen and will eat bacon and homemade waffles drenched in real maple syrup for breakfast and will gear herself up mentally for becoming Jessica Salt, because for her it's a character somewhat removed from her real personality. Sunny doesn't even like these people, but she supposes they are her friends. But the AVNs are not just an award show—there is a whole exposition surrounding this thing, the event room of the

Hard Rock transformed into a mecca of adult film. The girls will do so many interviews, most for online-only "news" outlets. They will stand at booths and promote products. This thing is really for the fans, and so they'll pose for pictures and sign autographs and engage in witty banter both with the fans and with each other for the fans' sake. Sunny likes her fans. She is excited to meet them and let them meet her. The girls will wear nice dresses, and on Saturday, the night of the awards, they'll wear *really* nice dresses. There's this whole red carpet thing at the Adult Video News Awards that's not unlike the Oscars, except with a level of tastefully exposed skin and an ability to not take itself so damn seriously that the Oscars only wish they had. Sunny will present the award for best direction to Vixen, who last year began to do less in front of the camera and more behind it and has big things on the horizon (that is not a pun). Sunny will win two of the four awards for which she is nominated. She will win Performer of the Year. She will not tear up when she accepts this award because she does not tear up, ever, not anymore. Silly will win most outrageous sex scene for a spontaneous double-vag session with two of the largest male talents in the industry. An interesting thing to note about porn is that some of the largest male talents' penises are insured for up to one million dollars by the talents' agents or contracting studios; this, Sunny reasons, makes no sense because it's not like if the thing is lopped off any amount of insurance money is going to be able to pay for a new one. Silly will also win an ensemble award for Best Big Butt Release for *Big Oily Asses 22*; there is no anal intercourse in this film—it simply stars starlets with shapely but firm posteriors. Silly does kettlebell swings three days a week. Jennifer will win no awards at all, although she is nominated for Best Fem-Dom Strap-on scene with one of the girls with whom she's rooming; it is, of the fourteen scenes she filmed last year, her favorite, the one she most enjoyed making. She tends to play the submissive in her personal life, so playing a dom was a nice change of pace, one that really turned her on and let her explore who she is deep down as a person, and her excitement in the scene is almost tangible as you watch it. There will be parties, and Sunny will attend a few and will smoke some pot with her friends. You would think there would be more sex at an adult entertainment expo, but there's really not that much, just some. The whole ceremony and related coverage will air in a 90-minute edited version on the Showtime television network the following week and will be rebroadcast a handful of times thereafter; it will be available On Demand until sometime in May. The award statuette, by the way, a Lucite block with a mannered simple engraving of an embracing man and woman, is named Woody; there is nothing explicit about it—it's really quite beautiful, to be honest.

From the front passenger seat there begins to sound a phlegmish snore, and it's clear that, even if she was meditating before, Jennifer is definitely sleeping now. "I have to take a piss," Silly says abruptly, as if she's been waiting to say it but didn't want to break the stillness and now Jennifer's harsh log-sawing has finally given her permission.

"I could use a snack," Vixen chimes in, looking up from her magazine, "and a bottle of water, and I mean I might as well use the restroom too, then."

When you're on a road trip and need to stop to use the facilities there is always either a rest stop coming up very soon and you happen to see the sign for it just in time, or else you've only moments ago passed the last one for the next fifty miles. In this case it's the former, and in less than five minutes Sunny is parking in front of a small outpost in the middle of the Nevada desert. Immediately Vixen and Silly open their doors and jump out of the vehicle, walking hurriedly toward the building. Jennifer does not wake but keeps snoring; her head lolls to the right against the door and a stillicide of saliva drops from the edge of her pinkly full lips. Sunny considers waking her but decides not to: she'll get her a bottle of water and a snack from the vending machine in case she's hungry when she wakes of her own accord. She pulls her aviators from a compartment between the car's two overhead visors made specifically for storing sunglasses—she doesn't usually wear the sunglasses while she's driving because the blue of the windshield's tint is a more-than-sufficient anti-glare barrier—and pops them on her face as she steps out into the hot hot world. Her phone is not in the left pocket of her jeans where she left it; it's fallen, as it tends to do, into the little niche in the door. She bends over, fishes for it, feels the metal and glass.

The rest area is a quaint little oasis: Three other vehicles in the medium-sized parking lot, two of them beige minivans. Three large palm trees that are not indigenous but have been planted by the Nevada Highway Commission to provide shade for weary travelers. A twenty-or-twenty-five-square-yard patch of grass, kept green by the thrice-daily ministrations of an industrial sprinkler system, the schedule of which is posted on a nearby sign so any travelers who wish to picnic on the lawn are informed of when doing so may lead to their lunch's soaking. A playground (really just a swing set and a set of monkey bars) on which two children cavort. There's even an area for pets with one of those poles with what looks like a birdhouse on top, except it's not a birdhouse but a dispenser for complimentary animal-waste disposal bags and complimentary plastic gloves, and under it is a trash can in which to deposit the waste. A pudgy man in shorts and a white polo frolics with his dog, a black shin-high labradoodle. The dog makes Sunny think of her cat, who she's left for the week with a kind neighbor on a floor one below her own apartment. There are large rocks and several cacti scattered about the area.

Sunny snaps a picture of herself in front of one of the palm trees and applies a filter and shoots it off onto the internet. It uploads slowly; reception is faint here.

In the bathroom she finds two stalls, one occupied and one open. She takes the free one. As she sits she recognizes Silly's sneakers underneath the stall's wall. Why the architects of bathrooms almost never extend the structure all the way to the floor is a mystery. "Silly?" Sunny says. "That you?"

"Yeppers." Their voices echo echo echo.

"Where's Vixen?"

"She was gonna get a popsicle out of one of the vending machines."

"Oh. Huh. I didn't see her out there."

"Yeah, well."

The awkward silence that comes from sharing a public restroom with another person.

"So, listen," Silly says, the sound of her bodyweight shifting on the other side of the plastic laminate board.

"Yeah?"

"Um, thanks for, y'know, driving and stuff today."

"It's no problem." This is something we say when people thank us—it's no problem—as if thanks are handed out only when the person being thanked has seriously inconvenienced herself.

"No, but I mean it. I don't think I could have kept my sanity coming all the way here on a bus full of oversexed women just looking for a party."

Sunny notices that there's very little toilet paper left on the roll in her stall.

"Which, I realize, is pretty much myself I just described, sure, but that's something I've been thinking about a lot lately, I guess. Myself, I mean."

There might be just enough.

"I've actually been thinking about—" There comes from Silly's stall a gentle tapping sound, like a kitchen knife on a cutting board, and then an inhalation followed by a cough.

"You okay?" Sunny asks.

The cough continues for a moment. A deep sniffle. "Yeah, I'm fine. Thanks for asking."

Sunny reaches for the toilet paper, but then Silly starts talking again, so Sunny stays her hand, not wanting the sound of the roll's unraveling to be taken as a rejection of the conversation.

"I haven't told anybody this yet," Silly says, "not even Jerry. So please don't tell Jerry."

"Don't tell Jerry what, Silly?"

"I'll tell him, is what I mean. I want to be the one to tell him, of course."

"Are you like pregnant or something, Silly?" It happens sometimes, a porn star conceives. But it's almost always a result of intercourse a starlet's had in her personal life, not on set; the pornography gods are solicitous that way.

"No. Noooo. Dear god, no. I could never be a mother right now. I'm not even twenty yet."

Sunny taps a foot on the linoleum.

"But I am thinking of retiring. From the industry."

"Oh."

"Yeah. I mean, maybe. I've been giving it a lot of thought."

Sunny can't see herself retiring any time in the near future. She enjoys her work too much. Even though it's often difficult and grueling and the long hours in heavy makeup sweating under hot lights become more irritating than exciting after so long, she enjoys it. It's often fun (that is, it's the most fun she's ever had in her not-that-fun life), and she learns so much about herself. "How long have you been performing, again?" she asks.

"Eighteen months. I started literally on my eighteenth birthday."

"That's right. I remember."

"My first scene was with you."

This Sunny doesn't remember. She's worked with Silly a handful of times, and she remembers the first time, but she doesn't remember being aware of the fact that her first scene with Silly was Silly's first scene.

"So, yeah, I just wanted to say thank you, I guess. For all of it. It's meant a lot to me. Changed my life in a lot of ways."

"Well, I'm glad I could be a part of it, then."

"Thanks."

Sunny hears the toilet paper roll on Silly's side unravel, so she finally reaches for hers as well and finishes up. There's just enough.

As they're washing their hands in two side-by-side sinks with annoying faucets that you press the button to turn on and that are supposed to shut off automatically so you don't have to press the button again with your clean hands except they keep shutting off after two seconds which is not nearly enough time to rinse your hands of soap so you end up holding the button down with one hand and rinsing the other one by itself and then switching out, Sunny asks Silly what her plans are.

"I think I'll go to school," she answers, drying her hands with a coarse brown paper towel. "For art. I've applied to a few places, and I've been accepted to a couple, and I've got money saved up for tuition now. And maybe I can spend some time with my family. I've barely seen them this year, been so busy."

"That all sounds good," Sunny says. "I think things will work out well."

"And maybe when school's over I'll pop back to LA and do a couple shoots for old times' sake. With you maybe and Rico and Eric."

Sunny nods. She does not repeat the oft-cited maxim that, once you've left, you've probably left for good.

"But first," Silly says, grinning, "the AVNs! It's going to be a great time. And you're going to win, like, all the awards, I'll bet."

In the rest building's foyer, where there are three vending machines—one of beverages, one of ice creams, and one of things like chips and candy bars—Sunny buys two bottles of water and a Diet Dr. Pepper and a bag of pretzels.

Outside the heat accosts her. With the button on the key fob she pops her car's trunk from a distance. The sun reflects off the white of the Audi like another sun, dulled only slightly by the coating of dust on its exterior. She pulls her aviators from the top of her head back over her eyes as she makes her way to the car. She rifles through the trunk, pushing aside suitcases, looking for the plastic grocery bag of snacks she packed this morning. She finds it. She grabs three cherry-bran granola bars. She calls out, "Does anybody need anything from back here while I have this open?" Nobody answers, so she shuts the trunk with a womph.

Suddenly Silly is beside her. "Hey," she says, "have you seen Vixen and Jennifer?"

Sunny realizes she's locked the beverages and pretzels in the trunk, having set them down there while searching for the cherry-bran bars. She searches her pocket for her keys again. "Jennifer's asleep."

"No she's not. Not anymore. She's not in the car."

Sure enough, the front passenger seat is empty, but the door is locked. "Hmm."

"And Vixen, too—I don't know where she went."

"They're probably just both in the bathroom. I'll check on them." Sunny sets the snacks on the car's roof.

"I'll come with you."

The women's restroom is empty, both stall doors swinging freely open on their hinges, creaking and squealing. Sunny suggests they check the men's room because Vixen likes to use men's restrooms sometimes. To mix things up, she says, shake the world awake. So they check: the room is not unlike the ladies', except with one stall and two urinals and far more permanent-marker scribblings on the wall than in the ladies' room; the fluorescent lights overhead flicker—one of the bulbs is dying or has a loose connection; one of the sinks' faucet is leaky and the water drips into the porcelain; but there is no one in here. The foyer, too, is still empty, save for the vending machines and a community cork board with nothing posted to it. Outside once again they circle the building; on the other side of it they find an RV-sewage-pumping station and a janitor's closet in which there is only a mop and a mop bucket and a mop sink and a couple spray bottles each of bleach and Windex. In the parking lot Sunny's car is still unoccupied. All the vehicles that were in the lot when they pulled in are still here. There is the man throwing a tennis ball for his dog to chase. No clouds. Clear blue sky. Flat cracked desert sand all around, visibility beyond the highway for hundreds and hundreds of yards: little green-brown shrubs (banana yucca, they're called), Joshua trees every so often. The children playing on the monkey bars. The sound of the children laughing.

The World Is Ending and There's Nothing You Can Do About It, But That's Okay Because It Happened Before and You Didn't Even Notice

IT IS DARK. *IT* IS dark. Both it and *it* are ambiguous and vague and impossible to define beyond the reference point of the present moment. It sort of pulses through your brain and your veins and through your blood. Both your veins and your blood. This is not a contradiction; so many things are contradictions, but this is not one of them because this is real. It's like it is your blood and so it pulses through your veins and you feel it, but you also feel it deeper than that, deeper than the blood; it pulses through the blood the way the blood pulses through the veins the way charge pulses through a string of copper and completes a circuit. It pulses through itself. Through you.

This is what they call a bender. You do not make a habit of it, but tonight it happens.

First drinks and music and more drinks. Shots of things

and then shots of things. Mixed together. Inadvisable. Do it anyway.

The first shot sweet and strong and sharp on your tongue and down your throat and in your belly like fire. The second also. The third. Hey. Hey! Do you want some of this!

No. No, not right now. I'm good.

Dancing. The sort of dancing where hips grind on hips and pelvises gesticulate in concentric circles, the center of the pelvises' circular movements growing closer and closer to the middle of your being. Merging with this stranger who dances in front of you in the room, in the room's upper right quadrant, the reference for calling this the upper right being when you walked into the door after the bouncer let you in. So you walked in and then to the bar on the left and downed the three shots and declined the other stuff and moved over to the other side and by the back wall and danced. With the stranger you danced. You felt the expansion of tissue. The smell of perfume and alcohol. You danced for maybe twenty minutes or an hour or all night.

You're back at the bar, thinking about thinking. About the lights and that time you were in the kitchen trying to cook an omelette and dropped it when you tried to flip it and it spilled from the pan and onto the countertop and the floor and the stove's electric burner, filling the room with the smell of burning. The memory is triggered by the guy behind you with the joint hanging from his lips, glowing ominously in the darkness.

It's dark but there are so many lights.

The guy with the joint pushes past you, bumps into you. You do not feel. He orders drinks.

You sneak in behind him and take the drinks and he says whoa there hey, and you don't care and give him cash. I'm not the bartender. You don't care. You give him more cash. You don't know what it was he ordered except that it's drinks and you down it all, both of them—there are two—first one and then the other, in seconds. And he watches you like what. You put the glasses down and pat him on the shoulder and say thanks and he eyes you sexily or so you think. He does not grope you. You've never actually been groped before, groping here being defined as the unwanted grasping of your body part or parts by strangers. You always thought there'd be more groping. You've never groped anyone either, groping again being defined in the unwanted sense. Thanks, you say again but you're already back to dancing on the other side of the room.

You wonder if you should try breakdancing, like clearing a spot in the center of the dance floor and breakdancing. You decide against it because a.) you've never breakdanced before and b.) this isn't exactly the music for it. You wonder if breakdanced is the correct past tense of breakdance. Maybe it's brokedance. You've never brokedance before. The drinks are really hitting you now. You are floating across the floor. You are on top of the room, upside down on the ceiling, above all the people, looking down at them. You are better than them. They are nothing.

You're in the bathroom looking for drugs. There are always drugs in the bathroom. The thing about clubs is you can always tell what kind of club it's going to be by how the bathroom is set with respect to how easy it is to do drugs in. Some of the clubs make it really easy, like they put mirrors with little shelves under them in all the stalls, and you can almost always find a razor blade sitting on the shelf or on the back of the toilet. Your experience with razor blades is not limited to dance club bathrooms, but it is limited. There are no razor blades here. There are no mirrors or little shelves in the stalls. Do you have any blow? Do you have any heroin? Do you have any Molly? Do you have any acid? I'll pay you. Thanks. Ooh, that's probably good stuff isn't it?

You tap the top of your phones together, exchanging money for goods via hand and electronic signals. It's some sort of pink pill that they give you and you pop it whole, swallow it dry. It does nothing for you. It isn't real.

Back on the dance floor you wonder if you're too old for this. Everyone in here is like eighteen, nineteen, and you are . . .

You move around. Sway. Undulate. Oscillate. Swing and roll and shake. You grind and bump. You move. Your moves are ugly. All the moves are ugly and what are you doing here and where are the people or person you walked in with—because you came here with someone, at least you think and remember you did, and they disappeared or were wiped from existence or never existed—and where can you get more drugs and you're back in the bathroom now with your tongue in some woman's mouth. In the bathroom it isn't dark but light. Bright. Very.

AND HOME AGAIN

"SO . . ."

"I'M STILL READING."

"OH."

Back in New York, in the same cafe in Tribeca where they'd first sat down to talk what like five years ago now? Bread and Whippo. Jonathan's plate is empty, a smattering of crumbs and a smear of mustard where a sandwich used to be. His parents' house is sold. Merrell's veggieburger sits on the opposite side of the table, uneaten save for one bite, but the fries are mostly gone. A pretty waitress takes Jonathan's plate and refills his coffee from a silver-and-glass carafe. She drops a few packets of sugar on the table. Jonathan smiles at her and nods and reaches for the sugar and the waitress doesn't move. She's staring at his arm, at the burn scars. He looks at her and she sort of jumps back and dips her head, embarrassed, but she shouldn't be embarrassed; if anything Jonathan should be embarrassed because this sort of thing happens a lot, but he's not. He smiles at her again, his smile as sincere as he can make it, trying to put behind his smile a message like, Don't worry, you haven't offended me and I'd still like to sleep with you. He doesn't know if he gets the message across, but the waitress walks away.

Jonathan empties a pack of sugar into his coffee, stirs. "Well . . ."

"Still reading. Almost done."

Outside the cafe the sidewalk is busy. Pedestrians with umbrellas. Pedestrians with wet dogs. Panhandlers. A street musician playing a trombone with remarkable skill and sincerity. A taco truck on the curb, its line of patrons a consistent five-people long. Rain falling from the sky in a drizzle. Droplets of water landing on and then running down the window by which Jonathan and Merrell sit.

Merrell sets the stack of papers on the table.

"Okay, so, well . . ." Jonathan says.

Merrell looks down at his burger with surprise, as if he forgot it was still there. He picks up a knife and begins cutting the burger in half with a deliberate sawing motion. "I don't understand why you couldn't just send it to me. Why make me sit here and read it?"

"I wanted to gauge your reaction."

"And?"

"And what?"

"Just and."

"That's what I want to know from you, Mer. I'm supposed to ask you that. You're supposed to finish reading it and then I'm supposed to say, expectantly, 'and . . . ?' "

"Right." Merrell picks up one half of the veggieburger and turns it over, as if examining its bottom bun for flaws.

"So?"

"I finished reading it."

"Yes. And?"

Merrell bites into the burger, chews, talks around a mouthful of food. "It's okay, Jonathan."

"Okay?"

"I mean it's not bad, but I don't think I can produce it."

"What? Why?"

"Because well first off it needs some work. A lot of work. And then aside from that, this thing would be expensive to put on, really expensive."

"What do you mean 'needs some work'?"

Merrell is looking at his burger again, holding it up to the light and scrutinizing its composition before taking another bite. "The main character, for example, she—"

"What about the main character?"

"I was just about to say what about the main character. You knew that. You heard me say 'The main character, for example,' and then you cut me off. Why do people do that? Cut people off in the middle of conversations and ask for information that clearly was about to be provided if only they hadn't cut off the other person."

"Sorry."

Merrell smiles around black bean patty and bun. "It's okay. It's just, why do people do that, I wonder? It seems counterproductive. Like a subconsciously deliberate step backward. Like they don't actually want to hear the forthcoming information, so they step in and ask for it, hoping to delay it paradoxically."

"Um, yeah. Well. So then, what about the main character?"

"She kind of seems like the sort of person who would cut in and ask for information that's clearly about to be provided."

"Uh huh."

"You see what I mean?"

"I'm not so sure that I do, Mer. At all."

"She seems a lot like you, Jonathan, is what I mean. I mean your first play, part of what made it so good, is how unlike you it was, how dispassionate the relationship was between you, the writer, and the play's main characters. You were nothing like them, and in fact they were nothing like anybody, really, they were so very singular—"

"There were two of them. Three if you count the father as a main character."

"Yes, but I mean that each of them was singular, like on their own. Like individually. Like each one was unique and interesting in a way different than the rest, and this character here isn't. This script that I just finished reading has one main character and that main character is a lot like you."

"Well but she's a woman."

"That doesn't matter. She doesn't act like a woman. She acts like Jonathan Bread has acted the last three years. She acts like someone who maybe lost her parents in a bombing and maybe lost a body part or two and has gone through some serious trauma and/or traumas."

"She has. Gone through traumas. That's the point."

"But that's *my* point. None of this works. It's all too . . . self-indulgent. Too sappy in a self-referential way. And even if the people watching the play don't know that, explicitly, as in even if they don't know what happened to you—and let's face it, most of them probably don't because playwrights, or play producers for that matter, are, if anything, very minor players on the scale of celebrity—they can still feel it. This script drips with self-pity."

"I . . ." Jonathan was not expecting this. The play on the sheets of paper on the table between them resembles his life not at all. "I thought that was the point. The point of writing. The point of entertainment."

Merrell frowns, and he appears to Jonathan to be altogether a different person than the one who green-lit the production of *Sugarcane* almost half a decade ago. He takes the final bite of his veggieburger, chews, swallows. "Maybe that was the point, a long time ago. But it's not anymore. Anymore all people want is entertainment. Good and evil. Villains and heroes. Look at Hollywood. Look at the thriller novels on the most-downloaded lists. Those guys can't write worth a damn, but they can plot and they can pit a good guy against a bad guy and, because that is the struggle facing the world these days, because good versus evil is the struggle, that's what people want to see. People want to rally against something. To hate something in a public and collective way."

Jonathan thinks about this. It's certainly not false. He wants to hate, has wanted to hate since JFK, but has had no one to direct any sort of hate at. He signals the waitress. "But that right there is what this is about, Mer. Self-hatred. You said it yourself. The best plays are the ones where the protagonist and the antagonist are the same person. Where you go through the whole damned thing waiting for the villain—or, even better, the hero— to show up, and he never does, and you get frustrated and hate the thing until suddenly you realize that both sides were there in every page and both sides were you, which is why you hate the thing, because it's you. You hate you. That's what this is about." He taps the top of script with a thick finger. He is lying right now, sort of: he had no goal in mind when he wrote the play, no intention that it be about self-hatred, but he wants it produced, needs it produced, and he sees the opportunity here, the angle that might pique Merrell's interests enough for him to put out the money.

The waitress comes over from the other side of the cafe. She picks up Merrell's plate and asks if either of the men would like more coffee. Coffee is the thing that makes it all go 'round. Jonathan says no and asks for the check and as the waitress turns around he reaches out and touches her hand. She doesn't notice.

"My first play was good, Mer," Jonathan says. "You know that. Everyone loved it."

"The critics loved it," Merrell interrupts. "But there are only so many critics. They're not the ones who make the money for us."

"And so what if we do *Sugarcane* again, then? First. Like a primer to rouse attention. And then meanwhile we get this one ready and start it up maybe the year after."

"*Sugarcane* won't work. We already know that."

"You just said it was the kind of characters people—"

"No. I said it had characters that were unlike its writer, but we still know they're not the characters people want to see. And, frankly, it's not the story, either. Like I said, people are scared, and scared people need to hate or else their fear will consume them. That's the truth of it."

"Maybe." Silence for several moments. Silverware clanking against dishes throughout the cafe's dining room. It's a soup sort of day, with the rain and clouds and cool air outside, and so much of the clanking is the clanking of soup spoons against ceramic bowls. For a moment, the whole place goes up in Jonathan's mind, engulfed in fire, the people and the tables and the chairs and the soup, another bomb, and Merrell's face is the last thing he sees overtaken by the fireballs before he is, but then it all recedes back whence it came, and people are still eating and talking and waiting. "So . . ."

"So I'm sorry, Jon, but this isn't the play for me. But feel free to bring me something else, in the future, if you've written it."

Jonathan smiles warmly. "Okay. Sure. Thanks, Mer."

"Except next time . . ."

"Yes?"

"Just mail it over to me. Or, better, email."

"Right. Ha."

The waitress brings the check over and places it on the table, equidistant between the two men. Jonathan reaches for it, but Merrell's hand gets there first. "It's on me today," he says.

The specificity with which Merrell spoke of hate at their lunch meeting surprised Jonathan. His therapist used to speak of hate in a similar way.

"Do you hate them, Jonathan? The men that blew up that terminal. The men that blew up your parents and took your eye from you and inflicted upon your arm such utterly unsightly deformity. Do you hate them? It's okay if you do. It's perfectly okay. It's natural, to hate those who harm you—it's natural and to a certain extent it's healthy. And I'll be honest with you, Jonathan—I'll be honest—if I had been there, and if someone had taken my family from me like that and exposed me to so much carnage, I'd probably hate them too, you know. I'd hate them."

It was here that Jonathan pointed out that, from a certain standpoint, he hadn't been exposed to any carnage because he'd been knocked unconscious by the force of the explosion and had remained unconscious for several days and therefore had seen none of the blast's aftermath; and also, he pointed out, we can't be sure, like one-hundred percent sure, the bomber was a man, or that the bombing's organizers were men, or that men were involved in any way.

"But it's likely, Jonathan. It's likely they were men."

His therapist insisted, when they talked, on reaffirming every few sentences that it was Jonathan he was speaking to, and not to someone else (even though there was no one else in the small room with the desk and the couch and the chair) by using his name, Jonathan, often. Jonathan. Jonathan. Jonathan.

It was likely, Jonathan agreed, that men were involved.

"And so then the question is do you hate these men, Jonathan? Well do you, Jonathan? Do you? Because I would. But then you know what I would do? Don't you? Do you know, Jonathan? I would get over it. You have to get over it. You can't spend your entire life wallowing in hatred now because your parents died and you lost your eye. Boo-hoo. Get over it. And you may think . . . this may sound like . . . I may be coming across as harsh, Jonathan, in the way I'm telling you all this, but I'm not. Harsh, that is. I'm being tough because that's my job. I can't be tough like this with all my patients, of course, not all of them. Some patients, if you do so much as even nod your head when they say something self-deprecating, will pretty much go and kill themselves right then and there. I've had patients jump out that window. That window right there with the big green plant in front of it, and in fact that's why the plant's there, because I always used to open that window, but then patients would start jumping out of it, and but still I kept opening it out of a force of habit, a habituary force, a need to open the window, which is something we'll talk about later, needs, and so I put the plant there to inhibit my opening of the window, or at least to remind me, when I go to open it, that, hey, bad idea, people will jump out of this window. Which is why it gets stuffy in here. Except that was all a lie. Nobody ever jumped out of that window. My wife bought me that plant when I moved into the office, and now I have to water the damned thing. But my point, Jonathan, is I don't have to pussyfoot around with you because we've already established that you're way beyond the desire to kill yourself, which is a good thing, because now we can delve into the real work. Starting with hatred, which I know you feel for the men who blew up that curbside luggage area, because who wouldn't. Feel hatred, that is."

Jonathan then reaffirmed that he felt no external hatred and that they should therefore move on to other topics, things he did feel and would like to get off his chest, and that also his therapist talked more than Jonathan had been led to believe a therapist was supposed to talk. Jonathan fired the therapist at the end of that session.

Across the street and down the street four blocks Jonathan goes before descending into the bowels of the city, down into the subway system where people go when they want to get somewhere far away from earth and yet so close to humanity, so close. He stops at a MetroCard vending machine to refill the piece of paper in his wallet, the flimsy little ticket. He puts nine dollars on the card, enough for three rides, maybe four. He might use them all right now. He might get on the F and take it all the way to Six, and then maybe he'll walk up into the city and decide he's not ready for that yet and turn around and reenter the turnstile and board the J for Nassau Street because he really likes the name Nassau. And then maybe he'll hop on another one after that and take it somewhere else. Maybe he'll go to Brooklyn. Maybe he'll go to Broadway and see *Matilda* or something and weep. Maybe he'll catch a movie. Maybe he'll hunt down a crab roll or a seafood buffet. Maybe he'll never go back to his little apartment again. Does he even still rent the place? He hasn't lived there in months. He doesn't like being back in this city, so alive is it with the constructs of civilization. So easy to get lost.

He slides his MetroCard into the little slot and the slot spits it back at him. The turnstile gives way as he pushes against it with his hips, almost thrusting. The subway corridors used to be so yellow, but now he takes out his phone and opens an application and hits a button and everything is turned up a notch—the lights, the colors, the closeness of it all. He bumps into a woman with a large handbag because he was looking down at his phone. "Sorry," he says.

The woman straightens her back and says nothing and walks a little faster.

Jonathan stands near the edge of the platform, waiting for the F to whisk him away. Over his shoulder is slung a brown canvas bag, inside that bag his computer and the script that's just been denied. Jonathan thought it was good. He was proud of it. He wrote it at his dead parents' house in his misery and he thinks now it probably isn't very good at all. He's washed out. He takes out his phone again and slides a slider with his thumb. Now the whole world is washed out, or at least it's split right down the middle. Depending on how he shifts the muscles behind his eyes, the subway station is either black and white or yellow or both. The walls are either grey or the color of putrid flesh. Even in black and white everything still smells like urine.

"Please stand away from the platform." A disembodied voice.

The lights of the F train fade into existence. Brakes squeak. The train, though, is still far away, is not yet in front of him. There is still time. Jonathan has not backed away from the platform's infinite edge. He needs to step forward. Maybe this time he'll get it right.

Brighter the train's front lights get and behind Jonathan are people moving forward. They have all just arrived. No one ever arrives early enough to wait for the train, to impatiently think, *When is it going to get here?* But instead they are fluid, the blood of the city pumping through its veins. If he adjusts his bionic eye Jonathan can see their warmth. They arrive just in time to think, *Oh, there's the train. I made it. It is here*, and to move forward through its doors without ever stopping. Except for Jonathan—he's been waiting. There are only a few more seconds to do what he has to do. Brakes squeal as the F train enters the terminal. The woman with the large handbag who he bumped into is nowhere around; she was heading for a train farther down the terminal, maybe the G or the C, but not the F. The F comes every seven minutes. Jonathan takes his canvas shoulder bag off his shoulder and steps forward to the platform's very edge. He turns the bag upside down and empties the papers within and the laptop within onto the tracks and then the train is there on top of them, ripping the papers to shreds or whatever and devouring the laptop's metal frame, and in front of Jonathan the doors open and he steps in.

His key still works. The apartment smells rejected.

He hasn't spoken to the super in three months but was

making automated rent payments while living in his parents' house. Things are like he left them.

He turns on the lights and turns up the digital thermostat, even though it is not cold, and grabs a dusty tumbler from one cupboard and a dusty half-empty bottle of brandy from another and pours. It is 5:37 PM. He caps the bottle, drinks from the tumbler, uncaps the bottle, pours and drinks another and recaps the bottle again.

Maybe he should get a dog.

When he was thirteen he and his parents had a dog, a boxer with a hint of black lab. Midnight fur with a nose that looked like it had been dipped in snow and pointy ears that sat flat but still sort of hung back on the side of her head. A tail that had been dipped in stars. Knee-high and warm. Excitable and excited always, except when she was sleeping or you were sleepy and needed a pillow to rest your head on and she'd provide that pillow in exchange for a scratching of her pink and white belly. She died at three, hit by a car, even though never before that day had she wandered into the street alone.

Jonathan leaves the capped bottle of brandy and the dirty tumbler on the counter.

Off the bed he rips the sheets and comforter, and off the pillows he tears the cases, and all—sheets and cases and comforter—he throws into a garbage bag, which he sets by the door to be taken for laundering tomorrow. From the bedroom's closet he produces a new comforter and new sheets and new pillow cases and realizes that they're probably just as stale as the ones he's torn off the bed. He walks into the bathroom and pisses, eyes closed, starting and stopping, missing the bowl by a couple inches twice. He doesn't zip his pants but instead takes them off and tosses them by the shower and wanders back into the bedroom. He does not draw the curtains to let the twilight in. He collapses onto the bed. He stays there for thirty-nine hours before getting up and showering and purchasing food and a new laptop.

WHY YOU KEEP GOING IS MORE IMPORTANT THAN WHY YOU STARTED

STANDING IN LINE, WAY IN the back of the line, last in line for a small handful of moments until more people get in line behind her, Rachel Gilpatrick has been wanting to ride this particular ride all day.

When her friend from the fast food restaurant where she works part time first called her and said, "Hey, I've got an extra ticket to Kennywood amusement park. You wanna go?" Rachel at first wanted to decline the offer—she isn't one for amusement parks—but then she remembered that they had recently opened up this new ride at the amusement park that the friend had the tickets to, and it was just like the ride at this one other amusement park that she'd been to about three years ago with a whole different group of people in a whole other life, and so she said yes, she'd love to go, against her initial inclination. And now she's here in line, finally, for the attraction for which she specifically came, and the rest of the group—the initial friend and three others whom she hardly knows—are tired, they said, and so they're sitting this one out. It's likely that after Rachel finishes this ride the day will be over and she and the rest of the group will leave, maybe grab a bite to eat on the way home. Maybe they'll stop at Applebee's. The group will have to drop Rachel off at her home because she doesn't have a car. There are probably a few hundred people in the line ahead of her. Probably three hundred. Maybe two-fifty. All kinds of people.

This particular attraction that Rachel's been waiting to ride isn't a roller coaster, per se—it's better described as a thrill ride. How the ride works is that it's this big wheel with seats all around its circumference (about forty seats, according to Rachel's eyes, which then raises the question of why the hell this line is moving so slowly, and the only explanation for that is that one or both of Rachel's counts is wrong, i.e. there are less than forty seats around the circle's circumference or there are more than three hundred people ahead of Rachel in the line, or possibly both, and so for a minute here Rachel begins to doubt her ability to eyeball numbers—either way the line is moving slowly, painfully slowly), and the big wheel has a dozen large metal spokes that meet at its center and merge to attach to one end of a metal rod, the other end of which is affixed to another rod, this one parallel to the ground, hundreds of meters above the ground, the ends of that one each being attached to two more rods that jut downward in a diagonal fashion and act as legs and are buried deep into the ground and held in place with thousands of gallons of cement. When the ride is activated, the circle swings in a large pendular arc, the apex of the arc being so high that those riding in the wheel are almost upside down, while also rotating on a ball bearing mechanism between the spokes and the tall metal rod in the center. The whole thing is very cool, and in Rachel's experience the feeling of being on this sort of thrill ride is nothing short of exhilarating. Last time she was on a ride like this she could, for a few minutes, forget everything else in her world, and that's something she wants to experience again, which is why she was willing to come to this amusement park with a group of people she barely knows and certainly doesn't like.

It will be a while before she gets to the front of the line and is able to board the ride, though, at least fifteen minutes by her potentially untrustworthy estimate, and so she's got nothing to do while she waits but watch the people around her.

It's a funny thing about amusement parks that even though there are thousands of people there, there are always certain people that during your day at the park you see over and over again in the lines, like somehow you're making the same decisions as them about which rides to ride and when to ride them, like your minds are in some sort of thrill-seeking sync. For Rachel Gilpatrick today it's been these young adults that are in the line in front of her now. There are four of them, three guys and a girl. The girl looks about Rachel's age, maybe a couple years younger, and has long dirty-blonde hair that she's pulled up into a pony tail, presumably to keep it out of her eyes on this sunny but windy day. Rachel has been having hair troubles of her own today, troubles that have been almost the sole preoccupation of her thoughts ever since she and her group first arrived at the park and one of them took a picture of her on a cell phone and then showed her the result and she noticed that her long hair, which is brown and actually isn't that long but the bangs of which still manage to cover her entire forehead, really is noticeably thin, which she's been afraid of for over a year now, and in the photograph, which was taken at such an angle that the top of her head is visible in the shot, her scalp can be clearly seen through the hair in several places. The preoccupation with her hair got even worse when the group went on a water ride—this boat that travels on a track up a hill and then plunges towards the water below, creating a massive splash that soaks everyone in the boat and also any parkgoers who happen to be standing on this nearby bridge—and her head was downright soaked and her hair hung in her face and stuck out to the side and became tangled within itself, and when she went into one of the park's many restrooms after riding the water ride she caught a glimpse of her reflection in the mirror and realized that, when wet, her hair was stringy and wiry and her pale white scalp was visible all over, and so she decided, fuck it, she's just going to shave it all off tomorrow. And so now all day that's what she's been thinking about: shaving her head, embracing her thinning hair, becoming a voluntary chrome dome, wondering if her head is even the right shape. If men will think she's attractive anymore. If men ever thought she was attractive or if her pudginess has repelled them. She's never had a boyfriend, after all. She's eighteen years old.

The girl in the group that Rachel's been running into all day has a long ponytail and is very thin in a way that Rachel is jealous of, and her skin is tan and plastic yellow sunglasses hang from her shirt's plunging v-neck collar. The three boys with her all look more or less the same: red hair, freckles, whiskered chins, backwards ball caps that say "Braves" on them even though this amusement park is in a suburb of Pittsburgh, t-shirts with street-art style prints on them, torn jeans, tennis shoes. It's likely that the three young men are brothers, if not triplets, but their age is harder to pin down than the girl's. They can't be much older than her, but it's obvious that they are, indeed, older. And yet somehow the girl comes off to Rachel as far more mature than them. It's clear to Rachel, who admittedly isn't great at social cues, that this girl is in a sexual relationship with one of the brothers, but exactly which one would be damn near impossible to tell by anyone just now seeing her the first time with the way she's flirting with each and hanging her arms around the necks of each individual brother in turn and looking into his eyes when she gets tired of standing, which she's been doing a lot of today, and which Rachel knows she's been doing a lot of because she and the three young men have been in several of the lines Rachel's been in, and Rachel's been standing a lot today, too.

The line to the thrill ride scoots forward suddenly and by a large amount, and now Rachel is standing in this dimly lit wooden tunnel.

So Rachel can't help but stare with more than casual interest at the young girl and the three red-haired young men and create a story for them.

She first saw them way back at the beginning of the day only a few minutes after the park opened at 10 AM. The girl, whose name Rachel imagines is Stacey because she looks like a Stacey, arrived at the park with the three boys. In Rachel's imagination Stacey is currently dating Rob, the younger of the three brothers but only by a few minutes because the brothers are fraternal triplets. It's weird that the distinction when it comes to twins, triplets, etc. is identical or fraternal, because even if they're identical, they're still fraternal because they're brothers, and fraternal means something like in the manner of being brothers, assuming of course that the twins, triplets, etc. are male; if they're female, they should, Rachel believes, be called sororital twins, which, sororital, isn't even a word, but that's a whole separate issue. Sometimes Rachel's weight really bothers her and the hair thing is not helping.

So Stacey came to the park this morning with the three boys, the boy Rachel imagines being named Rob being Stacey's boyfriend. Even though Rob is her current boyfriend, the other boys, for whom Rachel has not been able to come up with believable names, have all dated her at some point in the past. The first thing they did after arriving at the park, besides purchasing their tickets and then using the bathroom, which is the actual first thing pretty much everyone does when they first arrive at an amusement park, was decide to ride the Sky Rocket, the first attraction most people choose to ride when visiting this park because it's located almost directly by the entrance and so gravitating toward it is just a natural thing. The line for the Sky Rocket was short because the park had just opened and the majority of the day's visitors had yet to arrive, so they were able to bypass the queue setup and rush to the ride's boarding building-type-thing, although they were yelled at, and indeed threatened to be evicted from the park, by a park attendant, a late 20-something man in a red park shirt, for jumping over the metal line dividers, which was still considered line jumping even if there was nobody there, man.

Stacey, in Rachel's mind, actually wasn't too happy to be there at the park this morning. She enjoyed being with Rob and all, but after everything that had happened in the past, Rob's brothers were the people she was least interested in spending the day with, and they tended to treat her, even at the beginning of the day, with a general disrespect, a disrespect that even Rob showed to her, but that she was in that instance oblivious to because of the hormones of teenage lust or whatever you wanted to call it. In line for the Skyrocket the oldest of the triplets asked

Rob loudly if Stacey still gave head as good as she did when he, the oldest triplet, dated her.

Rachel's never had that sort of physical contact with another person before.

"Come on, man," Rob said, laughing, while Stacey looked irritated.

"I'm jus' playin'. I'm jus' playin'," the oldest said. "Tell your girl to lighten up." And then he looked at Stacey and said, "I know you miss me."

And then they boarded the Sky Rocket, Rob and Stacey sitting in the row second from the front and the other two in the very front row, the most coveted row on roller coasters despite it being the row where all the bugs hit you in the face. That was the last Rachel saw of them on that ride because she was directly behind them and so when she and her group boarded and rode and then got off, the boys and the girl who she imagined was named Stacey were long gone.

To be fair to amusement park bugs, it's actually you who hits them; they're just trying to live their lives.

Now the line for the thrill ride that Rachel's been waiting to ride all day moves forward again. She's in the middle of the tunnel. She can hear an automated voice on a loudspeaker outside but can't make out what it's saying, not even close.

Rachel saw the group of young adults again an hour after the Sky Rocket, at about 11:30 AM, in the somewhat-long line for the Jack Rabbit. Stacey and Rob were both soaked from head to toe, but the other two were dry. Rachel imagined that they must have been on the Pittsburgh Plunge (the aforementioned ride that's a descent into a pool of water) at some point between the Sky Rocket and the Jack Rabbit, and in fact it was likely that it was the only ride they'd been on in that time, because the process of standing in line for and then riding the Plunge and then moseying on over to another ride and standing in that line and riding that ride would have taken too much time, and but then Rachel wondered what they'd done between the Plunge and the Jack Rabbit, since while there wouldn't have been time to ride another ride, there would still have been plenty of time to do *something*. Rachel decided that they must have ridden the Plunge twice, then. Although that didn't explain what the two dry boys had been doing in the meantime.

Standing in line for the Jack Rabbit, one of the red-headed boys continued to harass Stacey, asked her again if she gave head to Rob the same way she used to give it to him, and then he told her she really did give good head and he missed it, and then he looked at the third brother and said, "Didn't she give good head, man?"

The third brother just grinned, his pathetically thin and pale mustache curling up with his lips.

Rob hit both brothers on their shoulders with playful fists. "I said come on, guys, leave her alone." During this exchange no one used names, so Rachel as she watched continued thinking of them with the names she'd assigned them in her head.

Stacey looked more annoyed than before. Her shirt, Rachel thought, might not have been the best choice for riding water rides. Rachel doesn't have this problem because her breasts never quite developed.

And then they were on the Jack Rabbit, this time at the same time as Rachel, who rode with her friend from work. The friend tried to make pleasant conversation with Rachel while the Jack Rabbit's operators went through a set of routine safety checks, but Rachel was distracted by the issue of her thinning hair and failed to respond to most of the friend's small talk. And when the Jack Rabbit started, going from zero to 120 in 3.7 seconds, nobody talked and everybody except for Rachel screamed with excitement and manufactured fear.

She saw them again a few hours later, this time at the Thunderbolt, an old wooden coaster, one of the oldest in the country, and there she saw something that surprised her. Rob wasn't with the party, but instead it was just Stacey and the two older brothers. Stacey wasn't speaking to either of them, and she looked downright pissed and offended, disgusted even.

Back in the present, the line moves forward again and Rachel and the young people, on whom her attention is still fixed, her reverie barely broken by the queue's progression, are outside the tunnel. On the other side of the tunnel are three long lines of people standing in a zigzag pattern, waiting, and Rachel realizes that the wait is going to be even longer than she thought. She can hear words coming from the loudspeaker near the ride as riders board, but she can't make out more than muffled intonations.

The thing about the Thunderbolt is that, because it's such an old coaster, the ride is bumpy. On the wall near the area where you board the ride is a big wooden sign that says, RIDERS MUST RIDE IN PAIRS—NO SINGLE RIDERS, which really isn't fair to have the sign placed there because once you've gotten to the point where you can see it you've already been standing in line for several hundred feet, including a set of stairs.

Stacey and the two obnoxious brothers saw the sign and Stacey groaned and threw her arms up and said, "Forget it. You guys ride. I'm done."

The brother who Rachel imagines is the oldest, the one doing most of the day's harassing, grabbed Stacey by the arm, and Stacey shouted "Get off me, asshole!"

Several people turned to see what the commotion was, but then the brother who'd grabbed her said, "Wait. You ride—I'll sit this one out."

"No, no," she said. "You guys ride. I'm fucking done. This day was a mistake."

"Please," the oldest brother said. "I insist. I insist."

They argued for several long seconds about this, and it didn't seem like Stacey was going to soften her position.

The older of the two brothers looked at his sibling, his face imploring, genuinely pained. The younger brother shrugged as if to say, "Sorry, Bro. I've got nothin'." But then he paused.

The younger brother turned in a circle, looking at the rest of his fellow line-goers until he spotted close by a young boy of about twelve with a young girl about the same age. He said something quietly to the two kids that Rachel couldn't make out, and the girl looked at the ride with longing for a moment and then looked back and shook her head. The younger brother reached into his pocket and pulled out a five dollar bill and said something else and held it out to the girl, who smiled and took it and kissed her little friend on the cheek and left the line. The younger brother stood up and turned to Stacey and pointed at the twelve-year-old boy. "This here is Jake. Jake's gonna ride the Thunderbolt with you today. His girlfriend said it's okay." And Stacey actually smiled.

Now, a few hours later, the girl who Rachel imagines is named Stacey hangs from the shoulders of the guy who she imagines is named Rob. The other brothers are again making sexual jokes about Stacey, but when they do it now, she's just rolling her eyes in response, something in them gleaming playfully and mischievously and hinting at alcohol and at the night to come.

And so Rachel Gilpatrick waits in line. The sun is setting over the river because the sun always sets over water. The line moves at a glacial but steady pace, every ten minutes or so growing shorter, Rachel getting closer. She can see the ride beyond the queue, can observe that the holdup is that every time the time comes for new riders to board, a significant portion of the new riders struggle with their seat's safety harness and belt mechanism, so the ride's two operators have to make their way around the circle and help the confused riders, one at a time, with the equipment.

In the eastern sky the moon rises from behind the trees. The eastern sky grows darker, bluer, a little less real or more real or something that Rachel can't pinpoint. There are two small girls beside Rachel. She's now on the final zag but the girls are still on the zig. They're with adults, but the adults are paying them little attention. The girls stare at the attraction in awe as it swings and spins and swings and spins. One of them looks frightened, and the other says, "Scared?"

And the first one says, "No, I'm not scared. You're scared."

And the second one says, "I don't get scared. You're the scared one, you weenie."

"I'm not a weenie. You're a weenie."

"Weenie."

"Weenie!"

Back and forth they try to insult each other, throwing the insult like a verbal wiffleball: softly and ineffectively and without malice.

The ride slows, stops, lets off its passengers. Those standing at the front of the line shuffle their feet, push against the gate, ready for their turn, but one of the operators holds out a hand as if to say wait, please and opens another gate to the side. A woman in a wheelchair is pushed through by a friend. She's pushed up to one of the circle's seats and with her arms pushes on the wheelchair's armrests so her body hovers, and she swings up and over and into the ride's seat with practiced ease. She pulls the harness down and fastens the belt with neither trouble nor confusion. Her friend wheels the wheelchair next to these little cubbies where riders are supposed to leave belongings at your own risk, and then she joins the woman on the ride.

The operator opens the gate. Parkgoers pour through. By the time the gate is closed again Rachel is only ten people behind the very front of the line. Next time will be her turn.

Operator one looks at operator two, signals an all-clear with an upward thumb.

Over the speaker the message which before was muffled. Rachel can hear it now, not exactly crystal because sound equipment is not first on most amusement parks' list of priorities, but clear enough:

"Heeeeelo riders! Welcome to the . . . *spppfft* . . . be advised that any loose items or articles are not permitted on this ride. If you have any loose items or articles please place them in one of the designated bins by the wall or leave them with a non-rider. Sandals, flip-flops, and other unsecured shoes are not permitted on this ride. Please leave your shoes directly beneath your seat and pick them up when the ride comes to an end. Keep your arms within the vicinity of your seat at all times and do not pull up on your safety harness. Thank you and enjoy the ride."

Rachel watches as the ride spins up first and then begins to swing. She watches it move before her. She stares, transfixed until it's over and her turn to board.

Through the gate now. The sky is dark. All things told she stood in line for maybe sixty-five long minutes, alone amongst all these people. The seat is hard and uncomfortable like they always are on thrill rides and she sits with her spine in pain against it. She snaps the buckle into place, pulls the steel and foam harness over her head and to her chest. This is not comfortable. Feet dangle. Again the poor-quality prerecorded message. A black lady is in the seat next to the left of her on the circle, yelling, presumably at her companion, whom Rachel can't see because of the circle's curvature, that the companion is a pussy and this ride ain't that bad at all and you'll see.

Again the ride begins to move, this time with Rachel gloriously on it. It swings and spins, slow at first, building momentum, mechanically powered but still at the mercy of simple physics. It picks up speed. The arc of the swing grows until at the top Rachel is nearly upside down and she can see the river and the rest of the park and the stars all in the same sweeping view. She can see the sky opening. There are stars up there. She wonders about the red-headed young men and the girl whom she imagines is named Stacey and decides that however their night ends is how their night will end. The black woman is yelling, "Oh shit! Oh shit! Oh shit!" Rachel feels the free fall. There's that sense that at any moment the pendulum could snap and the giant metal circle with all the seats and riders could just be launched to who-knows-where. The wind is cold against her head, blowing her thin hair. When this ride is over Rachel will go get something to eat with her group and then she'll go back home to her father. Bernard is divorced now and is a full-blown alcoholic. A few months after Rachel's sister ran away, her father walked in on Rachel's mother and Uncle Randy fucking. He had a massive heart attack that nearly killed him. He would be incapable of taking care of himself if Rachel weren't there to keep an eye on him. When Rachel was fourteen years old she went through a period where she cut her arms with a razor blade almost daily and no one noticed. Rachel thinks back to the redheaded boys and the girl who she imagines is named Stacy. How much of them is real? Now the black woman is screaming, "This ride is titty! This ride is titty! This ride is titty!"

ADULT

FOR THE FIRST THREE WEEKS after she left Pittsburgh and hopped on the Greyhound to New York City, Melissa Lynn Gilpatrick was officially a runaway, at least from a legal standpoint, although as far as she knows the police never pursued her or tried to bring her back home, but she likes to imagine her family, her father at least, tried to find her, like maybe he called the police and they said she was too old for them to bother; her decision was hers, maybe the police had said. Then she turned eighteen and called her high school and requested the paperwork needed to withdraw herself, and they emailed her the papers and she used a computer at the New York Public Library to fill them out—save for the portion requesting her current address, which she didn't have at the time, staying as she was those first few weeks in a shelter for battered women, pretending to be a battered woman in solidarity with the other women and children in the shelter—and sign them electronically, and then she closed that email account so she wouldn't be bothered by messages from anyone who had it ever again. Her phone stopped receiving cellular service two weeks after the last day she showed up for work at the call center, although she could still use it to connect to WiFi in coffee shops.

The day she turned eighteen the very first thing she did was find a local branch of the bank she banked with and had her stepmother removed from the joint savings account they'd opened when she first started working. This was easier than it should have been—Melissa signed Polly's name and the banker did not ask for ID. By virtue of the fact that her stepmother had never let her spend her own money, Melissa had, after a few months' work, just over five thousand dollars saved.

Through one of the volunteers at the battered women's shelter Melissa found a tiny sublet in SoHo for eight hundred dollars per month. She didn't know enough about the city then to appreciate that finding any apartment at that price was a miracle. She signed a month-to-month lease with the subletter, paying the first month's rent and a security deposit in cash. The place had brick walls and one very small main room plus a bathroom and a two-burner stove, but it came furnished with a futon and a table, and Melissa bought two plates and a skillet and a saucepan and a small set of water glasses and, eventually, a pair of nail-clippers. When first setting out on their own, everybody always forgets they'll need their own pair of nail-clippers. With an address now she opened a checking account and got a debit card and applied for a credit card which she vowed to use only in emergencies, emergencies she hoped would never happen but she couldn't be too careful because her life had for a minute there turned into one big emergency, hadn't it? At first Melissa didn't see the studio most days until early morning, her nights spent at any club that would give her alcohol without checking her I.D. At a club called Sparks, about a month after she ran away from home, she met a group of four women a few years older than her who took her under their collective wing. "Well aren't you just adorable," one of them told her on the first night she met them when they found her sitting alone at the wood-top bar ordering a vodka-something while trying to sound like she was supposed to be ordering it. "Don't let them give you the well liquor here," another of the women said. "They water it down in a way that's just shameful." Melissa didn't know what the difference was between well liquor and any other kind of liquor—in retrospect, her naiveté in certain matters was obvious to probably everyone but herself—but the women would let her have none of it, buying her three Stoli martinis that night. Stoli sounded at the time to Melissa far too masculine a name for a woman to be drinking, but what did she know? She did not tell the women her story, and they did not ask. They knew only that she was young and new to the city. She got their names but forgot them promptly. For several weeks she followed them to all the hip places. She never called them (she still had no working phone) or saw them outside of the city's nightlife; they would simply as they left each club or party make plans with her for next time, and she would go according to the plan, and they would be there, ready to help her live. They gave her marijuana, which she thought was okay. They gave her more marijuana, which she thought was better. They gave her Molly, which she got so high on she couldn't remember the night before and decided it was an experience she might be cool with repeating on limited occasions. They gave her cocaine, but she couldn't get past the idea of snorting something through her nose and thus never tried it.

Melissa bought new clothes, just a few outfits, nothing too

special and yet still far nicer and sexier than she ever had before. In these clothes she felt confident, stronger. In her independence she was brave and capable and powerful. She felt lonely only sometimes. She did not miss anyone.

At a club called Ethel's or Easel's or something like that, she met a man. He was tall and dark and all of those usual things, maybe thirty years old, handsome, with a chiseled jaw because why not, and he wore a suit that was either dark blue or black but looked dark blue under the club's azure lights, and he seemed to beckon to her in the shadow of the dance floor's electric pulse. After the weeks of exploration, Melissa still did not feel herself a natural dancer—she was awkward and had no rhythm and her body didn't want to move—but under the influence of most things she found the music had a way of possessing her, controlling her, moving her. The man's name was something, he told her; she did not hear it. He moved her hips against him. It was time, she felt, and so she yelled "Hold on a minute!" over the bass and moved to the bar to order a very large glass of very cold water. She drank it, patted her cheeks, and then found the man still on the floor; he had not moved on to anybody else. She took his hand and asked if there was somewhere they could go. They took a cab three or four blocks and an elevator up a dozen stories and he did not yet touch her, but upstairs, once they arrived in his apartment, she kissed him. It struck her then that this was her first kiss. It tasted more like salt and food than she'd been led to believe and less like cinnamon or peppermint. The first time he did not remove his pants and she did not remove her clothes but simply pushed out of the way what needed pushed out of the way, and he did not use protection but pulled out when he was ready. Then they had a glass of wine and talked about everything but themselves.

"You've been in New York how many weeks now and haven't been to any museums? I'm surprised."

"I know. I know. I really need to get to the Met, I'm told."

"Well the Met is obvious," he said. "You should go, of course, but there are other, better museums in the city. The Frick, for example. I'm a member of the collection and could . . ." he trailed off. Melissa said nothing. She didn't know for sure what it was he had started to say—probably that he could take her along or get her in for free one day—but they both knew that wasn't what this was.

The second time, they both took off all their clothes and he wore a condom. Also the third time he wore one. She slept that night in his big white bed in his big white apartment. In the morning he called her a cab, kissed her on the cheek. She did not see him again. Neither did she see again the women with whom she'd been hanging out the last few weeks. She'd left them behind at Ethel's or Easel's the night before and had no number or address at which to reach them, and while she went out on her own a few more times, she did not run into them. She slept with two more men, only one of them more than once. She stopped going to the clubs regularly soon after that—her time in that scene, she felt, was already over.

After two months in the city, Melissa had spent thirty-five hundred dollars of her five grand. She needed to do something about cash flow, didn't she? And as nice as the respite from work had been, she did not feel whole. She'd never felt whole, of course, and never exactly would, but she had to keep searching for wholeness. She couldn't forever spend her days sleeping and her nights cavorting with the so-called glitterati. It was not sustainable. They weren't even the real glitterati she'd been cavorting with anyway—the real glitterati didn't hang out in clubs with security lax enough to let minors in or with bartenders dumb enough to serve them alcohol. She needed to get a job. She was prepared for the search, but she was not looking forward to it. She went to the library (she had a library card now, having her own address, and felt liberated every time she handed it over along with a stack of books to a librarian instead of having to sneak the books into a bag and make off with them like a criminal) and used their computer to type and print a résumé. She fudged the details a little: she included her old friend Jessica's family friend's deli under work experience, even though he hadn't hired her, and she skewed the dates she'd worked at the call center so it looked as if she'd spent an entire year there, and under reason for leaving she put simply "personal"; she had no references so she made up three names and three Pittsburgh phone numbers; under skills she typed that she was personable, hard-working, good with computers, passionate about everything she set her mind to, and comfortable talking to people on the phone; she included her Twitter profile at the bottom for good measure. She printed the résumé. She did not have high hopes. Her plan was to secure an interview, somewhere, and then bank on the fact that she was new to the city and young and full of life. And in the meantime, while she waited who knew how long for the job search to play out, she'd live as frugally as possible, pay for only rent and food, eat ramen noodles if she had to—she could get by for at least a couple months that way.

She was hired as a barista at the first place she tried. It turns out New York is always hungry for baristas.

The place was quaint and warm and popular with the city's cadre of students and young professionals. The pay wasn't a ton or anything, but it was enough that, as long as she worked full-time hours and volunteered to pick up shifts when someone else called off, Melissa wouldn't have to touch the rest of her savings. Melissa fell in love with exactly two things in New York City, and both affairs were sparked as a direct result of working at that coffee shop.

Melissa's first serious affair was with tea. A perk of the job was that baristas received free coffee or tea—their choice—each week. The first week Melissa chose coffee, even bought a coffee pot so she could make coffee in her apartment, and they gave her a full pound of single-origin from the Sidamo region in Ethiopia (which she learned as part of her training at the coffee shop that Ethiopia is where the coffee bean originated, so this was supposed to be, like, good stuff). She'd never liked coffee when she lived back home. She drank it sometimes, whenever her father made a pot he didn't finish and she got curious, or after that party when she had that hangover, but each time she couldn't see why people drank it. But now—now might be different, because she was an adult now, on her own, independent, and coffee, what was supposed to be the *best* coffee, struck her as the sort of thing she should be enjoying; but she did not enjoy it. She took home another pound of coffee her second week, this batch from somewhere in Argentina; she did not like it, either. And so her third week she took home a bag of loose-leaf black tea and brewed it and, though she found it bitter, liked it much better than the coffee. She brewed a second cup, letting the bag steep not quite as long this time, and found it not bitter at all. From there she tried all kinds of teas: reds and white and Pu-erh and herbals made with things like cardamom and dandelion and even chocolate. She educated herself deeply about tea, about origins and varieties and histories, about ceremonies and brewing methods, and she started educating her customers about tea, too. After just a month at the coffee shop, she received a raise, and the owner asked her if she would become the shop's official tea buyer. Could she bring in better teas than the ones they were selling now? Maybe teach a workshop on tea from time to time, like maybe monthly? She said yes with enthusiasm. It seemed like tea might be Melissa's thing. She'd always wanted to be one of those people who had a thing.

Melissa's second serious love affair in New York City developed concurrently with the first and was with a person, a woman. Melissa met her at the start of her first day at the shop, about an hour before it was scheduled to open for the morning. The owner made the introduction.

"Melissa, this is Evangeline. She's one of my very best baristas and she's going to be responsible for training you over the next week or so."

"Oh," Melissa said. "You're not training me?" She'd liked the owner, a middle-aged, balding man named Ramit, as soon as she'd met him, as soon as he hired her and smiled his very white smile.

"No," he said, "No no no. No no. I'm not in the shop much, you see. I'm opening an Italian restaurant in the East Village—very exciting, something I've been waiting my whole life to do, a dream come true, you see—and it's keeping me very busy."

"That sounds wonderful," Melissa said, finding it impossible to not be interested in Ramit's endeavors. "When will it open?"

"Oh my, oh my. Soon, I hope, but there's still so much to do. I'm still courting potential chefs, and the decor has to be finalized, and then the menu, and then the decor will probably have to change to match the menu, and then there's finding the best sommelier . . . . But anyway, Evangeline is wonderful. She's been here for almost two years and knows everything there is to know about the place. I will, of course, drop in, from time to time, but Evangeline is my right-hand man these days. Don't know what I'd do without her. She'll take good care of you. Good care. But I must go now. I have to go. I found out just this morning that the upholstery for the restaurant's chairs is all wrong. Oh, and how am I ever going to come up with a name for the place . . ."

When he'd left, Melissa finally looked at Evangeline, who smiled at her. "Let me start by showing you around."

"There's no one else here," Melissa said, while Evangeline led her behind the bar. It was just after 7 AM; the shop opened at 8.

"We usually operate on a pretty small staff, just two or three people at a time, usually. Just one, sometimes, although Ramit tries to avoid that as much as possible. It'll be just you and me this morning."

"Just us?" Melissa said, sounding more nervous than she'd meant to.

Evangeline smiled. "Just us. Don't worry—we're not too busy in the morning. Places like Starbucks open earlier than us and are much faster, so they get the morning rush; we get the people who have time to slow down and care about their beverage, so we get fewer people. There's a bit of a pop around noon, lunch-break time, but another barista will be in by then, so there will be three of us for that."

Melissa must have still looked nervous, because Evangeline said, "Don't worry, I have a feeling you can handle me on your own until then." And then she winked.

Melissa blushed.

All morning Melissa struggled to keep her eyes off Evangeline. All week she quickly looked away every time

Evangeline caught her staring. Melissa knew Evangeline was older than her, but she didn't know exactly how old—twenty-four? twenty-five?—and she found herself wanting to know that and more, and she must have been more than a little obvious about this desire because on the Friday of that first week, while they were closing up together, Melissa cleaning the espresso machine and Evangeline counting the money in the register, Evangeline said, "Hey, do you want to hang out?"

"Hang out?" Melissa said. "Like a party?"

Evangeline laughed. "No. Ha. No party. Just me and you, drinks, talking. Et cetera."

Melissa paused her dismantling of the espresso maker. As far as she could recall, this was the first time in her life someone had asked for her exclusive company. "Tonight?"

"Yeah," Evangeline said, still chuckling. "Tonight. Like in a few minutes here when we're finished."

Melissa stood for a moment very still. There was something unidentifiable deep inside of her that in this moment she had to choose to overcome. "Yeah. Yeah, okay."

"Okay then. That's what I'm talking about."

Two hours later they were in bar a block away from the coffee shop. It was Melissa's first time in a place like this bar, dingy and dark with loud rock music playing in the background, the air smoky, but not really smoky because nobody inside was smoking or was allowed to smoke, but it felt like it should be smoky and therefore was—there was some sort of haze in Melissa's periphery. There'd been no cover to get in. The place was only half full on Friday night. The drinks were better, much better, than the drinks in any of the clubs she'd been to. Melissa sipped something with tequila and Goldschläger that the bar's menu said was an original concoction called a Marry Me, which

Evangeline had ordered for her so she wouldn't have to risk being carded.

Evangeline was twenty-four. "I came here, to New York, when I was eighteen, for school. I wanted to be an actor. I still do. I mean, I *am* an actor. You should always, I've learned, talk about yourself as if you already are what you want to be—things come quicker to you that way."

"What have you acted in?" Melissa asked.

"Well, nothing. Yet. Besides student productions and one-off little stage shows. I'm still in school, you see. I'm finishing up my BFA at the Tisch at NYU. I'll be done in a month, in June."

"Congratulations. You must be"—Melissa didn't know how to carry this sort of conversation—"excited."

"I am excited. Very excited."

Not only was Melissa inexperienced in holding a conversation like this one, in figuring out how to learn about a person, but it didn't help that the person about whom she wanted to learn she also found extremely attractive. There was something about the pink stripes in Evangeline's dark hair, about the ring in her left nostril, about the way she balanced it with light-colored, loose-fitting tops and tight jeans. Her eyes were nothing special, but for some reason they were what Melissa liked most: there seemed to be experience in them, age.

"It took me longer than I originally planned," Evangeline was saying, "to finish school. I took a semester off to save money. And I extended the course load of my last two semesters to four, to make things easier, so I could balance work at the shop with education. And it didn't help that the American education system is fucked, that it's all so fucking expensive."

"Yeah," Melissa agreed. This was something she'd read about, and from her reading she could cobble together an opinion. "The government needs to step in and help cover the costs."

"What? Fuck no. That's the last thing we need, more government. If the government got more involved in education the future of every student would belong to them. There'd be no one left to officiate future change because their sponsors wouldn't want an overturning of the system."

That made sense. Evangeline was smart.

"And that's not to even mention art," Evangeline said. "Degrees like mine would be a thing of the past. It would be freaking *1984* in this country. Almost already is."

"I've read that book!" Melissa nearly shouted, jerking her head up from the Marry Me, the tiny black straw, which she'd been playing with, catching in her teeth embarrassingly. She pulled the straw out, rolled it between her fingers in a way that she thought maybe looked sophisticated.

Evangeline laughed. "It's so overrated, isn't it, that book?" she said.

Melissa frowned. She hadn't thought so. From what she'd always understood, *1984* was a classic, but maybe there was something she'd missed. "So overrated," she said.

"Of course I've never actually read it, though, but if only Orwell were alive today, imagine his reaction to the world."

Melissa wasn't sure she understood, but at the same time she wanted this woman, older than her and artistic and with pink in her hair, to make a kind of sense, to be wise about the world, someone Melissa could learn from. So she agreed with her. "What kind of books do you read?" Melissa asked.

Evangeline was drinking a beer in a bottle. A local microbrew, she'd told Melissa. She took a sip as she answered. "I don't really read books, except for plays, but even those I'd mostly rather see, because it's the acting that I'm interested in as an actor, not the writing, you know? Even my news I'd rather get from people like John Stewart or Stephen Colbert than newspapers. You watch them?"

"I don't have a TV," Melissa said.

"Well, of course. Right? I mean I don't either. I watch my TV on the computer like most people."

"Yeah. Except I don't have a computer either. I'll probably get one soon."

"So then what do you do? When you're not working. You're not in school, right?"

"No, no school."

"You plan on starting in the fall, then."

Melissa was not about to divulge to this older, smarter woman that she hadn't completed high school, that she'd dropped out a few months before the end of her senior year. "Probably. Although I might take a year off first. See what happens."

Evangeline nodded, sipping her beer, which along with Melissa's Mary Me was almost empty. "You might be better off that way, what with the way the education system is."

"Right," Melissa said.

"Wait, though," Evangeline said. "But wait. You're how old? You're only eighteen, right? When did you finish high school?"

"Um, I was homeschooled, so I finished early."

Evangeline nodded again, even more approvingly than before. "So you're probably better off than most of the world, then, avoiding the whole fucked education system all together."

"I guess I am."

"And your parents?"

Melissa started. "Um . . ." And suddenly she was telling her story. She might have hammed things up a bit, might have made it sound more like her parents kicked her out than that she ran away, that she didn't have a choice, and she left out that she had a younger sister there, in that other place, whom she'd left behind, but telling the tale was invigorating, and when she was done she couldn't imagine why she'd been inclined to lie about it only moments ago. Maybe it was because, up until now, she'd assumed New York City didn't care about her past. And maybe it didn't, but could it be that some people did, that Evangeline did? Sure, if given the choice, she would prefer not to talk about it at all, but when asked wasn't it best to be honest?

Evangeline put a hand on Melissa's. Her fingernails were clipped short, painted purple. There was nothing electric in the touch, but there was warmth in it, comfort. "That's very brave, you know. You're very brave."

"I guess. I guess I am." Melissa hadn't thought of herself like that, but maybe it was true.

"Religion sucks, doesn't it?"

Melissa said, "What sort of acting do you plan on doing? After you get your BFA?"

"Stage," Evangeline replied immediately. "It'll take work, I know, but I'm going to be on Broadway. And then I'd love to move into movies from there too. Which is to say, I *am* in movies, right? Present tense."

Melissa smiled. Why not? She could live with present tense.

"Do you want another drink?" Evangeline asked. "I'm going to get another beer. These are my treat tonight."

Melissa said yes, she would like another drink, but not another Mary Me, which had been disgusting, she'd decided now that she was finished drinking it; she'd love one of whatever Evangeline was having. And so they drank, two more drinks each, dark, heady draughts that Evangeline said were "the best beer in the city," and they talked, and then they went their separate ways.

A week later they were sitting in Evangeline's apartment, her male roommate, Barry or Bart or Bertrum, out of town for the weekend visiting his family in Rhode Island or wherever. "Some people think it's weird when they find out I have a guy for a roommate," Evangeline had said on that first night in the bar during their final round of drinks, "but it's not because I don't exactly go for that sort of thing, I tell them, trying to be obvious but roundabout at the same time because people aren't always comfortable when I reveal that little detail to them, even in this city," and then she'd winked the same wink she had winked when Melissa met her the first morning at the coffee shop. They were watching musicals that Melissa had never seen (on the roommate's TV) and drinking beers and eating sushi. Evangeline was a vegetarian, except that she ate fish because "fish are ugly little fuckers; they don't even really count as animals." Melissa had recently started thinking about becoming a vegetarian, too.

First they watched *The Phantom of the Opera*. Evangeline at one point said she'd seen the Lon Chaney version and she really liked the changes Andrew Lloyd Webber had made, the way he'd made it his own, and one day she would star in one of his plays. Melissa, who had checked out of the library and read earlier in the week the original novel by Gaston Laroux, did not clarify that Andrew Lloyd Webber's story was a faithful adaptation of the book, that he had invented nothing. During the film a tension seemed to materialize in the room, something chilling and intriguing that Melissa had never quite felt before: little tendrils of sexual energy tickled her during "The Music of the Night," and during "The Point of No Return" Evangeline put significant effort into explaining the song's meaning, that the point of no return to which the characters referred was sex, like the actual act of fucking, and so the implication was that the viewer wasn't sure whether the song meant that The Phantom and Christine had already fucked on the night he'd whisked her away or whether they just wanted to. Melissa could have sworn Evangeline had done that wink again.

While they were watching musical number two, *Sweeney Todd*, Melissa felt the heat turn up inexplicably to a thousand. Evangeline moved closer to Melissa on the couch, saying this one always creeped her out and so she felt comforted by the contact of another person while watching it. Melissa never did see the majority of the film, because without even deciding to she turned her head and kissed Evangeline on the mouth. Evangeline pulled back and said, "Maybe you're a little young."

And Melissa, stunned and embarrassed, said, "I . . ."

And then Evangeline asked her, "Have you ever kissed a woman before?" And when Melissa said no, Evangeline said, "Let me show you how." And they made out while Helena Bonham Carter and Johnny Depp sang about how brilliant their respective characters were.

They took things slow. They did not have sex until two weeks later, at Melissa's place in her tiny bed, Evangeline complaining playfully of a lack of toys and mentioning that Melissa had a lot of education in her future.

In June, Evangeline finally graduated with her BFA and her roommate graduated too and thus moved away to take some job in Cuba, where apparently big strides were being made these days in sustainable energy research. Melissa and Evangeline were fondling each other on Evangeline's couch when Evangeline mentioned that she wasn't sure what she was going to do with the apartment now, because she still needed another roommate, at least until her acting career took off— she couldn't cover the rent on her own with the money she was making at the coffee shop, even if Ramit had essentially made her the manager now. "Maybe . . ." Evangeline said, "but, no. Never mind, that's silly."

"What is it?" Melissa asked, rolling one of Evangeline's nipples between her fingers.

Evangeline hesitated for another moment, but it didn't seem like real hesitation. "You wouldn't want to, I don't know, move in with me, would you?"

Melissa grinned. "Of course I would. I would love to. If you want me to."

"I definitely want you to."

They kissed, both laughing.

The moving process was quick and painless; Melissa had very few possessions that required transferring, and because she was paying month-to-month on her place in SoHo she had no trouble leaving. On her first night in the apartment she now shared with Evangeline, while they lay in the bed they'd just christened, bathing in the afterglow, Melissa almost said, "I love you," right then and there but held back because she wasn't sure saying it would be appropriate or if it was even true yet, but either way she was happy.

And like that she was in a real relationship. She felt more like an adult than she ever had before, and from that adulthood, from the fact that she'd achieved it in only a few short months on her own, she derived a smug satisfaction. If only Bernard and Polly could see her now, what they would think.

She and Evangeline worked a similar schedule at the coffee shop, so they were rarely one without the other, but this didn't cause a problem for them; on the contrary, Melissa felt like it only made their relationship stronger. Customers who were in the know about the situation commented often on what a great couple they were. Ramit, when he found out that his two favorite employees were romantically involved, was ecstatic: "Now if only I could find a man who completes me the way you two complete each other," he said, sighing wistfully, his eyes a little tearful. And the fact that they both worked at the coffee shop made certain things even easier, both of them benefiting in certain ways, ways like Melissa being able to cover things at the shop on mornings when Evangeline had an audition, or Melissa being able to pick up takeout from the vegan cafe down the street on her own on her way back to the apartment so Evangeline could rush home early to get started on a script of a commercial she'd just been sent, the audition for which was tomorrow morning can you believe it and they just emailed me the script today, or Evangeline being able to schedule dinners with actor friends and directors in whose projects she was trying to land a role on nights when Melissa was teaching one of her tea seminars so as to "minimally impact the time we get to spend together." There was a grand symbiosis at play in the universe, Evangeline liked to say: all the little particles fit together so perfectly.

Months went by. Ramit's restaurant was set to open in August, but August came and went. October, he said, it would open in late October now, because an inspector discovered a corroded set of pipes in the plumbing system and the whole thing would have to be replaced, necessitating the removal of large sections of two walls, in order for the water the pipes produced to be considered safe for cooking and human consumption. And the head chef, impatient, left. But then

Ramit, who was pouring all his money into a restaurant that it seemed would never open, money that came not from the profits of his coffee shop, which made not nearly enough to sustain a high-end Italian bistro, but from an inheritance, met a man who not only thought Ramit was just the greatest person in the world and wanted to be both his business and his life partner, but who also knew an Italian chef who had once come *this close* to being awarded a Michelin star. And so it was in January that Melissa and Evangeline were sitting in Ramit's Italian bistro, Antonito's ("the freshest thing to come to the East Village since that gluten-free bakery," according to the *New Yorker*), on the night of its grand opening, both dressed in black and Melissa having decided to try high heels for the first time in her life. "I plan to get very very drunk tonight," Evangeline had said in the cab on the way over. She'd had no success landing an acting job since graduating, not a one, and it was getting to her, and it was getting to Melissa, too, but in a different way. Evangeline's hair was without the pink streaks these days.

They dined on tofu-chicken soy-parmesan in a tangy tomato sauce with a side of capellini with olive oil and oregano. They drank red wine. Evangeline drank several glasses of red; Melissa drank just one—the more Evangeline drank lately, the less Melissa wanted to. Ramit appeared during dessert (tiramisu, which Melissa declined but Evangeline, who when drunk seemed to forget she was a vegan now, devoured), his arm inside the arm of a man with very short thin grey hair and thick glasses. "Ladies," Ramit said, "this is Merrell, the man I haven't been able to stop telling you about."

"Oh, please," Merrell said, pretending to hide embarrassment with his hands, "I hope he hasn't told you *too* much about me."

Melissa smiled graciously. "I'm afraid he's told us everything."

"Oh my, oh my. So you must have a terrible impression of me already, and we've only now just met."

"The impression we have is that Ramit likes you very much." Where Melissa had learned to be so charming she didn't know; it wasn't her natural disposition, but she'd become good at faking it when she met someone she liked. "Isn't that right, Evs?" She called Evangeline "Evs" now, for some reason.

"Very much so. The impression."

"Yes, yes, well . . ." Ramit said, his embarrassment childlike and endearing. "Oh. Evangeline!" he said. "That's right. I almost forgot. Merrell is a producer, on Broadway, and he's got this big new thing in production, and I told him all about what a wonderful actress you are and he thinks you should come down and audition for it on Sunday."

Merrell smiled. "Yes, absolutely. You both should come down."

"I'm not an actor," Melissa said. "Evangeline's the—"

"No no, you should do it." Evangeline put a hand on Melissa's arm. "You should." She looked at Merrell and Ramit. "She should audition. We both will."

"Wonderful," Merrell replied. "We'll see you Sunday then. Ramit will give me your email addresses so I can make sure you get the script beforehand."

The cab ride home from the restaurant's grand opening was uneasy, the discomfort inexplicable.

They auditioned, both of them, first Melissa and then, while Melissa waited for her outside the audition room with a half-dozen other hopefuls ("other" not entirely accurate, because Melissa was hopeful of nothing and had auditioned because why not), Evangeline. Ten minutes after she'd gone in Evangeline came out looking unhappy.

"What's the matter? How'd it go?" Melissa asked.

"It could have gone better. I think I blew it. Let's just go home and fuck."

They were fucking more than ever these days. Evangeline would come home from an audition and they'd fuck. Evangeline would go to dinner with someone with whom she'd gone to school and who was trying to get people together for a project; she'd come home and they'd fuck. The phone would ring and Evangeline would pick it up and nod while being told she hadn't gotten a part and she'd hang up, and then they'd fuck. The sex was angry. Brutal. On both sides. Evangeline taking out the frustrations generated by her becoming-more-and-more-obvious-it's-not-gonna-happen career and Melissa taking out frustrations generated by she had no idea the hell what. Maybe Melissa's anger was merely a reflection of Evangeline's anger; maybe it was coming from something else deep inside. Whatever the source, it made for fantastic sex. They never talked anymore. Had they ever really talked to begin with? About each other they knew so little.

Evangeline did not get a role in Merrell Whippo's play. Melissa was cast as a member of the chorus and asked if she'd be interested in understudying the lead.

"I'm happy for you," Evangeline said as they lay one night in bed after one of the most intense sessions they'd ever had. "I'm really happy for you. I think we should break up."

Melissa said nothing for several minutes. She did not cry or sniffle, and she blinked only twice.

"What's the matter?" Evangeline asked her.

"Do things ever feel broken to you?"

"All the time. Like nothing works the way it's supposed to,

or the way you think it's going to. Why, I sometimes bother . . . I sometimes wonder . . . I sometimes wonder why we bother to expect anything to happen at all."

"That," Melissa said. "Sure. But it's not exactly what I mean. I meant broken as in, I don't know, shattered. *Crash!* Y'know?"

"Like glass."

"Like glass."

"I guess, sometimes."

"All the time, for me. Today anyway. Probably won't feel that way tomorrow. But then maybe I will again the next day."

"Do you want to fuck again?"

"Can we use the purple one?"

"Of course we can use the purple one, and the coconut-flavored."

"Well then sure. Let's do that then."

Forty-five minutes later, drenched in sweat, both. Bedsheets on the floor now, on the hardwood floor with its bumpy parts and its rough parts and its knotholes. They'd never fought, ever. What they were to each other was something nobody else was to anybody.

"So you think we should break up, Evs?" Melissa said, on her side, her arms pulled together, cheek pressing against her hands leaving an imprint.

"I think I hate you."

"But in a good way?"

"In the very best way."

There were also in-between moments—moments aside from the first meeting and the night in the bar and the movies and living together and the grand opening and the audition and tonight. There had to be, because that's how things work: chronologically. There are no gaps in the record, only the things you don't know about, the parts of the narrative they choose to not tell you.

When you're with someone, all you can think about is leaving them.

They fell asleep at midnight. They lived together three more weeks, until production started and Melissa, making $1,600/week (plus an extra $33/week because of the understudy thing), moved into another studio apartment not unlike the one she'd miraculously found when she first arrived in the city, except this one was a little smaller and unfurnished. She left the coffee shop. Ramit was sad. Who would be his tea expert now? Maybe she could still teach the tea workshops once a month—he'd pay her. For three months she rehearsed, was fitted for costumes, was refitted for costumes when costumes were redesigned. Not long into the rehearsal process the play's writer, Jonathan Bread, asked her out, and she accepted but made it very clear over dinner (during which she did not drink) that she wanted nothing serious right now; she slept with him that night; he asked her how old she was and she lied and said twenty even though she would turn nineteen only a few days before the play opened; she did not feel bad for this lie because he could have checked the casting sheet to verify her age if he wanted to. He meant nothing to her. Nobody had ever meant anything to her. He was nice enough. He'd written a good play.

PARTICLES

IN THE FUTURE, A QUIET will descend upon the universe. A calm. A peaceable notion. And in those days the kings will have died and gone away. And in those days the universes will have no king, and everyone will do what is right by their own eyes and by their own hearts, and they will lay down a kingdom that will never be brought to ruin, or some shit like that, and there will be infinite possibilities.

Maybe it will be raining outside in Los Angeles and Eugene Apollos will be approaching the world-famous coffee shop on the Silver Lake portion of Sunset Boulevard. Maybe he will have with him no umbrella, having forgotten it, perhaps at the hotel or in the cab or on the plane or back at his family home across a continent and an ocean where his wife is waiting for him to return like she always is. Maybe his peacoat's collar will be turned up against the water.

There, at a table in a corner near the bathroom, waiting for him, will be Jonathan Bread, maybe, reading on a tablet, the latest model from some massive technology company, his head low, his breath invisible. Maybe on the table: two coffees. Apollos will want a scone but then he'll notice the scone that's already there, untouched for him. From his shoulders he'll remove his coat and fold it over his arm before approaching and putting a hand on the back of the chair. "Sorry I'm late," he will maybe say.

The simulated *click* of the tablet being locked. Look up. A smile. "It's okay. The coffee just arrived now anyway. I swear it takes them ages to make it."

"Pour-over, though, yes? That does take time."

"Sit down. Sit down."

How these two will have come to, maybe, know each other, to be the sort of friends who meet for coffee on rainy days, and how they will have both come to be here on the West Coast at this exact time on this exact day, is obvious. I will not spell it out for you.

Apollos will maybe sit down, and as he does maybe the bones in his legs will creak because he is old and growing older, and maybe his spine will thank him as it meets with the support of the wooden chair, their congress—the chair's and the spine's— an intimate one. Or maybe he won't feel any aches or pains at all.

"No one takes the time to make good coffee these days," maybe he'll say.

And maybe Bread will agree: "No one takes the time."

Maybe Bread will rest one leg over the other's knee like his father used to and put his hands behind his head, intertwining them. Maybe Apollos will comment on Bread's new bionic eye, upgraded only last month to an experimental model by doctors on the East Coast.

Maybe Bread will say, "It's like having a microscope in my

head. Forty-x micro lens on the end of this thing. Increased frequency at both ends of the spectrum, too. And it looks just like the real thing."

Maybe Apollos will comment on a new hit television show.

"She's wonderful in it," is what Bread might say in response, because he is a humble man these days.

"Indeed she is, but it's your writing, too. Without the writing . . ."

"She's wonderful in it." And then maybe Bread will say, "And *your* work, Doctor. How goes it?"

"We're making progress. We've begun to replicate the anomalies in the lab, and of course we're not able to account for some of the more random variables, but if we can replicate them, we can figure out their cause, and if we can figure out their cause, we can figure out if we can stop them."

"That's good."

"I fear the answer is one the world may not want to hear."

"You're doing good work, Doctor."

"When I get back we're turning on the new collider."

"That's great news. I'm glad you got your funding."

"It's all very exciting. Imagine, Jonathan, the world reduced to its smallest parts, ready for us to play with, ours to take and throw about and . . ."

Maybe the coffee wasn't there before like we thought it was but maybe it will arrive at the table now and maybe Apollos will take a sip and maybe it will be the perfect temperature so that it doesn't burn him. "The sample I collected yesterday will certainly aid our progress. And I'm even writing another book about it while I work. It's really just an outline."

Maybe Bread will have lost some weight. Or maybe he'll be fatter, living it up. Maybe he watched movies for weeks on end after buying that new laptop and when they found him he had bedsores and was dead.

Maybe Eugene Apollos, after laughing and sipping coffee for a while and telling stories, will go home and kiss his aging-but-healthy wife on the mouth when she greets him at the airport, and he'll take her out to dinner, and he'll scoff at the people at the tables around him with their heads bowed low, thanking for their meals an entity they believe in but only pretend to understand.

Maybe searchers found in the desert the severed head of one of those two girls that went missing a while back.

Maybe the problem is that for your entire life the world has been in black-and-white. Monochrome. This thing you've wandered through and wondered about and have not understood the kodachromatic depth of.

Maybe this is a joke.

Maybe Eugene Apollos will be assassinated, *The Prehistoric Christ* the catalyst for a new jihad.

Did you know that, on the scale of atoms, objects never really touch? *We* never really touch. One atom's electron clouds push away the other atom's electron clouds. My electron clouds push away your electron clouds. More than 99.9 percent of the matter of any atom is concentrated in its nucleus. The sensation of touching is really just invisible force fields overlapping and repelling each other. Touch is repelling. Touching is just the opposite of what we think it is. Maybe Bread and Apollos will just sit there, then, avoiding further conversation, while the chatter of the people around them drones on into the spaces between us all.

I still don't know who I am—did you think I would figure it out? This was never about You or Me. Maybe it never will be.

But even though atoms never touch, in the hearts of stars the repellent forces of their nuclei converge, and with this they become something new: this is fusion.

ABOUT THE AUTHOR

Shawn was born in San Diego, California, in 1990, where he lived until he was seven.

In high school, he won several awards both as a writer for and editor-in-chief of his student newspaper, prompting him to study journalism before deciding that his passion for writing was better directed at fiction.

He is the author of three books: *The Flute Player*, *Brand-Changing Day*, and *Particles*.

Shawn currently lives in Helena, MT, with his wife and their cat.

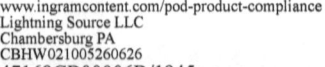